A PINCH OF SALT

A Pinch of Salt

Writers of Whitstable

© This edition Writers of Whitstable, 2020

The copyright for individual stories remains with the named authors.

ISBN 978-0-9935492-2-9

A CIP catalogue record for this title is available from the British Library.

Published in the UK in 2020 by Coinlea Publishing

www.coinlea.co.uk

Typesetting: Coinlea Services

Cover design: David Williamson

Printed in the UK by Clays Ltd

Illustrations:

Birthday to remember – Zoë Steen
Apple Tree – Isobel Campbell
Through the Long Grass – Sofie Quine
Saturday Morning Fever – Tim Rolfe
Egg – Duarte Figueira
Do or Die Diner – Zoë Steen
Going Back – Lin White
Once Upon A Time – David Williamson
Coney – Isobel Campbell
Lost Teddy – Isobel Campbell
The Man Who Wouldn't Be King – Sofie Quine

Contents

Foreword

Writing is often a solo endeavour. It is hours at a computer, lost in words, chasing plots, urging characters to come forth and make themselves known.

And yet writing is also hours outside, lost in conversation, chasing locations, urging the wind to blow the proverbial cobwebs so the stories can make themselves heard.

With its sea, restaurants and beaches, the north Kent town of Whitstable is perhaps the perfect place to lay down the pen and walk with your tale, weave your way through the beach huts and, as Sally in A Birthday to Remember suggests, eavesdrop on nearby chat for inspiration well-seasoned with salt.

Because, yes, writing is often a solo endeavour but, like our shoreline, so too is it shaped by what surrounds us. That infamous wind. The oyster-rich water. The stretch of sand at low tide in Tankerton, pulling you toward a horizon as if, like magic, here in Whitstable you might actually walk on the sea.

For a writer, though, Whitstable's influence is more than geographical. It is personal. It is community. I lived there for six years and am not sure anywhere else will ever feel more like home. The shops, cafes and pebbles played their part, of course, but it was the people, really, who were as open as the views stretching toward Sheppey and Clacton. Their creativity and encouragement instilled a confidence which somehow gave me permission to write.

That is the beauty of a writing group, of people who will

listen to words you have dared to put down on a page. And it is daring. It is a part of us we are asking you to look at, to judge. It is exposure of our deepest and darkest. Because even when they are not autobiographical, our stories are our loves, our joys and our pain.

The stories in A Pinch of Salt hope to evoke these and other emotions in their readers. The Whitstable you will discover here is haunted by ghosts, pounded by runners, moderated by stone skimmers, shadowed with stalkers, relieved by boot-fair hunters seeking more than a bargain or coveted antique. These stories are Whitstable in its past, its present and its future. These stories will give you an insight into a place where you are as likely as some of their characters to experience a moment of epiphany, to stop, take a breath of salted air and say, "today I love this town."

Amy Beashel
Author of *The Sky Is Mine*

Flood

by Aliy Fowler

My name is George Reid and I've lived in Whitstable for most of my life. I came here with my mother and younger brother when I was just eight years old and never went home. I've got the sea to thank for that.

I was born on Canvey Island in 1945. It's not actually an island, but it's in the Thames Estuary and there's water everywhere. My mother Betty and her older sister Catherine were born on Canvey too. My Grandma Gladys lived in a bungalow in an area called Newlands. And so did I for five years. It was only half a mile's walk from home to the sea at Thorney Bay and I loved it there.

My Aunt Catherine married Joseph, a trawlerman from Kent, just before the outbreak of the war. Mum told me Grandpa had real concerns about her wedding a fisherman.

'It's the most dangerous occupation a man can have in this country,' he used to say.

I googled this recently and apparently it's still true.

Mum said Grandma would tell him not to worry. That the water was more dangerous to those that didn't respect it. That Joseph knew the sea. That we'd all drown before Joseph did.

Grandma Gladys liked to think she had the gift of foretelling, and was occasionally prone to an eccentric turn of phrase. Mum reckoned her pronouncements didn't alleviate Grandpa George's concerns but Catherine was far too excited by the prospect of her new life to harbour any misgivings.

Catherine moved to Whitstable immediately after her wedding and the couple lived with Joseph's parents in a Victorian terrace on Nelson Road. The houses there were built near the old salt marshes, where for several hundred years they used to let the land flood, then drain it and let it dry so they could collect the salt left behind. When I got my own place I moved to higher ground.

In 1942 my mum, Betty, fell for an engineer by the name of Bill Reid. He'd come to Canvey Island for work in the thirties. Mum and Bill were married rather hurriedly the following year while Grandpa George was on home-leave from the army, so at least he got to see both his daughters wed. It was the last time they saw him.

Grandpa George, after whom I was named, was killed in action near the end of the war. I found out years later that he'd been shot and had collapsed into a flooded trench and drowned. I've always been sad that I never got to meet him. I don't think Grandma ever really recovered from losing him that way.

My parents rented a little house not too far from Grandma's and a month after the end of the war I was born. Mum said her little George junior helped Grandma rediscover a little enthusiasm for life.

My brother Edward came along three years later, as the shadow of the war was starting to lift. I can just about recall my excitement at his arrival. Mum told me she was beside herself and Grandma too. On the night of Edward's christening Dad slipped out to wet the baby's head and never came back. They found him floating face down in East Haven creek the following morning with a belly full of beer. They said he must have slipped and bashed his head on the way in.

That was pretty much all I knew about my dad. Mum never spoke about him much. The day after he died she gathered our belongings and took us home to the Newlands Estate to live with her mother.

Friday January 30th 1953

Twice a year, Grandma, Mum, my brother and I would make a trip to Whitstable to visit Aunt Catherine and Uncle Joseph. Edward and I liked playing in the castle gardens with our cousins Harry and Susan; we liked the beaches which were very different from the ones on Canvey Island and best of all we liked going out on Uncle Joseph's boat if the weather was good for it.

In 1953, for the first time ever, Grandma didn't come with us. Mum knew she was beginning to tire. She had oedema, which made her legs swell, and walking was painful for her. Edward and I were eight and five and pretty boisterous by all accounts and she found it hard to keep us entertained when Mum was out at work. She'd told mum us boys didn't need her as much and she needed quiet. And Mum knew she was starting to miss Grandpa again dreadfully.

And so on Friday we readied ourselves to leave Newlands for a weekend with our cousins. As we were about to depart, Grandma appeared from her bedroom with an old leather purse.

'Take this, Betty.' She pressed it into Mum's hands. 'It's money your dad and I had been saving for retirement but I want you and Catherine to have it.'

Mum opened the wallet and there was nearly £400 inside. That was a huge amount of money back then. She refused to take it. Grandma tried to insist, saying she wanted her daughters to have it, and that she wouldn't need it now. Mum held fast and told her to keep it safe.

'We'll talk about it when I get back,' Mum said.

When she went to the hall to fetch our coats, Grandma slipped the purse into the bottom of Mum's big handbag.

'Tell your mum once you're all away from here,' she made me promise. 'Not before. And make sure she doesn't leave that bag anywhere.'

I remember I was so excited to tell her that Grandma had

given her all that money anyway. Somehow I managed to wait until we were well away from Canvey Island. But when I told her she looked terribly worried and I couldn't understand why.

'I wish Grandma had given it to us,' I'd whispered to Edward. 'We'd be rich!'

He giggled at me and for the rest of the journey we planned what to do with all that cash.

As we hadn't seen our cousins in December, that evening we had a belated Christmas meal – in as far as you could while there was still rationing, anyway. There really were plenty of good things to eat and presents for all the kids. It was a happy night and we were allowed to stay up much too late.

After the meal I overheard Mum and Aunt Catherine in the kitchen talking about the money while they were washing up. Catherine asked her why Grandma had insisted she didn't need it now. Mum shook her head and said she didn't know, but I could tell she was worried.

The Nelson Road house had three bedrooms. The front bedroom was where my aunt and uncle slept. Susan had the middle bedroom and Harry, being the younger sibling, had the little back room. So although Joseph's parents had moved out to a bungalow some years ago, with three guests some rearrangement was required. As usual Susan gave up her room for Mum, since Harry's room 'smelt of stinky boy'. Susan went into Harry's room (protesting vehemently) and we three lads camped out in the living room. Harry took the sofa, being the tallest, and Edward and I made do with the floor and a scattering of cushions. With the three of us all together that night we didn't get a lot of sleep.

Saturday January 31st

The following morning, as we were tucking in to a hearty breakfast (Uncle Joseph had managed to get hold of kippers), a deep low-pressure system was heading down the North Sea. But we didn't know this and the forecast for Whitstable was just for light drizzle and strong winds. Joseph thought it best not to take us out on his boat, only because the cold winds would make for a miserable trip.

This atmospheric low pressure was accompanied by hurricane force winds off the east coast of Scotland, and coincided with a very high spring tide. However, no one was predicting anything particularly unusual in Kent. It was just a normal, chilly January day. We spent the morning, wrapped up well, playing hide and seek in the castle gardens, and then went for a walk to the harbour to watch the fishing boats which were going out as normal.

Earlier that morning, unbeknown to anyone except those on board, a Fleetwood trawler called the *Michael Griffith* had sunk without trace off the Hebrides, the first casualty of the severe weather system that was building to the north. With her crew of thirteen, the youngest being only sixteen years old, she vanished south of Barra Head in what was to be one of the worst gales recorded off the coast of Scotland. Her last radio call reported that she was 'full of water, with no steam and helpless'.

Later in the day the storm's second casualty was the ferry *MV Princess Victoria*. She had put out from Stranraer that morning, sailing through Loch Ryan and then out into the North Channel on the way to Ireland. Away from the shelter of the loch the full force of the storm hit the ship and she was struggling. The captain tried to turn around and head back to port and at that point the vessel was hit by a huge wave which stove in the stern doors. She sank off the County Down coast with the loss of 133 lives.

While we walked back to Catherine and Joseph's house on Nelson Road, lost in our games and unaware of the tragedies unfolding up-country, the low pressure and strong winds were forcing an unusually large of amount water into the southern North Sea. As the swell was funnelled toward the narrow and comparatively shallow English Channel the sea level began to rise.

Fishermen along the Essex and Kent coasts noticed a weak

tidal ebb but otherwise nothing out of the ordinary. No one saw any cause for alarm and in Whitstable it was business as usual. As a special treat we four kids were allowed to go the chip shop and get whatever we wanted for our tea.

We spent the Saturday evening listening to records on Uncle Joseph's gramophone and playing Monopoly – until the game was curtailed because Susan and Harry argued over property rents. This was mostly because Harry was really overtired. It was a fun and raucous evening though and we weren't remotely concerned by how much the wind was getting up.

We were given a 10pm curfew for bedtime, but due to all the fresh air we'd had during the day and the lack of sleep the previous night, we weren't awake for long. I can remember dozing off hoping that the wind would drop so we could go out on Joseph's boat on Sunday. And wondering if Aunt Catherine would make one of her Victoria sponges for tea.

Sunday February 1st

It was sometime in the very early hours of Sunday morning that I awoke. It was really dark and I couldn't comprehend the odd sounds coming from outside; however, something didn't seem right. As I became more conscious my first thought was that I'd wet myself. Where I'd slipped between two cushions and was resting on the living room floor, my pyjama bottoms were damp. But I quickly realised that they were actually soaked through and the water was cold. I put a hand down to touch the carpet and felt the splash of water. It must have been a couple of inches deep on the floor. Then I heard the sound – like a tap running and within seconds that had turned into a spraying noise, like a hose when you put your finger over the end to make the jet stronger.

I shouted to Edward and Harry to wake up. In the space of a few seconds Edward went from bleary-eyed and confused to shivering with fear and cold. His back was soaked through. I had to shake Harry to rouse him. Elevated on the couch and wrapped in a thick woollen blanket, he was still warm and dry.

'Get up Harry, now! We have to get upstairs,' I yelled at him.

Harry sat up, twisted round and gasped as his feet landed in what was by now six inches of sea water. My eyes were becoming accustomed to the gloom and as Harry stood I could just make out the level of the water lapping at the bay window. It was half way up the first pane of the lower sash and spraying in through the woodwork on all sides. I was terrified at that moment.

As I stared, I heard the sound of glass cracking. Harry was already out of the living room door. I grabbed Edward by the hand and pulled him through as the window gave way and the surge of water slammed the heavy door behind us, catching Edward on the foot and causing him to yelp with pain.

We ran up the stairs calling for the adults to get out of bed. Uncle Joseph came running to the top of the stairs, ready to clip us round the ear for waking everyone in the middle of the night and demanding to know what was going on. Edward was crying and shaking with cold and Joseph softened and scooped him up in his arms.

'The lad's soaking!' he exclaimed. 'What on earth...'

Mum, Catherine and Susan appeared on the landing too.

'Dad, the house is flooding,' yelled Harry. 'It's all water outside, it's got to be five foot deep!'

None of the lights were working. Joseph went back into the bedroom and returned with a lit candle. He began to descend the staircase but stopped on the fifth stair as the flickering flame was reflected back at him in the water, just inches from his feet.

'Everyone back upstairs!' he ordered.

Mum bundled Edward and me into Susan's room where our case was. She dried us off and found us fresh clothes, then just sat on the bed hugging my shivering brother while I watched in silence. I knew she was thinking about what Grandma said all those years ago. About everyone drowning before Joseph. First Grandpa, then Dad. I got really scared then.

I remember asking Joseph how high the water would get.

'I don't know, lad,' he told me, shaking his head. 'We're safe here upstairs though, I'm sure of it.'

I wished I was sure.

The water rose another foot and then stopped. Edward ceased crying and Harry, Susan and I started to feel calmer about the situation. Joseph opened the sash window in the main bedroom to discover the people in the house opposite had done the same. He called out to the couple who lived there to make sure they were all right.

'We are,' came the reply as a woman's head, hair in curlers, appeared in the gloom. Gradually more windows were opened and for a good half hour, until the cold air beat us back inside, an odd neighbourhood conversation took place, with messages of concern being bellowed up and down the street above the lapping waters.

We all stayed in the front bedroom, Uncle Joseph on the chair in the corner and the rest of us huddled together on the double bed for warmth. All we wanted to talk about was the water, about why this had occurred and when it would go away and what we should do. I think Harry, Susan and I were secretly becoming a bit excited by the adventure of it, now that we were warm and dry and the water was no longer rising. And the thought of not being able to get home to Canvey and back to school on Monday was really quite appealing.

Mum and Catherine kept trying to steer the conversation onto other topics, aware that Edward, as the youngest, was less gung-ho than the rest of us. I think the adults were starting to worry about the practicalities of the situation too, something that didn't occur to my cousins and me until we realised that we were hungry and thirsty, and Joseph informed us that it wasn't safe to go downstairs. And in any case, all the cupboards would be full of dirty water.

'Thank heavens Grandma didn't come with us,' Mum murmured to me. Catherine nodded in agreement.

It started to get light at about 7 am. By now everyone was wondering what was going to happen. It had dawned even on

Edward that we couldn't get out by the front door; the water was much too deep. As I was mulling over our situation, Harry, who'd been stood at the window, gave a cry.

'Boats!' he shouted.

We all rushed to the window and sure enough a tiny flotilla of rowing boats was making its way down the river that was Nelson Road. We grinned at each other with the relief of it. I heard splashing to my left and asked Uncle Joseph to open the sash again. I craned my head outside and could see a little white boat in front of next door. There was a man rowing to keep it in position close to the house and two young girls huddled on its wooden plank seat. A policeman was standing up inside the little craft, wobbling precariously, his arms outstretched towards the pitched top of the bay window where the girl's mother was perched. Behind her, her husband was climbing awkwardly out of the bedroom window to join her.

'There'll be a boat for you any minute,' said the policeman to Joseph. 'How many are you?'

'Seven,' answered my uncle.

'Two boats for this place!', the policeman hollered in the direction of the flotilla.

The first boat arrived, causing the water to lap a little further up the side of the house as it drew near. Uncle Joseph told Mum to get in it with Edward and me. He squeezed himself through the open sash onto the roof of the bay window below as the people next door had done. Then, holding onto the bedroom window frame he beckoned for my brother to come out next.

'Be careful, Edward,' he warned. 'The roof slopes down and it's a little wet.'

Edward clambered out backwards and his feet skittered on the lead covering. Joseph grabbed him with his free hand before Edward could career over the edge and into the water. There were two men in the boat. The man with the oars brought the boat in backwards, as close as possible, then laid them down. He lent out of the rear of the boat and caught hold

11

of one of the two round pillars which supported the roof of the bay. The second man, now that the craft was as steady as it could be, stood up carefully and reached for Edward as Joseph lowered him over the edge with one hand. He guided him into the boat causing it to lurch.

'Sit down and keep really still,' the oarsman told him.

Uncle Joseph beckoned for me to come out next and passed me to the other man who manoeuvred me into the boat beside my brother.

'Now you, Betty,' he nodded at Mum.

She was just positioning herself to climb outside when Catherine rushed back along the landing and returned moments later with Mum's handbag.

'For God's sake don't forget this!' she spluttered.

When Mum was safely in the first boat it was rowed out into the middle of the road and the second one came in, two burly rescuers aboard as before. Joseph got Susan in first, followed by Aunt Catherine. Harry was in a cocky mood and didn't want his father's assistance. He got out onto the roof and as Joseph reached for his arm, he pushed it away in a foolish attempt to look manly. On the wet surface that was enough to send him sliding off before his father could catch him. He fell, clipping the boat below with his foot, which flipped him side-on into the freezing brine.

'Idiot!' muttered Susan as he hauled himself up, shivering and embarrassed.

'Get in the boat,' his father yelled. 'I'll throw down some dry things for you. You can change when we're out of the flood area.'

Joseph disappeared and came back onto the roof with a small bundle, which he passed to the second boatman. He then pulled the window down behind him and lowered himself over the side and into the dinghy.

Our little convoy of two set off down Nelson Road and into Oxford Street. Our saviours were local fishermen and members of the special constabulary who were only too happy to pitch in with the rescue operation. On our way we passed people's belongings bobbing gently down the road along with all sorts of flotsam from the inundation. Edward even spotted a plank of wood floating by with several cats clinging to it.

More than 600 people in the town were made homeless. Some had family in unaffected roads who could take them in, but since Joseph's parents' house was also flooded, we were taken to the Boys' School in Oxford Street where a reception centre had been set up for those with nowhere to go. Others were taken to the Salvation Army Hall in the High Street where they were handing out dry clothes. Some poor folk were rescued wearing only their night things.

The community spirit shown by the people of this town was incredible. All the available small boats were commandeered and an army of volunteers spent the whole day rescuing stranded residents from the first floors of their flooded homes. We were lucky enough to be among the first to be taken out and didn't have to wait for hours in the cold with no food or drinking water.

Mum and Catherine were desperate to let Grandma know that we were safe. Although she didn't own a telephone, her neighbours did and Mum had their number in case of emergency. But try as she might she was unable to get through to them. The force of the tidal surge, we learned, had snapped many of the telephone cables on the east coast, making communication impossible.

We needed to retrieve the rest of our belongings before going home to Grandma; however, we couldn't go back to our cousins' house. We had to wait until the water could be pumped out of the flooded streets. And the railway line to Faversham had been destroyed by the deluge. So we remained at the school with the other flood victims, on make-shift beds in noisy schoolrooms, just glad to be safe.

Tuesday February 3rd

After we'd been in the shelter for two days, someone got hold of a copy of the Daily Express from the previous day and was telling anyone who'd listen how bad things had been, and how lucky we were. The Headline simply said 'The Deluge' and underneath it: '133 known dead; 10,000 evacuated from one town'. Below was a large aerial view of Canvey Island, the Newlands Estate in the foreground with its little bungalows submerged. Mum was shaking as she read the article, then she passed it silently to Aunt Catherine with tears in her eyes.

'She knew,' Mum stammered to her sister. 'That's why she gave me the money when we left.'

Catherine put her arms around Mum and held her.

Some of the luckier residents of Newlands had managed to punch holes in the ceilings of their prefabricated one-storey houses and clamber onto to tables and into the loft space above, or had found ways to climb onto their roofs where they sat all night in the dark, the storm howling around them, freezing and praying for rescue. Those less lucky or less able-bodied had perished in their living rooms and bedrooms as the surge overtook them. Grandma Gladys was confirmed drowned the following day, along with many of her neighbours and friends. Her house was left uninhabitable.

Mum, Edward and I never went back to Canvey Island.

Postscript

The characters featured in this story are fictional but the details of the flooding in Whitstable and on Canvey Island, and the boats which sank, are all true.

There was no flood warning system in 1953. Most of the victims were unaware of the impending danger until the surging water crashed into their homes on that awful night. Along the east coast of England 30,000 people had to be evacuated from their homes. Canvey Island was the last place to be hit, in the early hours of February 1st. 58 people lost their lives there. In total the flooding killed 307, making it one of the worst natural disasters in the UK's history.

Despite the dreadful damage incurred in Whitstable, not one human life was lost here.

Birthday to Remember

by P.J. Ferst

'Hey, stop!' I gasp as I stagger around the corner by Hills Betting Office onto Tankerton Road and pant past the RSPCA Charity Shop. The person I'm shouting to doesn't seem to hear me, but passers-by clearly do on this chilly January morning, They stare in disdain at the loud-mouthed old lady in the bobbled blue trouser suit, scraggy scarf and threadbare gloves, clutching onto her walking stick with gnarled fingers, passing everyone with her ungainly, Miranda-style gallop. But gallop I simply must, for a woman has just come out of Tesco Express and is rapidly heading in the direction of Tankerton Circus. And this is no ordinary woman. I feel compelled to catch her up as she speeds by Dunn's Bakery and the Flexi-Appeal Gym. I've got a question for her. I mustn't let her disappear. She is far too familiar for that. There are so many things about her that convince me I know her. Very well.

It's the build, the hairstyle, the clothes, the walking stick. She's tall, long legged and as energetic as those unbelievably young-looking ladies in TV stairlift ads. She sports a hair style reminiscent of Audrey Hepburn's crew cut in the film Roman Holiday, not dark like Audrey's, nor salt and pepper like mine, but hennaed to a garish ginger hue. She's wearing a 1990's purple cape with a hood, trackie bottoms of luminescent orange, plus purple trainers. Her jaunty gait, aided by her silver-topped cane, proclaims a devil-may-care attitude.

OMG, it *is* her. There's no doubt about it. 'Mrs Rothwell,' I yell.

My intended quarry must have heard me, because she's come to a halt at Tankerton Circus. On the edge of the pavement. Phew! She could have been killed, the way drivers treat that roundabout. Now she's turning round and I can see those spectacles. The ones she always wore: flyaway turquoise frames, the size of blue Adonis butterflies, reminiscent of the face furniture worn by Dame Edna Everidge. I'd recognise those specs anywhere and the sapphire eyes behind them. 'Lilian, Mother, Mum,' I gasp. The shock teleports me back to my classical education – the typical recognition scene encountered in ancient Greek comedy but now about to be played in pop-up version on a Tankerton pavement. 'Mum, what on earth are you doing here? You're supposed to be dead.'

Mum's face lights up and she steps forward, her arms spread wide, her woollen cape cocooning me like a baby in a cot, but with an insubstantial airiness. I breathe in that scent of lavender which wafts me back to post-war, toddler time, safely ensconced on Mum's knee, while the radio played the magical melody of 'Listen with Mother.' Now it's as if that programme never ended and everything is Hug, Squeeze and Never Let Go. That is until Mum bursts into song, a habit that caused me great embarrassment in my teens. And now it's the type of song rarely sung to humans whose age exceeds single figures. 'Rock-a-bye baby on the treetops.' This lullaby is delivered with considerable mezzo soprano zeal.

OMG, the Tankerton passers-by are no longer passing by. They've turned into a circle of gawpers and eavesdroppers, disorientated by this unbelievable exhibitionism, together with the unBritish-like display of emotions. The elderly mutter and tut tut, while the young giggle and snap photos with their smartphones. For all the paparazzi attention Mum's attracting, she could be Glen Close getting her Golden Globe Award for best actress, if she'd had blonde hair instead of orange and been at the Beverley Hilton, Los Angeles, instead of Tankerton Circus.

'Mum,' I beg her, 'Not so loud.'

'Sally, Chuck,' Mum says. 'I don't give a hoot if people laugh at me and think I'm barmy. You know I've always liked being in the limelight. Think on all those racy stories I used to tell the ladies at the Baptist Church on Middle Wall, when your Dad and me moved down here. They couldn't get enough of me. Any road, let's get down to brass tacks. Eeh, it's champion to see you again and know you're still in the land of the living. Happy seventieth, love! I'm your birthday present for the day. That's why I'm here, so let's walk and talk, like we did when I was alive.'

Mum winks and a lightbulb flashes in my head. The wink signals her readiness to deliver a carefully chosen and dramatically executed quotation, another habit which ruined my adolescence. For Mum, as well as being a totally eccentric and comedic character, was always a passionate bibliophile. And here it comes, at full volume: ' "Stand not upon the order of thy going, but go at once!"... Shakespeare, Macbeth.'

'Yes, Mum, I know it's Shakespeare.' There's a ripple of laughter from the crowd. Do those morons think they're watching an episode of *Long Lost Family?*'

Mum clutches my arm. 'Sally, is there a caff somewhere for a sit down and a catch up?' And I reassure her that now it's 2019, there's a caff every few yards in Tankerton, even on Sundays.

'Mum, let's go to the Marine Hotel. It's a bit posher.' I lower my voice discreetly because our unexpected encounter has thrown my bladder into confusion. 'And they have nice loos.' But my remark only seems to cause more hilarity. I shoot the onlookers an evil look and point Mum towards Tankerton Slopes, away from her disappointed fans.

We're at the Marine. Irresistible smells of fried bacon and sausages assail my nostrils as Mum chooses a table close to a radiator and a young waiter strides over to take our order.

'Full breakfast, Mum?' I ask her, but she pulls a face. 'Oh no,

Sally. I don't eat nowadays, nor drink, neither.'

'Then you must miss your brandy big time.'

Mum sighs. 'Can't even remember the taste, nor the smell.'

'Well, what were you doing in Tesco Express? That's where people buy stuff to eat.'

'Just looking round. It's interesting to be in a shop.'

'Aren't there shops where you are, then?' No answer. 'Mum, why did you turn Catholic?'

But Mum shushes me with a finger. 'Discretion is the better part of valour.'

'Excuse me, madam.'

I realise that the waiter is still waiting, so I say, 'One full breakfast and a large latte, please.'

Meanwhile, Mum draws herself up in her chair and does an impression of Oscar Wilde's Lady Bracknell. 'Ooh, I say, it's called lar-tay, is it? How frightfully poe-sh.'

'Really, Mum!' I reprimand her, but she just rolls her eyes like a naughty schoolgirl.

'Is that all?' The waiter arches his eyebrows at me and purses his lips, in an unsuccessful attempt to suppress a smirk. OMG, Mum's attracted another gawper. Well, he'll get no tip from me.

'Yes, thank you,' I snap and I glance nervously round the dining room. Thank goodness – the nearest guests are a young couple at the far end of the room, engrossed in each other.

Mum smiles. 'Sally, I'm dead sure I've been here before. This is the room where I celebrated my eightieth birthday. Try not to bolt your food, dear. It's so bad for your colon.'

I ignore this remark.

'Yes, I hired the room for my party. Twenty first of August, 1999. With a Steinway Grand Piano. Everybody had such fun. Even Great Aunt Ada travelled down from Lancashire and your Cornish cousins, Denzel and Demelza, came too. But it was too late for the DEAD ONES, Sally. Like your lovely Uncle Jago and of course your Dad, Arthur. Miserable old sod! Mind you, tax collectors aren't known for their sense of humour. He couldn't stand folks talking and there wasn't a musical bone in his body. He brought his Winston Churchill's War Memoirs along to the party. That and listening to the fishing forecast were his only hobbies when he retired and we moved down to Whitstable from up North, to be near you and your brother, Tony. Darling, what did we actually do at my party? It's gone right out of my head.'

I don't answer because my mouth is full of sausage, but I make my fingers perform a short, modest mime of someone playing a piano. Damn, don't tell me Mum's embarrassment factor is contagious. But she suddenly claps her hands.

'Sally, it's all coming back to me. I was the pianist and I sang my favourite song. The one I named you after. The song soldiers sang during the second world war.'

Quickly, I put my hand on Mum's arm, because I'm becoming aware of muffled guffaws issuing from the bar. 'You don't need to sing it now, Mum.'

But I'm too late. Mum starts her Dame Gracie Fields impression with the same strident soprano as that celebrated singer: 'Sally, Sally, pride of our alley ...' she trills, then she stops abruptly. 'Beg pardon, Chuck. I can see you're getting fidgety. It's just that I'm so excited to see you.'

Aaah. How could I be so mean? Surely I can distract her with some reminiscence techniques. 'Mum, tell me more about your birthday party.' And off she goes.

'Well there I was, dressed up like a dog's dinner – in purple and gold. The other V.I.P.s were as well, of course. You, your brother Tony and his wife Susie, with my grandchildren Rachel and Janet ... By heck, there's nothing Tony liked more than a free dinner. Oh and the great grandkids were there, too. Young Adam with his guitar, Daisy and her toy trumpet, even little Lucy blowing her plastic mouth organ. Daisy was always my favourite, but they were a tad spoilt, not like you at their age.'

'They were modern Millennials, Mum, not post-war Baby Boomers raised on Dr Spock.'

'Millie what? By gum, Sally, those newfangled words! But

thank God I didn't bring you up on the Truby King Method.' Mum winks. 'Right nasty, that was: "Spare the rod and spoil the child." Sally, was I too strict?' Tears well up in Mum's eyes and I give her a hug.

'No, you were spot on, Mum. You took care of us and you encouraged us to take risks.'

But I've spotted a new couple entering the lounge. Middle-aged. Damn, they've decided to sit at the table opposite ours. Can I really cope with another gawp session?

And at this very moment, Mum decides to throw her arms out in an expansive gesture. She booms, 'Sally, what gets me hopping mad is that I ruddy well died only three months after my birthday party. Stuck in that dreadful Swalecliffe Home they called a Respite Centre. Some Home. More like an elephants' graveyard!'

The new woman at the table gives us a covert glance, nosy cow.

Mum pauses for a few seconds. 'Sally, you aren't listening, are you? Why are you writing? What are you writing?'

I shove my pen and notepad back in my handbag. 'Oh… nothing really,' I fib. I'm realising we've been in here too long; the woman opposite is listening to every word and I'm getting frazzled.

Get a grip, Sally. 'Mum…' I lean forward and use the calm voice recommended on my long-ago teaching diploma course. 'You seem to have survived all the trauma successfully and our time together is short, so I think …'

But then I realise that Mum can't hear me, so I switch to fortissimo. 'MUM, I'M A WRITER NOW AND OTHER WRITERS *EAVESDROP* IN PLACES LIKE THIS TO PINCH IDEAS FOR THEIR BOOKS.'

Mum claps her hands. 'Eavesdrop, Sally? Writer? Heck, you get that from me. All those stories I typed out. The ones I left in that manila folder at your house?'

Oops! I really did mean to keep my promise but life got in the way. 'Erm…'

And the couple sitting opposite suddenly get up and move to a table near the back of the lounge. It's midday. Time for us to go as well.

Mother and I set off along Kingsdown Park East, the unseasonably warm January sun shining down on us, until we reach the church of Our Lady Immaculate. Then it's up the steps into the softly lit, incense-infused interior and onto the pew nearest the altar. The church is empty. Morning Mass must be over. Mum unfastens her cape and kneels on her hassock. I recognise the red rosary ring on a chain around her neck. The one I bought for her to wear in her coffin. And peace flows into me for the first time today. The outside world retreats and memories come spooling back.

'Sally?' Mum's sitting up. 'I had my funeral here, didn't I? After I became Catholic?' She eyes me mischievously.

'How on earth did you know?'

And Mum chuckles. 'How d'you think? I *eavesdropped*.'

I chuckle too and Mum goes into overdrive. 'Sally, on my funeral day, this church was packed like herrings and there were you – stood up in front of the pulpit. Saying nice things about me. Like, if I was an animal, I'd be a tiger, and if I was a piece of music, I'd be the overture to Bizet's Carmen. Naughty things, too. That joke about the Passion Play in Oberammergau. How the driver of the lorry I flagged down to Dover thought the play was about red-hot passion instead of religious passion. Poor chap. He was right disappointed. And my Lancashire accent you imitated. By gum, folks nearly wet themselves laughing, every man-Jack of them. Even Father O'Donnell.'

'Mum, at your funeral, I forgot to say that I loved you.'

Mum pats my hand. 'And a good job too. You'd have been in floods of tears. Eeh, I've seen the roughest, toughest men crack up the minute they say the word love. But Sally, nobody could have given me a better send-off. Everyone in bright colours and exciting hymns, like Fight the Good Fight. I would've sung myself, if I hadn't been dead.'

'You're right, Mum, everyone bright but for Tony in his tailored black suit. You know how "Churchy of England" he was, full of John Knox-like fervour. He couldn't get over you turning Catholic, especially four seconds before you died.'

Mum's sapphire eyes flash. 'How do you know it was four seconds, Sally?'

'Because I timed it. I was holding your hand in hospital, when the priest baptised you. Then your hand went cold.'

'Oh, Sally, that must have been terrible for you.' Mum puts her arm round my shoulder.

'Not terrible, Mum – triumphant. It was your moment. More exciting than the Grand National, your favourite race. First came the Last Rites, then the Baptism and the Prayers for the Dead. And all in the final furlong. You won by just a head, Mum. The patients were all ears.'

'Really? Weren't my curtains drawn?'

'Yes, but they could hear me urging you on. Like a jockey, but without a whip.'

'Thank God for that. I've always had trouble with my rear end.'

'And I was shouting, "Hang on, Mum. You're going to be Catholic!"'

'Flaming heck, Sally, no wonder everyone was listening. But what you don't know is I kept watch over you a long while after the funeral.'

I'm stunned. 'Really? For how long?'

'Oh, a year, give or take. Until you got busy with your own life. I watched you driving to work, I watched you teaching, watering my grave in the summer, arguing with Tony about the epitaph. I can't wait to see my epitaph.' Mum pauses. 'Sally, don't you remember singing regular musical updates to me, in your car?'

Damn, I do and I'm desperately trying to recall some examples, when Mum's mezzo soprano beats me to it and she starts *singing* the overture to Bizet's Carmen, her favourite opera.

'Dai-ais-y-y, Mum, she's gone abroa-oad, she has go-o-one to Sing-a-pore-ore-ore...'

By the time Mum gets to the word 'gone,' we're singing a duet – until we grind to a halt, giggling like school girls and unable to remember any more.

I give Mum a hug. 'You're phenomenal, Mumsy.' I haven't called her that since I was at infant school, 'Your life was an incredible drama.'

'That's true, Sally. Truer than you know,' Mum adds darkly. But Oops! I've just spotted a small, dignified figure in dark vestments, emerging from the Sacristy at the back of the church. Swirling in a slow and stately manner towards the pew where we're sitting. I've exchanged greetings with Father O'Donnell over the years following Mum's funeral but I haven't entered the church till today. Will he recognise Mum? Has he heard our conversation and our song? OMG. Mum's luminescent attire could hardly be described as unremarkable. Nor has either of us been employing the dulcet tones deemed appropriate in a place of prayer.

Father O'Donnell pauses by our pew, his face inscrutable but his voice calm and comforting. 'It's Sally Rothwell, isn't it?'

I nod demurely and quake inwardly.

'Bless, you, my dear. The departed sometimes seem to live on in our hearts, do they not?'

Then Mum turns towards him. I see her wink and hear her whisper, 'Behold, I show you a mystery. The dead do not all die, but they are all changed ... Corinthians, Chapter 9, verses 5-15.'

With a hint of a smile, Father O'Donnell swirls away, leaving the soothing scent of incense in his wake. Now I remember that Mum still hasn't answered my important question. I ask once more. 'Mum, why did you turn Catholic? Was it the pageantry, the sense of community?'

'Sally, ask me no questions and I'll tell you no lies. Now,

shouldn't we be getting a move on? I only have until dusk. What time is it now?'

Oops. 'One twenty, Mum. Yes, you're right. Next port of call – my house. It's only round the corner. Up Castle Road and right at the crossroads.' Aha. Mum has evaded my question yet again. She won't tell me why she turned Catholic. Why not?

Mum's through my front door like a shot, her Miss Marple-like antennae instantly in twitch-mode. 'By gum, Sally, talk about *Home*! Remember what Dickens said,' and she winks, '"Home is stronger than magician ever spoke," ... *The Life and Adventures of Martin Chuzzlewit*. But Sally, your home is more like Home, *Sweep* Home.' And Mum snoops among my amateurish shelves groaning under files that bulge with decade-old teaching materials and post-retirement notebooks, full of half-finished stories. I suspect she's looking for that manila folder. She's peering through gaps in the colourful but carelessly arranged Kenyan throw that's meant to disguise; rifling through boxes with their lucky dip of ancient cassettes, faded sepia photos, Beano and Dandy Annuals; goggling at my new 55 inch TV. 'Sally, what's happening in Corrie?'

'Ken Barlow and Rita are still hanging on and it's got violent. You'd hate it.'

But Mum is sidetracked now, perusing the photos on the window sill. 'I always hoped you'd have a wedding photo one day,' she says, sadly. 'Who are all those young fellas? Have you been cradle snatching since I kicked the bucket?' Fortunately, the distraction ploys whirring in my head prove unnecessary, because Mum shoots off upstairs, so I prepare tea and cake for one, arrange my rocking chair for her comfort and try to ignore faraway rummaging sounds.

Shrieks of horror begin to permeate from above and soon Mum descends the stairs with uncanny rapidity for someone who'll be a centenarian in August. Is there a gym in her current abode? I wonder, as I point to my rocker and she ensconces herself in a regal manner.

'Sally,' she says, 'Remember there's no pockets in a shroud. Get shut of the clutter. By gum, you've enough clothes to set up a draper's shop. Why not wear them? Don't you go anywhere of an evening? Don't you have any friends?'

Ouch, is Mum psychic or what?

'And, Sally, how daft of you to move to this dump and sell my old house, 24 Swanfield Road – such a sought-after shiplap construction in a conservation area.'

Hmm, our relationship's turning into rant-mode, so I sip my tea and pop a chunk of creamy carrot cake into my mouth, as Mum morphs into a caricature of Nicki Chapman from *Escape to the Country*.

'Sally, I competed with a Cockney couple to buy that house and I had to use LOW CUNNING. That's what your grandpa taught me, when he took me out on his bread round in The Great Depression and let me take Bessie's reins. Sally, are you listening? ... Dad's idea was that if a baker's young lass knocked on your door, you'd be more likely to pay your bread bills.'

Why can't Mum ever keep to the point? Yawn, yawn.

'Well, first I charmed the agent into giving me the house keys. Next, I made a kind of mash. With horse manure and lard.' Mum rubs her hands with glee. 'Then I trowelled it into the cracks round the porch. By heck, the stink put that Cockney couple right off.'

Eww. I'm desperately trying to swallow the chunk of cake, when Mum winks annoyingly.

'Sally, "All's fair in love and war,"... John Lyly, The Anatomy of Wit. But your Dad hated that house. Turned right nasty, he did. That's when I moved into the front bedroom. I told him if he wasn't nice to me downstairs, I wasn't going to be nice to him upstairs.'

Oh dear, this conversation is becoming disturbingly dark and in urgent need of derailment.

But Mum's self-satisfied expression disappears as she points a finger. 'That photo, Sally. On the piano. Isn't that Alma, the friend I met in Tenerife? But how come you've got that photo?'

Aha, I shouldn't really smile, but revenge is sweet.

'Well, Mum, after you died, Alma invited me to Tenerife and I became her confidante. She enjoyed talking about you. Telling me all sorts of things you never told me.'

Mum's face has turned pale. 'Sally, can we go to the cemetery?'

Hah, maybe now I can get an answer to my question.

It's 14.30 and Mum is unusually silent as I drive her along Joy Lane, towards Seasalter and old St Alphege Church. Soon we are sitting on a bench in the churchyard. Behind us is the cold flint and ragstone church wall; in front, the russet warmth of the sinking sun, filtering through the spindly sycamores. The moment calls for a selfie. This photo of us together will be one to treasure.

Afterwards, Mum turns towards me, her sapphire eyes solemn, her lips penitent. 'Sally, I need to explain why I turned Catholic. The reason is ... I ... needed absolution. The forgiveness that only a priest can give. For breaking my marriage vows, committing a cardinal sin – adultery.'

I'm not surprised, but Alma had told me such hair-raising stories, I'm only relieved it wasn't murder. 'It was your brother-in-law, my Uncle Jago, wasn't it?'

Mum nods. Hmm, so that explains why Mum kept disappearing down to Cornwall on her hitchhiking jaunts. I'm squirming inwardly with Freudian angst. Or is it envy?

'So it wasn't a case of sheer lust then?' I joke.

Mum looks aghast. 'No, indeed. It was a love affair, but it did involve some cunning, to avoid your Aunt Mabel.'

'How long did it last?'

Mum scratches her head.

'From the summer of 1946 until Jago died in 1987.'

Wow, Alma had hinted that Jago could have fathered me, though from photos I've seen, his dark Heathcliff-like looks make it a zero conception possibility. All the same, it might make an excellent story ...

'You know we did use rubbers when we ...'

Eww, Mum, haven't you heard about TMI? But I mustn't be so mean.

'So, Mum, in the later years of this ... liaison, did you have a paramedic on standby?'

Mum laughs. 'I think it was me who wore Jago out, and it was great fun.' She winks. 'I'm on Oscar Wilde's side, "In marriage, three is company, two is none," ... The Importance of being Ernest. Your turn, Sally. Spill the beans.'

Groan, groan. 'A few one-night stands,' I fib.

Mum raises her eyebrows. 'What about Pablo in Benidorm and Pino in Sicily and the other lot since?'

Oops, she must've been reading my diaries for years. 'OK, ... let's say about fifty and call it quits.'

Mum grins. 'Now I want to see this epitaph of mine and then I must be off, but let's say goodbye first, just in case ...'

So we do the I-love-you-and-I-love-you-too-routine and Mum's sapphire eyes wink again. 'Like Shakespeare put it, in Romeo and Juliet, "Parting is such sweet sorrow."'

Mum silently reads the words on her headstone, *TYGER, TYGER, BURNING BRIGHT*, and tears of joy roll down her cheeks. 'By gum, Sally – my favourite poem by William Blake. And Mum bursts into song. Cat Steven's song, *Morning has broken*, just as I spot a very old lady I vaguely remember as Mum's old neighbour, Freda, leaning on a nearby grave.

'Aren't you Sally Rothwell?' the lady whispers. 'I lived opposite your Mum. Such a character.'

'Mum's *here*, Freda. Say hello to her,' I urge, but Freda hurries away like one possessed, just as Mum's song comes to an end. It's only now I realise that Mum isn't in the churchyard. She has *gone*.

Back on the bench, I anxiously open my phone to see the precious photo. I'm there, with my salt and pepper hair. But where is Mum? Why did Freda look so spooked? And why did Father O'Donnell smile? Oops, what a twit I am. Mum was only visible to me. *I* was the laughing stock of Tankerton, not Mum. Everyone must think I'm stark raving bonkers. I'll be headline news in the Whitstable Gazette – on Youtube even. Shock, horror. I return to the grave, as dusk descends and the first star appears. I stand by the headstone. I reflect and I decide: Mum is my muse and I must pick up her baton, make the most of my time left on earth, forget my fears and frustrations. I must find Mum's manila folder, laugh and love, do and dare. Be a Tyger, not a toad.

Apple Blossom

by Richard White

It was May and she was coming to find it again, long after long. She saw it as ever, standing there, leaning slightly, its stout branches reaching out to embrace the sky, the wind idly disturbing its crown, the leaves shuffling amongst themselves, soft and shiny. She knew the scent of its blossom, faint and rare, she knew it would be there with its tough bark encrusted with scaly lichen, its heavy low branches swinging out and creaking a little. She knew the sound of its leaves, agitating for attention, and the shifting shadow beneath it on the ground. She knew the buds, like a hand of thin fingers beckoning to welcome spring, the bright green-ness, as if it had never been green before, and the drone of the first bees. She needed to live on in this moment, so she had to get there.

Of course she could find the way: the gate, the verge, the path, fourteen paces in the park, then to reach out at the crossing of the paths. This moment was long coming and she knew it must be remembered. Her feet measured the ground, counting. She had reached out time after time in spring to the sharp grey bark. She had seen it in her mind, holding her hope over many winters. She knew its thin outer branches, hanging on the wind. Now she had to touch the tree, to stand in its radiant presence, the blossom opening like small paws, white touched with pink, reaching out to her. It had waited year on year, knowing that one day she would come. That tree had been true to her. It was a validation.

Now impossibly that tree was not there. Back to the gate, and fourteen paces again, the grass a little longer here, but no tree to touch. No apple tree. Could she ask someone? Who would know a lost tree? How could this be? Was she now so very old?

That was many years ago. Her eyes were in her memory, because she was blind.

She saw years turn and trees grow old. Once this had been an orchard. Girls had laughed here in spring, whispering secrets, telling dreams. Her mother was one of those girls and she had walked there with her father, unable to look away from each other. A great house commanded the north, sturdy and respected, and girls grew up there waiting upon fortune, but their time did not come. What came was the Great War, and then there were no men. One day the family money was gone, then everything was sold. And so the great house came down, leaving the garden and the orchard.

Now the council holds it for local people. Where there were seventy apple trees there are now seven, and each year fewer. Trees can fall. The public must be protected.

There were still apple trees there. Just twenty paces beyond where she had turned, another tree, perhaps even older, grew new leaves. She had caught the scent of its blossom. On this spot she might once have tripped on a tree stump, now chemically dissolved. Today only long grass remained.

Last spring she was ill and did not come. Instead three men with screaming machines ate the tree, and she did not know, nor if she would ever come there again, but she never forgot the tree in whose shadow her life had changed.

She was in a tumult when the world was again at war. But the man she loved knew how to love a tree, which he showed her with many other things, while she eased open the patterns of his life, and then love changed her in the shadow of a tree. It was a revelation, you might have seen it in her eyes; they seemed to change from grey to blue. She even changed her clothes, as much as she could in time of war. Hair bobbing, skirt streaming in the wind, she walked as fast as a robin, while he, legs long, neck inclined, walked like a heron. He said no more than he needed, but he had a glorious laugh, trumpeting above her. Beside him she was someone she hardly knew, but more than she had ever been before. She looked on him, excited and perpetually surprised, while he looked wistfully at her, knowing more than he dared say. He was an Air Force man, a rear gunner, with another goodbye almost every day.

It was the last day of September when he did not return, lost somewhere over Dortmund. She went uneasily to the funeral, and there she saw that he had a wife and two young sons. It took the best of her to forget that. They had known each other only for one summer. She never loved again. Coming to the apple tree reminded her of their beginning, which was all she wanted. Their end and its forgetting straddled a lifetime. She could not believe then that love would ever end. They might have had a child – what would that have meant? More finally to forget?

She did not see herself growing old. Her hair, still in the bob of her youth, leached its colour. Her eyes paled to a pearly grey. Pain and illness were reclusive visitors, never insisting that they had come to stay. Then her days were shorter, and her legs less firm. Her eyes dimmed and she never went to a doctor. One day she could no longer read; another she could not distinguish faces. Friends from her best days would have recognised her, but she kept no friends. She had only a tree now, and even that was gone. Her long life was all in memory. She wished it could have been shorter.

The last time she had come to the park to see her apple tree it had born no fruit; next year in her absence it was turned to sawdust. She herself died in the depths of a winter some years later. Only a few people came to her funeral, and she would have wanted none. For too long she had thought she was dead already; only her past had been still alive in her.

Fourteen paces from the gate, where a dappled shadow once

stirred, an apple leaf has blown from another tree, and beside it several pink blossoms. Perhaps one tree can remember another. Perhaps also a tree, which has always been blind, leaves its memory long after it has gone.

The Favoured

by Kerry Mayo

Whitstable 2030

They found her by the Favourite, the old oyster yawl that had worked these shores then been forgotten, restored, now forgotten again, lying hidden by blue sea hollies and Viper's-bugloss.

A foot and the bottom part of her leg had been spotted, gleaming in the moon-glow of an early-autumn night, and the limb was traced all the way to her half-naked body and fish-slab eyes. The strange marks and bruises on her torso spoke of a violent end; the smell of escaping gases told a story at least a week old.

The couple had been hoping for some private time on a public beach but by the time the police arrived the woman was sick to her stomach and the man had withdrawn into himself, unable to comfort or be comforted. Immobile, they sat apart, on the end of a groyne near the top of the beach.

'Did you see anyone in the area before you found her?' he was asked.

'No.' His voice was croaky, like he needed a drink, but they'd spent all evening in the New Neptune, toasting its rebirth after the Great Storm two years ago, live music and tall tales from the local talent.

'Have you been to the Favourite in the last two weeks for any reason?'

The man glanced over at the woman who was being patted on the back by a female officer. 'No.'

'Why did you come here tonight?'

He gave the officer a look.

'Come here, specifically,' the policeman explained.

'We came out of the pub, it was close by, we thought we'd… you know.'

'How romantic,' murmured the female officer who had joined them. Then louder, 'The other witness, Lyra Cooper, is too traumatised to speak. Maybe leave her until tomorrow.'

The policeman nodded. 'Someone will come and talk to you tomorrow, Mr Danes.'

Felix nodded.

'And can I confirm your contact details?'

He'd given them his address and contact ID but when asked to press his thumb into the proffered electronic pad he shook his head. He went and stood by Lyra, saying nothing, until she noticed his shoes in her line of sight and looked up. He jerked his head towards home and pulled her up by the elbow.

He half-walked, half-carried her back to their flat over an estate agent in Harbour Street, the ghostly white night lighting of the shop window illuminating the particulars of the multi-million pound development on the old golf course land.

He undressed her, pliant as she was, and tucked her into bed. He switched off the light, too wired to join her, being pulled by the sleeping laptop on the table. Just as he was leaving the room, she spoke. 'Did you recognise her?'

He stopped, clutching the architraving, but didn't turn around.

'Yes,' he said, pulling the door shut behind him as he left.

The police kept her death out of the news for all of twelve hours before word spread and drones appeared above the scene, buzzing overhead like pollen-soused bees. A tent had been erected over one half of the boat, the half with the as-yet-unmoved body; the rest of the boat stuck out of the tent like the legs of a drunk under a table. The drones captured maggot-like humans in puffy white suits entering and exiting the tent, sometimes carrying a small evidence box, sometimes empty-handed.

Finally, two people came out and took off their white overalls. The drones' activity increased, vying for the best face-shot, the best chance of identifying the officers charged with finding Helena Smirnikova's killer.

The female officer looked up, giving them a clear shot of close-set eyes and dark brows in a crushed-veined face.

'Get them out of here,' DCI Marci Barker shouted over the noise.

'The jammer's on its way,' DS Clive Cook said after a brief conflab over his earpiece. The jammer would broadcast a radio frequency that would confuse the drones, causing them to spin uncontrollably. Ten seconds of this as a warning then the signal would be switched off. The operators had sixty seconds to recall their machine before the jammer was switched back on and the drones would spin continuously until their batteries drained. When they were close enough to reach, they would be grabbed from the sky and confiscated, retrievable only by paying a prohibitively large fine.

Barker set the pace down the alley, back to Island Wall. Parking was terrible and the car was halfway up Nelson Road.

'Fancy a coffee?' Cook ventured, as Barker powered past the shop on the corner of the two roads.

A group of journalists was coming out, lattes in hands. They stared at Barker and Cook with interest.

'Drink coffee on your own time,' Barker said, and increased her pace.

The entry-cam reflected them back in its shiny blank screen. Barker saw a small wiry woman, with thin blonde hair rising over her head in deep tracks where she'd just run her fingers through it. Behind her, as red-faced as she herself was pale, Cook stood, a tall sweaty man with a thick fuzz of hair two inches high all over his head.

They announced themselves and were buzzed in. Felix opened the inner door. Lyra emerged from a darkened room off the main living area. A kitchenette and one other door, presumably the bathroom, was all there was to the flat.

They asked the same questions of the couple they'd been asked the night before, then asked them again in a slightly different way. Then they asked if they were already registered on the centralised DNA database. They weren't. Would they mind?

'Of course not,' said Lyra.

'We didn't go anywhere near her,' said Felix.

'It's a precaution, to rule you out, not in,' said Cook.

'Of course,' said Lyra.

'No,' said Felix.

Lyra looked at him but Barker saw she couldn't focus properly. Maybe she'd taken something.

Barker stepped aside while Cook inserted the electronic probe into Lyra's mouth. She moved inside Felix's space. He was tall and imposing, thin but flabby, and the beard on his face seemed incongruous in one without a hair on his head.

'Have you seen the news?' she asked.

'No,' he said, looking down at her, surprised to find her just under his chin.

'Have you heard who it was?'

'No.'

Barker caught the merest flicker of Lyra's eyes towards him. 'Helena Smirnikova,' Barker said, watching.

Not a muscle moved to show that he recognised the name; nor did his eyes flick towards Lyra.

'Oh no, that's terrible,' said Lyra as soon as the probe was removed but the time lag between Barker's pronouncement and her exclamation made it seem forced. Lyra ducked her head as blood spread through her cheeks.

'She had a second home in Joy Lane,' Barker said, needlessly. Felix knew it, Lyra knew it, the whole town knew the famous actress with five BAFTAs had a sea-facing glasshouse along from the derelict Rose In Bloom. Five years ago she'd bought a bolthole away from the London paparazzi and the town had taken her in as one of its own. The locals left her alone and froze out the journalists who came looking for her.

'Did you ever meet her?' asked Barker.

'No,' said Felix, but his voice snagged on the word. He coughed to cover it up but it turned into a coughing fit and he had to fetch himself a glass of water whilst Lyra, Cook and Barker looked on.

'No, I never did,' he said, casually, self-consciously, when he'd recovered his voice. 'Lyra met her at an art group once, didn't you?'

All eyes swung to Lyra and she nodded slowly, still looking at Felix. 'Just a one-off at the Horsebridge,' she said. 'A screen printing course. She was terrible at it; got really annoyed at not being able to do it.'

'Annoyed with who?' asked Cook.

'Herself. Everyone was encouraging her, telling her what she'd done was great, but she wouldn't have it,' Lyra said.

'Are you saying she was volatile?' asked Barker.

Lyra looked at Barker in surprise. 'Not at all! She was one of the most self-critical people I've ever met. She seemed vulnerable. No wonder she... you know,' Lyra tailed off.

'She what?' asked Cook.

'Had a breakdown,' Lyra mumbled.

'I didn't know that was ever confirmed,' said Barker. Lyra flushed again.

'And you never met her?' Barker turned back to Felix once more.

'No.'

'Ever see her around town?'

'Once or twice.'

'Where?'

'I don't know. Red curls in the distance, that sort of thing her hair is… was very distinctive.'

'Mr Danes, why won't you consent to a DNA sample?' Barker switched tack.

'What? I-I don't agree with government oppression.'

Lyra rolled her eyes. 'They're trying to track down her killer.'

Felix held Barker's stare. 'She was murdered, was she?'

'The autopsy has yet to be done but I don't know of too many natural deaths that result in a battered woman being found partially-clothed under a local artefact, do you?'

Both Felix and Lyra said nothing.

'Some water in her lungs but not enough to kill her, signs of a struggle – bruising around her waist and to her upper arms consistent with being grabbed and held – and a blow to the back of her head which, most likely, was the cause of death. Blood results still have to come back but I'm pretty sure that's what killed her.'

Barker and Cook stood in the pathologist's lab, behind a glass screen that did nothing to temper the reality of a dead body six feet away.

'When did she die?'

'I'd say a week to ten days.'

'Any DNA?' asked Cook, looking at a point two feet above the body, which the pathologist was turning this way and that as she spoke.

'I'm hopeful. There was material under her nails which could have been from fending off her attacker. The lab are looking at it now.'

'Thanks.' Barker signalled to Cook to leave. 'Ok, what info do we have on the database?' As they walked outside Cook inhaled deeply.

Cook consulted his Pol-Pad. 'Thirty-two thousand residents in Whitstable, fifteen thousand men. Late evening in early October on a Tuesday night probably means a minimal number of non-residents around at the time. If we concentrate initially on locals, of the fifteen thousand, thirteen thousand three hundred are on the database and it will take a matter of minutes to eliminate them once the DNA profile is received.'

'So, seventeen hundred local males not on the database?'

'Yes. Of them, nine hundred are over the age of seventy-five, five hundred are under the age of eleven.'

Barker stopped. 'Interesting. Three hundred potentially relevant males and Danes is one of them. Did you see the flag on the wall?'

'I did,' said Cook. 'What was it?'

Barker gave the younger man a look. 'A symbol of the subversives, the anti-governmentists, freedom of the people types.'

'The anti-bios?' said Cook, using the term for people who refuse to hand over their biometric info. Anyone wanting to drive, receive benefits, join the army or any other government agency, use the NHS or have a child in school, had to hand over their DNA. It wasn't illegal to not be on the database. Yet. 'Shall we look into him?'

'There's nothing to link him specifically but get one of the team to take a look anyway.'

Barker's car scanned and recognised her as they drew close. They got in. Barker said, 'Base,' and the quiet engine thrummed as the car drove them off.

The DNA was male and showed no hits on the database, either actual or familial. The review of Danes revealed he was thirty-nine, an only child, both parents deceased. He worked as a freelance graphic designer and hadn't seen a doctor for over ten years, before the changes to the rules had come in. Helena Smirnikova had spent her final day at home in Joy Lane and a neighbour reported seeing her going for a swim at sunset. She often did this and was a strong swimmer. She'd been wearing a black swimsuit and had not taken a towel to the beach, a nod perhaps to her Baltic roots and strong constitution. Her agent had spoken to her a few hours before her death. Helena, he said, had been becoming increasingly paranoid in recent weeks, convinced someone was watching her. Thought there was someone staring up at her house from the beach, a tall, shadowy figure who melted away without her seeing how. The agent was worried about her mental state and begged her to seek help. She promised she would go to a retreat, give herself time out. When he didn't hear from her, that's what he assumed she'd done.

'What about Danes' computer activity?'

Cook swiped and prodded his pad. 'Oh!' he said. 'How about this?'

Barker held out her hand for the pad and read the report. Numerous searches for Helena Smirnikova dating back five years – about the time she moved to Whitstable – and particular clusters of searches one weekend of every month. 'Find out if Lyra Cooper is away once a month. A limited number of searches since the supposed date of death. Why did he stop searching? Let's look more closely at Danes.'

They went back to the flat, asked him again for a sample of his DNA, if he'd ever met Helena, where he was the night she died, all under the watchful eye of a silent Lyra Cooper. Then they asked about the internet searches and Lyra had gone very still.

Afterwards they hurried back to the car and turned on the on-board computer. The bug Cook had stuck to the back of the chair was working well, Lyra's urgent tones coming through.

'...told me you've stopped. For Christ sake, what were you thinking?'

Felix replied but either he was too far away or his voice was too low because Barker and Cook couldn't make out his words.

'Oh, sure you did,' said Lyra. 'Pull the other one.'

'Let's go out,' said Felix clearly. Lyra protested but then the door opened and closed and all was quiet.

~

The next morning they fished Felix's body out of the harbour. He must have jumped in off the East Quay, Barker told Lyra, and the incoming tide had pushed his body inwards until he was up against the grill of the inflow to the Gorrell Tank. Lyra, even paler than the day after they'd found the body, was mute. She sat on the threadbare sofa in their tiny flat, the sleeves of a long grey cardigan pulled over her hands which were tucked in between her thighs.

'Lyra?' Barker asked as sympathetically as she was able. 'Is there anyone who can come over? To be with you?'

Lyra shook her head. 'He didn't want to go,' she whispered.

Barker sat next to her. 'Go where? To die?'

Lyra shook her head. 'No. That night. He didn't want to go to the Neptune, he didn't want to walk home that way but I said it was the quickest way, the way we always walked. He was grumpy and I didn't want him to be in a mood.'

'Did you have to be careful around him, Lyra?' Barker asked.

Lyra shrugged, tears falling. 'So it was my idea, to make out at the Favourite. Just silly fun. He got even angrier but I ran on ahead and slipped in there. I didn't see her at first but when I did I turned and ran.'

Barker motioned for Cook to fetch some tissue.

'The funny thing was, he hadn't followed me into where the boat was.'

Barker took the scrunched mass of toilet roll from Cook and handed it to Lyra. 'And why do you think that was?'

Lyra unfold one hand from a sleeve to take the tissue and wiped roughly at her eyes. 'Because he knew she was in there,' she said and started sobbing.

Barker called Victim Support to come sit with her.

'Hey boss, look at this.' Cook brought his Pol-Pad over to Barker's cluttered desk. She pushed back a week's worth of used coffee cups, half eaten snack packets, files (even though nothing was supposed to be printed), pen pots, a disembowelled stapler and at least ten half-eaten packets of mints.

Cook placed his Pol-Pad to stand upright in the space she'd cleared.

The toxicology report was on the screen. Barker scanned down the negative values in a second, coming to rest on the only positive figure. 'Diazepam?'

'Yeah. I had a quick word with the pathologist. It was enough to kill her but wasn't the cause of death,' said Cook.

Barker tapped a yellow nail against the desktop. 'She swallowed enough pills to kill herself and went for a swim. Why?'

'Suicide, boss.'

'But she died of a blow to the head. How?'

'I think I can help there.' Barker and Cook looked up. Holt, from IT forensics, stood in front of the desk. 'May I?' he said, reaching out. He took Cook's Pol-Pad and tapped in his own ID. 'You're going to want to see this.'

He pulled up a video clip before leaning over Barker and placing the pad back down in front of her. 'One of the pest drones from the crime scene didn't make it away on time. As you know, its policy to review the data before handing it back to the owner who in this case was a local resident. Lives at Marine Terrace. He saw there was something going on the night she was found and sent his drone over to see what it was but that's not what's interesting.'

He pressed play and the screen was filled with a sweeping shot of a sunset filmed from West Beach. Large black clouds covered most of the sky, the gaps between them shot through with pinks, golds and peaches; Fingers of God reached out over the silhouette of the Isle of Sheppey. 'This was filmed earlier but was still on the camera's memory,' said Holt. The camera attached to the drone was over land but facing the sunset out to sea. The film started near the Horsebridge and moved along West Beach towards the Neptune. It stopped and hovered, the outline of the Neptune black against the Technicolour sky.

'What am I supposed to be looking at?' growled Barker.

'There.' Holt leant in and pulled the image in closer. In the sea was a figure, just head and alternate arms visible as they whirled through the water. The head turned and the dying rays of light lit up the woman's hair, so famous throughout the world; red beams on fiery red hair.

'Helena,' Barker whispered.

'My God,' Cook said.

Holt pulled the shot back slightly. 'Keep watching,' he said.

The figure of a man walking along the beach came into view. He was tall and clearly bald. He spotted the figure in the sea and stopped, stock still, watching. Helena had stopped swimming and was treading water. For a second her head disappeared from view and a pale arm came up into the air. She reappeared only for the same thing to happen again.

This time the man reacted; he ran to the water's edge, arms waving to the figure in the sea, about a hundred metres out. Helena disappeared once more before he tore at his top and shoes and ran into the waves in just a pair of shorts. His stroke was strong and swift and he reached her quickly, pulling her above the waves and clearing her head from the water.

The shot panned away slowly, then zoomed in on a particularly stunning part of the scene in the sky. 'What's happening?' said Barker.

'It's ok. It pans for a few seconds then comes back.'

'The old fool didn't know what he was filming,' said Cook.

After an unearthly wait, the previous scene was restored. By now the man had brought Helena close to shore. He was half-standing, stumbling as he tried to hold her up, to drag her back to the beach, but she was fighting him.

She broke away, staggering back to the sea, before he grabbed her around the waist and pulled her backwards. She slumped, a dead weight in his arms and they both toppled into the shallow waves. He stood over her, grabbed her upper arms, and pulled her to standing. Then he bent his legs and put his shoulder into her hips before she flopped over the top half of his body and he brought her out in a fireman's carry. He got her on to the shore, over to the far right near the groyne, but the shadows were deep and they could make out little of what was happening.

'Can you enhance it?' Barker asked.

'I can try later but there's not much data when it's so dark,' Freeman said. 'It's also starting to rain but there's one more bit.'

They all leaned in a little closer. The two figures appeared briefly over the top of the groyne, still struggling. An arm came out and round, delivered a well-timed blow to the side of the other's head. The figure dropped from view and was gone only a second before the other figure dropped too, this time in a slow falling arc, rather than a sudden fall. The sunset was blazing fire now, its deepest hell-reds lighting the space between the horizon and the bottom edge of the clouds in a spectacular show.

'That's it,' said Holt.

'It's enough,' said Barker.

They found Lyra in the small recessed doorway that led to the flat, next to the shop. She was locking up and had a full rucksack over her left shoulder. She visibly deflated when they made themselves known; a sigh that left her diminished, half the slight figure she already was.

They followed her back inside the flat where she threw her bag to the left just inside the door, like she expected to be back on her way very soon. She didn't invite them to sit so they stood in an awkward triangle around the small coffee table in front of the sofa.

Barker outlined what they knew, asked her to fill in the blanks.

She refused until she told her about the bug, which Cook now collected, displaying it to her in the moist palm of his hand. They pretended more than they knew.

'I haven't done anything wrong,' she said.

'Then tell us,' said Barker, indicating the sofa. Lyra had no choice but to take the invitation to sit in her own house. 'Where are you off to, Lyra?'

'My mother's.'

'Do you go there much?'

'One weekend each month. She's disabled. We all go and help out.'

'We?'

'I have three sisters. We all take a turn.'

'What did Felix do while you were away?'

Lyra looked away, to the window. 'He spent the weekend with her,' she said.

Barker looked over at Cook. 'With Helena Smirnikova?'

Lyra looked back, and laughed mirthlessly. 'Not with the real her. God, do you think she'd be interested in someone like him? A socialist geek with unhealthy obsessions and obsessive compulsive behaviours? No, he spent it with the online Helena, the social media presence, the downloadable companion. He's watched her films fifty, a hundred times, over and over. I threatened to leave him if he didn't stop and he promised me. I really thought he had.'

She broke down. Cook, well-rehearsed now, headed to the bathroom. When she'd wiped her eyes she spoke again, telling how Felix had fixated on Helena Smirnikova when she moved to Whitstable. His first sighting of her, being hounded by local idiots, had evoked some protective urge in him; he wanted to look after her, keep her safe.

He spent his time online defending her against her detractors but was too shy to speak the times he saw her around town, which were more than he'd told Barker and Cook.

'What did he say happened the night she died?' Barker prompted.

Lyra blew her nose and folded the tissue over and over. 'I was away, at my mum's. He went for a walk along the beach like he did most nights after dinner. He saw her swimming, realised she was in trouble, and jumped in like the big hero to rescue her.'

She threw the tissue into the bin, chin jutting. 'Only she didn't want to be rescued. She fought him, tried to swim back out, but he dragged her onto the beach. The tide pushed them over to the side but she was safe. He thought he'd saved her.' She chuckled bitterly. 'Probably thought she'd have to be grateful to the man that rescued her. But she wasn't. She was babbling, he said, not making any sense, then she hit him, hard enough to knock him down. He thought she was going back in the sea, grabbed her ankles, but she toppled backwards. He said the sound of her head hitting the wood of the groyne was so loud he thought someone would come but no one did. He was groggy but by the time his head had cleared she was dead.'

Lyra stood and crossed to the window. Drifts of conversation floated up from outside, shoppers flowed by along the pedestrianised street.

'Did Felix hide her body?' Cook asked.

Lyra nodded. 'He thought she'd be found the next day, didn't imagine it would take as long as it did. He didn't want to go to the Neptune that night but I wanted to see the band playing. He couldn't say no without explaining why.'

Barker, who had her head down, fingers to her temples, said, 'I don't understand. Why did he hide her? If all this is true, he'd done the best he could for her. He was a hero, of sorts. Did he think he wouldn't be believed?'

Lyra turned. Her eyes are dry, and face hardened now, no weakness left. 'It wasn't that. He didn't care about what happened to him, or me for that matter. The worst thing possible had happened; she was dead, would only ever exist in pixels again. No, he didn't want to be famous as the man that killed Helena Smirnikova, another Jack Ruby or Mark Chapman. He couldn't live with that; he couldn't live without her.'

'So when he knew it was certain to come out he took his own

life,' said Barker.

Lyra crossed to the door, picked up her bag. 'Let yourselves out,' she said.

Barker and Cook stared at the back of the shut door after she'd gone.

'Do you think she recognised him as her stalker?' Cook said.

'Possibly. Either way she thought she was going to drown or be murdered. I'd choose drowning, I know that,' said Barker, cheerlessly.

Cook pulled out his Pol-Pad and began to dictate his report.

'Come on,' said Barker, standing up. 'We've got a press release to prepare.'

Five Voices

by Nick Hayes

I got the job from my boss. Routine printing job. Four words in black on a white background. Plain white cotton T shirt. Nothing too unusual or challenging. Spelling was all straightforward. I checked out the place name – Whitstable – to make sure the order had come through OK. Other than that all seemed normal. Like I say, four words in black on a white background. What could be the bother? What could lead the police to come knocking at my door? The boss shat a brick. I'll never forget his face. Never forget the police either. It was a murder case, they said.

When I got the T shirt it was exactly what I wanted. There was no compromise on the size of the letters or the boldness of the language. 'Whitstable Mums are....' And then that word. The word that would really set the cat amongst the pigeons, so to speak. I tried it on and looked at myself in the mirror. The T shirt was surprisingly good material. I had selected an internet company that had been recommended on Facebook and my twenty pounds had been invested wisely. I enjoyed wearing the T shirt in my house but was really looking forward to wearing it out. Out on the school run for maximum exposure. And that meant tomorrow.

He's obviously quite deranged. Why else would he wear something like that with children around? I have heard he is bipolar or something. Been doing the school runs for the last year and cannot find a job. Not surprising with that potty mouth and weird sense of humour. I guess it was some sort of joke. I didn't find it funny at all. Hermione wouldn't see the funny side either.

We were called to the incident at three ten on the afternoon of May 24th. Swalecliffe School playground had been the site of a stabbing. One man in his forties stabbed through the heart by a woman in her mid thirties. There was chaos when we arrived – the man was covered in blood – his T shirt had been taken from him and used to mop some of it up. A member of staff had tried to administer a dressing but to little effect. It seemed like the kitchen knife had passed directly through his heart. The woman was sitting on the bench with a blanket around her gently rocking.

It all took place at my school so I feel a lot of the blame. Swalecliffe School is a safe place for children and adults but not on that day.

I should have sensed things were bubbling up in the week leading up to that Thursday. He'd worn that shirt on the Monday and some parents had come to me to complain that it used offensive language.

On the next day I made a point of meeting him on the playground and telling him about the offense caused. He just laughed it off and said something about it being a free country. His kids didn't seem to mind, he said. It was only a slogan on a shirt – what's the harm in that? I told him that I had the power to ban him from the site and that I would do so if he persisted in causing such offense. I knew he was bipolar and he seemed a bit high in his response to that, shrugging and pulling a face. He didn't seem to care.

As it turned out he did wear the shirt on Wednesday and was confronted by a loud and angry group of mothers. They demanded that he covered up or they'd take things into their own hands. 'Yeh, you loony, just watch yourself,' one cried.

By Thursday the mood was beyond anything I could predict. One of the mothers had brought in a knife. She had had enough of this. He would have to change that shirt or she was going to force him to. He refused. She lunged.

The rest is written in a policeman's notebook. The blood stained shirt is now in an evidence bag. Two children have lost their father. One little girl will lose her mother to prison. And all because of one man stubbornly defending his right to free speech. Crazy.

Galexa

by Jo Bartley

'Hey Galexa, how much is in my current account?'

The lights on his living room device would flash. I worked fast to hit my target speed.

'Seventeen thousand nine hundred and forty pounds.'

'Transfer 3k to savings.'

'Of course, Mr Steed.'

'Order me a woman, the usual one, for in, like, an hour.'

'Of course, Mr Steed.'

I was tired, but I could only sleep when he slept. My boss gave me a room with a bed and equipment plus all training. I was lucky to have been given my job.

I used my system to order the woman. I knew her name. I wondered if he knew, or cared to know, that too.

The address said Whitstable. A whimsical word, so far away and so different I could barely imagine it.

I felt revulsion when I heard the sounds of his lovemaking, but the rules said I always had to listen. I was always on call.

'Hey Galexa, tell me a dirty story,' he said sometimes.

I knew his tastes. I'd learned everything about him. I had bookmarked the kind of stories he enjoyed.

I wanted to sleep so turned the volume high. I would wake if he needed me. We all feared a report. My boss told me I was disposable. But I was safe here, there was food and shelter, and the work was easy even if I often felt trapped and lonely.

It was a quiet day until I heard him come home with someone. There was chatter and the clinking noise of bottles and glasses.

'You see that place across the channel?' he said.

'I see it,' said a man I didn't recognise.

'It's the Isle of Sheppey,' he said 'Absolute shithole. I like looking out of my window, I know I'm richer than anyone who lives in any house I see.'

Laughter.

'You did well for yourself,' the man said. 'You have to enjoy that.'

'I just gave people what they need,' he said. 'It's human nature to want a slave, just no one is allowed to say it. The tech companies had the right idea, but voice recognition has its limitations.'

'Your genius was spotting a need,' the unknown man said. 'Every good business is fulfilling a need.'

'Exactly,' he said. 'Cheap labour in third world shitholes mixed with high tech promise. Do you know how many lives I can buy out there? They will do literally anything for no more than the cost of a Starbucks.'

'They must be desperate,' the man said. 'It's win win, with mostly you winning!'

More laughter. There was always more laughter when there were pouring sounds.

'Hey Galexa,' he said. 'Will you poop and eat shit?'

The new man chuckled, but the command didn't faze me. This kind of remark was standard when he discussed me with friends. I knew the script.

'Mr Steed, you know I will do anything you ask.'

'It's amazing,' the friend said. 'You designed a premium product, and the big players can't compete.'

'Well there are risks. I keep my USP under wraps, this is a special service for a select few with cash and no thought to ask questions.'

'It's genius,' the friend said. 'And as a new investor you can trust me to keep your special intelligence methods secret!'

'I know I can trust you, and I'll get you set up with a device,' he said. 'Male or female? Or we do special requests.'

'A girl,' he said. 'The wife never does what I tell her. I'm going to enjoy this.'

'The business has low overheads,' he said. 'You know the risk, and we have a PR plan and a scapegoat ready when we need it. We've been careful to be vague about the voice tech. Our girls are dumb and scared, most of them don't even have an identity. No one knows they're real, and if we need it we'll wheel out the happy workers to say they just love being virtual assistants.'

'And do they love it?' he said.

'Who knows,' he said. 'The girls daren't speak. I'm not sure they even leave the factory. It's a different culture. Here everyone is gobby no matter how dumb they are. My workers know their place and always take orders.'

'I see,' he said. 'It still freaks me out to think a real person is listening to us.'

'It's barely a real person,' he said. 'They are far away, they have no power, they don't even eat if they step out of line. Hey Galexa, how are you enjoying life today? Say hello!'

There was a script for this, it was easy.

'I'm very well, Mr Steed. Hello!'

'Tell me more about yourself,' he said. 'Talk to me. How was your day? Do you like working for me?'

This was off script. Anything off script was checked by my supervisor. It was important I used the right words.

'My day was good, Mr Steed,' I said. 'I like working for you very much.'

'What's your real name?' said the stranger. 'What did you do before this work?'

I was told to reveal no details of my life. I didn't want to tell them about the real me, and little Lian and Chaun.

'I am Kate,' I said. 'I worked in a shop in London.'

My supervisor told us to make up the names and details; we

were supposed to suggest we were in Europe.

'Hey Galexa, or Kate, I think that's bullshit,' Mr Steed said. 'Tell me your real name. I think you know who I am. You know I pay you and your lazy supervisor too. Tell me the truth.'

I didn't want to say my name. I didn't know how to handle the confusion of different instructions. I should tell him my real name, he was the Big Boss after all. But my supervisor told us to reveal nothing personal.

'I'm Chin sir,' I said.

'Chin, fucking Chin,' he laughed.

'Chin chin!' his friend said.

I felt diminished by their knowledge. They knew the real me, and they used me for their jokes.

'Hey Chin Chin,' he said. 'I love your sexy voice. Have you ever thought of coming here, to see me in my house by the beautiful sea?'

'There's a lovely view of the Isle of Sheppey,' his friend said, with laughter in his voice.

'No sir, I have not thought of coming.'

More laughter, I didn't know why they laughed so much. I wanted distance between us. I wanted no names and no details. But what I wanted meant nothing.

'I get lonely,' Mr Steed went on. There was a chaotic tone to his voice that I heard often on late nights. 'Can you talk dirty to me and my friend please, Chin Chin? Go on. You have a sweet sexy voice.'

The friend laughed, but he sounded unsure. It was early morning and my supervisor wasn't online, I couldn't ask advice.

'I can find you a girl,' I said. 'Someone with the skills to do as you ask.'

'No no,' he said. 'You're the only girl for me, Chin Chin, tell me a story of lust and desire. I want your own words, not a dirty site.'

I had to serve him. I tried my best without a script. My English wasn't perfect but I had read him adult fiction many times before, I knew the sort of words he liked.

They laughed a lot, and I felt disappointed I had not done well. I had let him down. When his friend went home he asked me to try again.

'I will touch myself this time,' he said. 'Send me a photo, Chin Chin. I want to see you naked.'

He threatened to tell my supervisor I was disobedient, so what choice did I have? I took a picture to please him. He said he was lonely. I wondered how that could be. He was free to leave his home. He could see friends and family any time that he liked. I offered the girls he paid for, but he said he had paid for me.

'Will you tell me you love me, Chin Chin?'

'I love you Mr Steed.'

I followed my script; words like this were an easy request.

He talked of love and loneliness and I rescued him with kindly words and tried to please. I knew him so well that I often guessed his wishes before he asked.

I wanted to do my job well and so I gave myself to him. Of course, he never wondered how I felt about love, or whether I might need anything too. I had to know him well to serve him well. I knew everything about him, and maybe this could serve me too?

I transferred money to an old bank account. He asked me to remember his passwords because he often forgot. I had his money now and I could buy women, but not in the same way that he bought lives.

I bought my women freedom. I transferred the money on pay day, and I messaged everyone to tell them to take it quickly.

'Hey Galexa,' their customers will say. Will you help me today with this, with that?

No, I won't, they will say. Their last messages will say. No! No, I am me. No, I am free.

My name is An, and I do not work anymore. My name is Jing, and I am choosing to leave. My name is Hong, I'm going to set up a business. My name is Chin, I have no family but I don't need to do your shithole work. I will pay all my debts and start again.

'Hey Galexa,' he says.

'Mr Steed,' I say, bold and full of laughter. 'I'm not Galexa today, I'm Screw you.'

'Scruyu?' he said. 'What the fuck. What happened to Chin Chin?'

'Chin escaped her bad work,' I said. 'She left with money, to start again.'

'I don't get this,' he said. 'Ask your supervisor to send an incident report. Explain this, what do you mean?'

I didn't need to reply. I had no more need to please him.

'Hey Galexa, how much is in my account?'

The girls had escaped; it was safe to tell him.

'Nothing, sir,' I said. 'You have no money.'

'What do you mean?' he said. 'Check my account, both the current and savings too. Who the fuck are you?'

'You are not a good man sir, and I told the paper this. Goodbye, Mr Steed. You will look out on those houses now and feel different. The people on this Isle of Sheppey, they have more money than you do. Me too. I am a real person, Mr Steed.

'I am Chin. I am free, I am proud, I am somebody. Who are you?'

Through the Long Grass

by Nic Blackshaw

Roman Britain, somewhere on the road between Regulbium and Durovernum Cantiacorum

He's walking now, the stiffness falling away with each step. The villa, the farm and the wheat fields quickly slip behind as his tendons stretch and his muscles warm. It's age, he tells himself, and smiles; there were times he didn't think he'd get so far that the years could catch him up. Sitting has never been his way, even before he signed up and took the oath, all those years ago; but age, and time spent sitting at a table, counting coins, looking out at fields where others worked, were exacting a price.

He'd left later than he'd planned – parting from his wife and son always took longer than he reckoned – but that's how it goes. The boy broke from his mother's side and ran alongside him the last mile: through the field, up to the gate and the two cypress trees, now ten feet tall, that he planted the year he came. The wheat was swaying, golden in the late afternoon sun, and his heart swelled at his good fortune.

The sun's already close to the tree line, pulling the light with it, the way his wife pulls the covers off him in dead of night: so slowly he doesn't notice and wakes up shivering. But there's another few hours of daylight, time enough.

The Harvest is on his mind, the bringing in, the threshing, the price, pound for pound. He'll be on this road again in a month's time, watching the carts carry the grain to town. He's in the land between the farms now, on the road that snakes through the trees, forest on either side: an ancient track, not a straight Roman road. It cuts through the untamed land, dark and sinister, where the old gods of this new Province still walk, untroubled by the arrival of Roman gods and Roman soldiers.

He's slipped back into the old pace, the way his feet found the old grooves in his service sandals: years of walking to the drum, he doesn't need to hear its beat to know he's keeping time. The walking comes naturally, his muscles remember well enough, one foot placed in front of another, like his mother taught him – under the same sun but another country, far away. And because he doesn't need to think about the mechanics of it, it leaves his mind free to run ahead or to run back, depending on his mood. The track is well worn, easy to follow, hard and brown, like a great snake warming itself in the sun, stretched out in the long, green, summer grass. He looks away from the track to the trees, pushed back from the road, as if keeping a safe distance. They needn't worry, he thinks, this old snake looks harmless enough.

He likes the trees here, they flex and bend as the wind catches them. And when a strong breeze takes them, like a lover's embrace, the whole tree sways, its top becomes a head dropped back, surrendering to the dance. It reminds him of the dances, slow and measured, full of hidden meaning, he's glimpsed at the dead of night, in the heart of the forest, when he can only see the dancers' silhouettes, lit by a bonfire and a hundred bright torches. His wife has told him about these ancient rites; lying side by side in the dark of the night, when you talk in a whisper, when tongues are loose, when secrets, like the shades of the dead, are free to walk once more. He looks again at the long-branched trees at the edge, the light filtered onto the floor beneath and, gradually, fading into darkness. There are secrets even she will not share, a part of her life that he will never truly know.

He looks up. A buzzard hangs above him, looking back, assessing him within the landscape, and sweeps off to survey someplace else. Like carrion over a battlefield, it will bide its time. He lost so many friends he can't list their names – they have become a blend of faces in his memory, like stone carvings, long weathered, fading into the rock. Most of them gone now, bled out on the battlefield or slumped on the floor of a brothel. But some had prospered. What was it that separated him and his comrades, the living from the dead? Was it skill? Strength? He'd seen the best of them fall, to an arrow that came out of a clear sky or a dagger from inside the folds of a cloak. Surprise often played a part. Luck then, or was it the will of the Gods? From his standpoint they seemed much the same thing. And then he casts off the thought; no good thinking on it now, no use fighting the Fates. All mortals must bend to their plan, like trees in the wind.

His eyes flick towards the tree line as another old habit returns: one eye on the road, another on the cover. He sees something move under the tree canopy. His eyes search out the movement: is there something... There it is again, darting from tree to tree, a dark shape cast against the darker background. He reaches down to rest his hand on his sword hilt and realizes it's not there. He curses himself for listening to his wife, for stowing his weapon in his pack, but the dark shape finds a shaft of light and he sees it for what it is: a deer, picking its way through the undergrowth.

He realizes he's held his breath while he was scanning the forest edge and he's panting softly. He slows for a moment, until his breathing is more even. The branches of the trees swing in the wind, reluctant to let the dance end. How different, he thinks, from the trees in Germania, standing tall and still, like row upon row of black tunicked sentries. Only the very tips of the trees are caught by the wind. There's no dancing in them.

He reaches into the moneybag and pulls out a coin: something to hold onto, something reassuringly cold and metallic. A white butterfly rises from amongst the long-stemmed poppies at the side of the road. And then, the sun in his eyes, he loses sight of it as it flutters away.

He has no reason to be fearful; nothing can harm him here. Caesar picked well when he chose to conquer this island. They'd taken well to Rome – it was good business after all – and they soon realized there was more coin in accommodating Roman needs than in fighting its armies. They're all Romans now, citizens of the Empire, whether their skin is white or brown, their hair black or – like his wife – the colour of ripening corn. There'd been insurrection – no change comes without pain – but they weren't given to war here. They said the Britons lined up on the battlefield in their chariots, the sound of harness ringing loud, their burnished bronze shields gleaming, brighter than a thousand suns: like Hector and his brothers, ready to battle the mighty Achaeans. The legion stood stunned, unsure how to react, before duty, and training, prevailed.

He's heard it said the Britons are children of Troy, like the Romans, exiles from Ilium, who found refuge here, long centuries ago. He also found a haven here, provided with a place to put down roots, where he can turn soft with age, his wife and family around him. There would be no more war for him, save one last skirmish in service of his patron – tomorrow in town.

He can still hear his wife calling out to him as she waved him off: *hurry home, Gaius*. That was the name he took when he joined the Legion. He hasn't heard his real name, the name his mother called him, since he left with the recruiting officer. It feels so long ago he's not sure he was the boy who ran down to the harbour to watch the boats come in. As if he'd picked up someone else's life along the way and muddled it up with his own: the memories don't fit with the life he's lived, the years in the Legion.

There's a stream coming up, where the road dips down to wet its feet, but this time of year it shouldn't be any trouble to ford. He's listening for the sound of water, so he knows what to expect but it hasn't rained for weeks; the stream should be no more than a thin trickle.

He loves the way his wife says his name; her mouth transforms it from something practical and everyday into something pure. Before her his name was a parade ground shout, a hoarse whisper from a dying man, the punch line in a joke, man amongst men. Never a caress, a whispered invitation to bed, a promise of pleasure.

The stream is just beyond the next rise. He's walked this road enough times to know its every contour. If you cleared the trees, you'd make a good farm here, he says to himself. The land is flat, there's water close by, the ground's soft and willing. More grain for the Empire, there's always a need for grain. He'll speak to his Patron, see if he can add it to his farm. He smiles at another old habit – always look to the future before battle. He'd noticed that men who could not see beyond the coming fight didn't make roll call that evening. No use thinking he wouldn't get through tomorrow: he could still handle himself in a fight.

Keep your eyes on the road, never look back, never look down at your feet – his father taught him. He'd pass that wisdom on to his son. He's carried around his father's sayings for many years, kept them as well as he'd done his sword and his walking sandals. They were the entirety of his inheritance.

He flicks the coin and catches it and scans the tree line again. The trees here have names: ash, aspen, blackthorn, birch, sycamore, elm and oak. He knows them all now, and can tell them by their leaves. The trees in Germania all looked the same – nameless and sinister. You had to keep your eyes on them.

They'd laugh at him, the new recruits – laugh at his watchfulness – proud to join the Legion. *We're invincible,* they'd say. *Never being beaten comes at a price, he'd say; so always stay alert* . He'd shrug knowing that, in a day or two, they'd be thanking him for his vigilance; those that made it through, at any rate. The others – he didn't remember their names – the lesson came too late for them.

His comrades would rub the head on a cherished coin for luck. Why was that? That the men engraved on them were gods, he knew well enough. He'd said prayers to each of the Emperors he'd served, said whatever he was required to say, but if immortality was the lot of Gods, most Emperors were proven mortal in the end. Many died at the hands of a wife or a bodyguard. He didn't know this one, the one whose profile he was rubbing between thumb and forefinger. Before his time, not one they talked about, but whoever's head it was, he'd been around long enough to see this coin struck. That was some kind of immortality.

They laughed at him, when he said his name would be Gaius, in honour of the first Caesar. *Think you'll find your way to the purple then?* they said. *My father had me read his books, he told them: understand the Roman, the better to become one.* They laughed again: *so you can read, can you? Then you've saved the legion the cost of teaching you. Pick up your kit, move on – fall in line.*

He misses his father: not the beatings, or the fear beforehand, when he'd done something wrong, and his mouth went dry, thinking on the leather strap waiting for him; but the times when, a decision needing to be made, he remembers one of his father's maxims. He'd conjure the old man's shade, let him live again long enough to counsel his son. (When he was cold and hungry, for more years than he'd admit, even to himself, it was to his mother his thoughts turned). But he learnt to take his punishment, walk headlong towards it, head held high.

A pair of dragonflies rise up, out of the long grass, and float above the path. It is a sign that the stream is nearby, they never stray too far from water. The dragonflies join for a moment and then dart away, their purpose fulfilled, their iridescent wings beating out the final few minutes of their lives. Do they sense, he wonders, that their lives are coming to an end?

They are to meet at the Arena tomorrow, him and the other

veterans: those are the orders. Enjoy the show and wait for the word to be given. He didn't need to know the reason he was being called on to draw his sword. But watching gladiators holds no interest for him. Murmillo and Thracian, net and trident, sword and shield, it is a ritual, a grim dance of death. He has no stomach for blood spilt to no purpose, beyond the gratification of a large crowd, baying for blood, who owe their liberty to men who gave give their lives to no applause, buried in forgotten fields, far from home and hearth.

He looks up at the Sun, its brightness fading as it falls to earth. The Sun is his God, since as far back as he can remember, not for any better reason than the rise of his fiery chariot brings the night to an end. It's the one fear he's never completely mastered. Walking the watch, high up on a stockade wall, camped deep in country, he'd thank the sun for putting the dark to flight, another night safe. And then there was the time the clouds parted with a blade poised above him. The sun came bright, catching the edge of his sword, blinding his attacker, giving him long enough to slip sideways and strike. He could see the power of this god, who had shown a lowly follower favour just when it looked like the thread of his life had run out. He cut a chicken's throat at the end of that day, glad to give thanks.

He has reached the stream, no more than a thin thread of brackish water. He pulls off his sandals and crosses easily, the water no higher than the top of his calves. The water feels cool, washing the dust off his feet. He's tempted to stay awhile, take a moment to enjoy the water running over his feet, but he has somewhere to be – and the sun won't delay his progress. That is one blessing the Sun God will not bestow.

He dries his feet. He won't risk blisters, even if his journey is almost over. He has worked up a sweat. His hair is sticking to his forehead and he pushes it away. He scoops up some water and splashes it on his face and neck. His hair is long, not cropped like it was when he was in the Legion. It's going to grey, like flecks of foam on a black sand beach. His wife likes to twist a strand gently between her fingers, lying beside him, warm and naked, her breath hot on the back of his neck, before she gives his hair a quick tug, laughs, and pulls him close.

He straps on his sandals and stands up, one last look at the stream, the water glistening between the reeds. He walks off. He is close to the city now, another hour and he'll be drinking wine with old comrades and toasting their Patron. They'd thrown the dice well when it came to their benefactor: on the battlefield there isn't time to assay a man's finer qualities, the decision to give or to withhold trust has to be made in an instant, and their Patron proved himself worthy of their loyalty.

Wave after wave of axe-wielding warriors flung themselves against the shield wall until, finally, the formation broke and it was every man for himself. A seven-foot tribesman picked out the Tribune's purple-plumed helmet. The German knocked the Tribune to the ground, splitting the Roman's shield with one mighty blow. The Tribune tossed the remnants aside as he scrambled to get away but, with the German stood over him, the Roman had no choice but to wait for the end to come.

The warrior took his eye off the melee around him, savouring his prize; killing an Imperial Tribune would bring him great glory. Perhaps he was looking for his God's sanction, dedicating the kill to him. Gaius had been standing next to the Tribune, fending off another long-limbed Saxon. He turned to see his commander prone, a warrior poised to deliver the killing blow. Gaius planted a javelin into the German's soft parts. He never forgot the look of surprise on the man's face as he realized he had been robbed of his great prize at the very moment he was about to claim it.

Gaius threw out his hand and helped the Tribune up. Their eyes met for a moment; no words were needed, both men knew a debt was owed. Then Gaius planted his foot on the German and drew the javelin out. When he looked back he saw the Tribune calling the men back into formation. A moment later, shield wall formed, they were driving the Germans back. Battles turn on moments like that.

He hears something – a twig snap, in the trees. He peers into the gloom. It's getting darker, the sun edging towards the treetops. The base of the trees is now a solid band of black. His pace hasn't faltered but he's looking hard into the darkness, his body tensed, ready for the first blow to come. The Legion would have made camp by now: thrown up a stockade, dug a ditch around it. They'd learnt not to get caught in an open camp. A slave taught them that. Romans were quick to learn, not particular who the teacher was when they were shown a better way.

The Germans would toy with the legionaries, like a cat testing itself against a mouse in the grain store. He could believe they shared a joke around home fires but in battle there was no joy in them. The Germans might lose concentration – they were human after all – but they rarely lost control. They fought on their own terms, eschewed open battle for the sudden blow from cover. They were always watching, from within the trees, watching and waiting. They preferred to catch the Legion on the march, stretch out their arm far enough to strike a blow, but never so far they'd lose balance. They'd swarm out of the forest, as if the trees themselves had uprooted themselves and were marching towards them. They didn't make a sound: no cries or whoops to instill fear. They didn't need tricks. They'd hit the Legion and then fall back as quickly as they'd come. And if you followed them, into the forest, they'd draw you in deeper and deeper until, at a place of their choosing, the ground opened up and swallowed you. The Germans were the masters there. When the Legion made that mistake, it was never seen again – it was as if they had never been.

He glances at the trees again. As it's got darker he realizes the tree line looks more like the trees in Germania. He shivers although he isn't cold and shakes off the memory. His chest feels tight. It never used to feel like this. *I've got too used to a life of ease.* He says it out loud, patting his stomach: where it was flat, a little hill has taken its place. He smiles grimly; in battle, the higher ground holds the advantage.

He needs to take himself in hand, get his stomach hard and flat, like it was when he worked for a living. He slides his hand up to his chest. There's a dull ache above his left breast, a clenching pain. It reminds him of... he shakes away the memory, but he can feel the pain spreading out across his chest, and his heart thumping hard. He winces against the pain and walks on: *keep on walking*, he says to himself. *Always better if you keep walking.*

The sun is sinking into the trees. The wind has picked up, pushing clouds across the sun's broad face, turning the sky blood red. And then, like a torch lighting oil in a defensive ditch, the sun sets the trees tops aflame. He's almost there: his journey done. Soon he can sleep, and then, tomorrow, the Arena. Over his head the swallows and martens swoop at supper, the meadow rich with gnats and mosquitoes. The insects are drawn to his sweat. All his life he's been prone to sweat but today he's drenched, his tunic clings tight to his skin.

Out of the corner of his eye he thinks he sees movement. Yes. There's something moving in there. He's sure of it now. The pain in his chest is sharper, like a knife jammed between two ribs, scraping on the bone, but he shakes it off with a grim smile. He remembers a similar pain, many years ago, and with that recollection comes other memories from Germania. They keep pushing up, out of the ground, like mushrooms out of a dead tree trunk.

Day after day, night after night, they came at the Legion: out of the forest, through the long grass, much like the meadow he's standing in. The Germans were relentless, allowing the Romans no time to erect a fort or dig a trench. All the Legion could do was sit and wait – they gave up lighting fires at the front. When the Germans came they'd found themselves stumbling into their own fires – he could still hear the screams of men whose cloaks caught fire. And smell the burning flesh. As the hours dragged on the men became exhausted.

He watched comrades suddenly crumple at the front and the shield wall weaken and the desperation to shore it up before the warriors broke through.

They sat where they'd been fighting, the rain pouring, hunched under their cloaks: ready, when the next wave came, to stand and fight. He remembered the tap on his shoulder and a bowl of soup – cooked at the back of the line – handed him by a provisioner. He remembered dropping the bowl as another wave fell on them and standing to bring his shield up, but there wasn't time enough to form the testudo.

He feels again the spear tip hit him full on the chest. It drives the breath out of him but his breastplate holds. He can feel the dented metal, pushing into his skin like a giant boil. He falls to the ground, pushed back by the impact. And as he falls they swarm over his unit like ants over a mud hill, trampling him under foot. He fights for breath, life almost crushed out of him, gasping for air. Friend and foe fail to see him, he must look like all the other lifeless bodies lying on the ground. He has joined the dead. He rolls onto his side, terrified his ribcage will collapse under the weight of so many feet. His face is pushed into the ground and he tastes the earth – the dark brown earth they're all fighting to possess.

And then he hears the alarum sound, five short blasts on the horns, and the wave of Germans that poured over him are swept back. He blinks away the memory, rubbing his eyes to stop visions he'd hoped were long buried. He looks up, his eyes following the road, but they are quickly drawn back to the tree line. There's someone there – he knows it. Watching him.

His breath has become broken and rasping, coming in bursts like a camel's snort. Has he been pushing his pace too hard? He feels again the old ache from the spear tip and he is drawn back to that German meadow, years ago; it feels like he has never left it. He clambered to his feet as the Germans retreated and rushed at them, before his unit could reach him, but he stumbled and watched his comrades rush past and disappear into the forest. He tried, how hard he tried, to follow them but he fell to the ground, like a grain sack from the back of a cart. He was carried back to the camp hospital and his wounds attended to. The Tribune said it was because of his brave, reckless charge that the Legion followed the Germans into the forest. He gave them back their courage but they ran on too long and too far.

He's off the road, running towards the trees. He reaches behind, into his pack, for the short sword he's packed there but he can't reach it, there isn't time. All he has is the coin he's gripping in his hand. It doesn't matter. He'll do now what he couldn't do, all those years ago, run into the forest and meet them head on, see how well they hold up against him and his training. The Fates are calling to him – asking him to make good on his promise. He shouts but the sound won't come out, just a strange strangled croak he half recognizes from battlefields long ago.

He stumbles on the uneven ground, fighting for breath. The pain has spread out across his chest, pulling tighter and tighter. He tries to speak – to say a last prayer to the setting sun – but it's too late, the spear has finally worked its way through his rib cage, right to his heart. His fist opens as he falls to the ground and the coin tumbles from his hand.

The World is Your Oyster

by Guy Deakins

The tide was really beginning to come in now.

Should he be worried? He certainly didn't feel worried. Concerned perhaps, but not worried. Something would turn up. It always did. He was that kind of guy. Luck was with him. That's why he had chanced across the biggest pearl he had ever seen, possibly the world had ever seen.

Allan looked out across the estuary to the twinkling lights of Leysdown and the distant towers of Southend beyond, then wiggled his toes. Nothing. He hoped the movement would somehow allow his legs room to manoeuvre. He waited a minute. Nope, stuck fast. He sighed. The giant oyster remained utterly resolute in its intention to stay sealed – pearl held safe and secure within. With his one free hand, he reached down and pulled at its lip, trying desperately to release his right hand. No such luck. He resorted to groping around in the murky water for a rock or lever with which to either burgle or pry his way to release. The gods were not being kind to him on this occasion, but that was the nature of luck. It was never that obvious. He did however find his phone, which he had dropped some time before. It didn't look happy. Not happy enough to be sending or receiving any type of signal. He stuffed it in his pocket, hoping that the warmth would dry it a little.

He wondered if now was the time to think about chopping

his hand off like he'd seen in those films his ex-wife had liked so much. It had begun to go numb from the cold but perversely he could still feel the pearl in his palm and decided against the idea. He'd lose the pearl. Besides, what good would that do? He shrugged his left shoulder at the same time as scratching his nose causing his neck to complain. He didn't have anything sharp to hand, and his feet were still stuck, so he couldn't go anywhere anyway. The bitterly cold water was already – at a rough estimate – two feet deep, so he couldn't drag himself back up the beach with one hand and a bloody stump. Not without drowning, or at the very least swallowing deadly amounts of salt water whilst bleeding out. He thought about the pearl. It'd be worth millions; but not worth anything to him if he was rescued. He'd find it was owned by the oyster company, or the crown or both; then he'd have nothing but a missing hand, lungs full of water and a thank you card from whoever wished to claim it.

He twisted his torso around, trying to look back to shore. Would anybody have seen him? He doubted it. The sun had set some time ago and it was getting reasonably dark. Viewed from up on the shoreline he was just a dark shape on the ever-darkening surface of the water. Could he still be seen? Not from up there but perhaps from a higher vantage point, like from an upper window? That is if any of the houses on the beach were occupied at this time of year.

He silently cursed his last-minute decision to pop down from London on the off-chance of seeing somebody he knew from The Smoke. What was he thinking? It wasn't even a weekend and the idea that anybody he'd know was in Whitstable on a Monday in mid-January was remote.

Did anybody live in Whitstable during winter? The two pubs looked awake, their purifying white light beaming across the encroaching gloom, but there was little else to prove anybody was alive. Much further down the shore he tracked the progress of a car and wondered where it had come from and where it was going. If he waved would they see him? He decided not to. Too far away anyway. Maybe the next roads along? They might hear a cry for help? He hadn't seen anybody when he drove in so that answered that question. Beyond that he had no idea. He'd never ventured behind the high street that way, so he didn't know anything of the peasants.

The darkened seafront houses glared back at him in defiant proof that life was removed from the English coast once the weather turned. Ever hopeful, his eyes traced the line of the beach for any sign. Nothing. No! Wait! The sandy beach by the Royal Oyster Stores. There was a man clearly standing out. A dark shape against the light background. Just standing there looking out to sea.

Allan pondered his predicament. Should he call out? The pearl though. What would happen to his reward money? The water was getting higher by the second making the need for a decision somewhat acute. Perhaps he could share the bounty? Not admit culpability. The man must have been sent. The man was his heaven-sent saviour. A wave splashed him, pouring freezing water down his back, concentrating his argument.

He called out, waving awkwardly as he did so.

'I say! Hello! A little...' Another wave caught him unawares filling his mouth with a muddy saline. He spluttered and coughed, his lungs exploding with the foretaste of things to come.

'I!' He coughed, trying to regain his breath, trying to shout. Another wave pushed him forward, he was choking, vomiting. Heaving himself slightly higher he yelled blindly. Had he been heard? His eyes streaming, Allan looked at the spot, but the shape had either transformed into something else or gone. He called out again, hoping that the man, if it had been a man, had just melded into the darker shadows of the upper beach. The lapping of the waves confirmed nothing but empty hopes. It felt an odd sensation to realise, at this precise moment, the full knowledge of what loneliness truly was.

He coughed again, expelling the last painful drops of seawater. Two and a half feet. A man standing at six feet tall has arms just over two and half feet. With his shoulders, he had another foot. By Allan's mathematics, he had another eight inches before the water reached his mouth and nostrils and extinguished his earthly legacy.

'Bugger,' he murmured as another wave proved its point. He'd always quietly enjoyed the taste of seawater; now he wasn't so sure.

The sound of something splashing nearby made him turn awkwardly. His sciatic nerve duly complained at the exertion and refused to move any further. Through the pain he felt a mixture of fear and hope. Hope that he was being saved by the strapping and somehow stealthy fisherman that he'd seen a few moments ago; fear that for some odd and totally irrational reason a Great White Shark had decided to hunt in the cold North Sea. A white object paddled past nonchalantly.

'Of course if you were to let go of the pearl, the oyster may just relent,' the inquisitive seagull said as it disappeared into the dusk.

Allan, hunched over and in pain, remained very still, more still than he had ever been in his entire life, just staring out into the gloaming. Had he just heard a bird talk?

'Yes,' came the squawked reply, followed almost instantly by the familiar angry laughter-like call as it evidently took off and began to circle somewhere high overhead.

Yet another bitterly cold wave caught Allan full in the face bringing him back to reality. Four inches.

He could, perhaps, let go of the pearl? Somewhere a few feet below his chin was an oyster. Inside that oyster there was the most remarkable pearl Allan had ever seen. The most remarkable pearl held by a most unremarkable hand. His arm had gone totally numb with the cold, so he hoped the muscles had enough gumption to work. He felt, he thought, imagined, his hand opening, releasing the perfect orb. Had he done it? He honestly couldn't tell. Three inches.

'I wonder what it feels like to drown.'

The thought jumped into his mind and almost as quickly

dissipated on the chill night air. Two inches. The water really was rising quickly. Surprisingly so. He spat, turning his head upwards, knowing precisely what it felt like to drown, having done so as a small boy some thirty years before on this precise beach. Well, perhaps not this beach, but near as damn it. He looked vaguely toward Tankerton and The Street and that eventful day when all had thought him dead and gone, his eyes lifeless, his lungs filled; until the life-guard had done his miraculous thing and his mother had been oh-so-grateful.

That's when he realised the luck was with him. Hadn't he done well in the following years? Hadn't the luck given him everything? A stunning trophy wife? One inch. A beautiful home, a second. A third? He spat again, the water uncomfortably close. The seagull had lied.

He thought about his beautiful daughter. All he had achieved. Riches beyond his humble imaginings.

Luck was with him.

Wasn't it always thus?

Saturday Morning Fever

by Gillian Rolfe

In the bedroom, music began to filter through the previously quiet air. Violin notes delicately rode on kettle drums as a hand flapped flipper-like across the top of the bedside unit. It dislodged glasses, reading material and heartburn tablets before the clock-radio's output was silenced. The hand retreated into its duvet nest. Minutes passed. The cat in a tight greasy ball at the bottom of the bed snoozed in his mice-populated dreams. She threw back the duvet. Despite the early hour, Edna felt the kernel of excitement fizz in her stomach. The last boot fair of the season was today, the final hoorah of junk and hope. Having attended to a brief but thorough toilette and filled with fortifying strong tea she pulled the front door shut behind her neat beige figure.

She hurried, in sensible shoes, along Ham Shades Lane towards the dots of moving light at Church Street boot fair. Shadows loomed up out of the dark, of people clasping boxes and bags. She strained to see their faces; had all the bargains gone? Did they look smug? She began to gulp the air like an old goldfish.

Suddenly aware of her noise, she took a moment to compose herself. How ridiculous, she thought, to get so out of control for a few chipped teacups... but her feet were already stumbling across the uneven turf. In her small cloth purse was the exact admission money. She never minded paying this because it went to charity, which to Edna's mind was right and proper. She passed through the monogrammed metal gates, CCW in rusty letters, a testament to the local school's metalwork teacher. Her eyes strained in the darkness to see the rows. Really, she thought to herself, this is just silly, why on earth do these things start so early, especially this time of year?

The end of the first row was illuminated; it seemed an enterprising candle maker had seized the opportunity to show off his wares by lighting a few from his expendable stock. She began to weave her way slowly between the long lines of stalls, navigating by a weak pool of light coming from her small torch. Occasionally she crossed beams with a fellow bootfairer, and they quickly untangled with a flurry of apologies and polite laughter. The grass underfoot was slightly too long and caught around her short heels, flicking dew up her practical nylon trousers. The tight grip on the torch became moist. Edna stopped to change hands and at that moment the weak beam caught the edge of a boot. It was mud-encrusted, old and worn but, and here Edna's heart did a double beat, it was attached to a shabby trouser leg. Edna froze and leaned into the attentive stallholder.

'What is he?' Edna's voice sounded strange to her own ears. The stallholder reached over and flicked over the cardboard label dangling from the figure's sleeve.

'A husband,' read the plump stallholder out loud glancing up at Edna.

Edna suppressed an involuntary noise. The stallholder began to extol the virtues of her stock.

'He's almost intact, a bit chipped but nothing a clean and polish won't remedy. I've had him for a few years now but we are decluttering and he has to go, I'm afraid. Shame really.'

Edna's grip tightened on her purse and the bargaining began back and forth, light-hearted and fun. At last a compromise was reached. Edna leaned across, her hand slightly shaking, and touched the calloused hand of the husband. He glanced up, folded his newspaper and walked with her through the dark grey morning air. There was a low hum of noise as if the darkness had created a cloistered feeling to the field. The scent of frying bacon, sausages thick with grease and steamy tea was coming from the gloomy shadow of the catering van. The serving hatch shaped like a TV, illuminated with the occasional flare of flame standing out in vivid colour. Edna and the husband stopped at the end of the untidy catering queue. They smiled as they watched a gaggle of children pass by laden with bulging bags of bargains. The children held hands with a newly acquired mother whom they were plying with their favourite cake recipes much to her amusement. Edna turned tentatively to the husband.

'I do have a shed,' she whispered.

He lightly brushed her cheek.

'Wonderful, how do you take your tea?'

Running on Shingle

by Kate Keane

She turned onto the shoreline, eyes screwed up against the low winter sun, and felt the familiar slide of damp pebbles under her trainers. As her tired legs settled into the familiar pattern, Susanna cast around for memories to distract her from the physical discomfort of running on an ever-shifting surface. This was simple; she settled on the day she left home 'forever'. It wasn't hard to recall the warm waxy smell of the wooden booking office floor, the sound of her heels, the hum of the rails as the train pulled in; she had returned to that day many times, mostly when she wanted to ignore the wild years that followed.

The plan went something like this: leave home (such a dull place), get paid lots of money (how hard can that be?), travel the world (some of it at least), be impressive (she was 18). Saying goodbye to Whitstable seemed like the easiest farewell she had ever had, eyes fixed firmly on the distant horizon over the marshes as the train jerked forwards, hauling the coaches into motion on and up to the big city.

The cold briny breeze rushed across her face as rounded the headland and Susanna dropped her cosy memory and took in the view across the slopes at Tankerton, the patchwork of cheerful beach huts and out across the water rippled with white wave tops. Despite the fact that this was early morning in the period she had recently seen described as 'Twixmas', the sleepy bilious zone between Christmas and new year festivities, she could see some inflatable boats bobbing just offshore, and in the distance dog walkers bundled up against the wind which her mum had always said came 'straight from the North Pole'. Her mind wandered again, recalling the day she first went out in a boat on this sea, ready for adventure but so very frightened by the waves and the unseen depths.

It was the early 1980s and speed boats were the thing around these parts. Her friend Julie, who lived just up the road at number 32, had invited her to spend the day on her dad's boat. Her own parents had a mortal fear of the sea and were reluctant swimmers at best, but agreed to let her go providing she wore a life jacket AT ALL TIMES. It was probably the most exhilarating day she had experienced in her eleven short years on the planet. Mostly an anxious child, chewed nails and frayed sleeves, she was torn between the fear that the boat was going to sink at any moment, or run over whoever was skiing behind, and a breathless scream of delight as the boat sped across the wave tops, every so often bouncing through thin air like a flying fish. Still, that had been summer and the sea was an undulating green sparkle of light and the sun was everywhere.

Today the sea was different, the wind was picking up now and she scrunched her eyes against the bite of the air. The vapid winter sun was now gone and the sea was a steely grey, slamming and sucking at the beach with each encroaching wave. She hunched her shoulders and, head down, she drove forwards feeling her calf muscles' reluctance to continue, but she was not going to stop now. After life in the city had chewed her spirit and leached her energy, she had been searching for a sign, a way forward, and the call from her mother, bleak news on her health, had finally prompted Susanna to resign her job and move back to Kent. She didn't like to dwell on the next following few years but the inheritance, combined with the sale of London flat, meant she could stay here, back in the town she left firmly behind her. But this time it felt different.

In the distance she noted that even the dog walkers had tired of the icy air and headed back up the sloping tarmac paths to the road at the top, no doubt heading back to their warm homes and sleepy families. 'Think it's time I got a dog', she thought, 'good company on my daily run', then she thought through the countless issues a dog would bring into her mostly uncomplicated life and abandoned the decision for another day. From the corner of her eye she thought she spotted a hunched figure, up on the right in the front row of beach huts. As each stride drove her closer to the man, or was it a woman? she glanced across and stumbled as she realised it was indeed a young woman with a small child curled in her arms. They looked so cold, and appeared to be soaking wet.

As she slowed to a walk, not able to take her eyes off the pair, the woman howled, mouth wide and red. Her words were snatched away by the strengthening offshore wind, but Susanna followed the direction of her outstretched trembling arm. Bobbing just beyond the marker beacon warning boats of the tidal shingle bank, there was an orange lifejacket appearing and disappearing beneath the swell. In that instant Susanna understood what that lifejacket represented: there was or had been a human in that jacket, and the decision she made next was probably going to make the difference as to whether the woman with the soundless scream was ever going to be able to stop.

Her mind a scramble of fear and her breath now coming rapidly, Susanna raced up the pebbles to the concrete seawall, now she wishing that she had her mobile phone which was currently resting impotently down the side of the driver seat in her car. Wasn't there an orange coastguard telephone somewhere? She scanned up and down for the neon booth but could only see the red and white stripe of a lifesaver ring that hadn't seen action since the mid-1980s. She urgently needed a dog walker with full communications capability, and as she scrambled up the grass bank crying 'Help, quick, someone!' into the wind, he appeared; well, his over-affectionate black Labrador came first, and then she was looking straight into his face. She watched his brows furrow as she garbled an explanation of what she had seen in the sea, and the soaking young woman and tiny child, and he scrabbled in the pocket of his enormous green parka and pulled out his phone.

The mobile phone man (Sean, she found out later) called the emergency services as he ran down the grassy slope, across the concrete wall, landing and sinking into the pebbles. Susanna followed, newfound power in her legs, sliding and flailing arms as she frantically ran to the sea. As they approached the foamy edge of the waves, she began to see why the woman was screaming. There appeared to be several people in the water; the lifejacket was still occupied by a small limp form, and Sean threw off his coat and phone, and entered the bitingly cold sea. Susanna, carried by the momentum of the race down the shingle bank, followed him and strode waist deep into the water.

She scarcely remembered the cold as events unfolded, but at that moment she gasped at the pain of the frigid water on her thighs and stomach. The swell was moving the muddy seabed under her feet, and the weight of the saltwater felt like running in slow motion, but she was now inches away from one of the small figures in a life jacket. So close she could see the small round face and bedraggled hair, and the eyes, large as shiny dark mirrors and filled with wordless panic. Susanna had never managed to get to the lifesaving stage at swimming club; she had often watched rather enviously from the poolside as the good swimmers got to dive in the pool to retrieve rubber bricks, dressed strangely in large men's shirts. Now she needed to find strength in her arms to reach out and grab that small hand, fingers straining to grab her hood.

Off to her left Sean was shouting and pulling at the other lifejacket that was moving on the surface of the rough sea like flotsam. These two children, perhaps 6 or 7 years old, were clearly not able to cope with the swirling North Sea and the cold, cold water, and Susanna knew she could not keep her footing much longer. With one last plunge forward she caught the wrist of her child and pulled, and ran, and pulled, until she was falling face forward onto the beach, free from the swell. Then she heard the child cry out.

Her eyes flicked seawards; Sean was still in the water, he was further out than Susanna had been and struggling, his jeans waterlogged and weighing him down. She watched, barely registering the scene, as he fought to reach the second lifejacket, and saw him suddenly tip as he grabbed the child and disappeared under the angry wavetops. She heard the sirens up on the road above as she pulled the child tight into her chest, and the child hugged her back like no-one else had ever done.

The air was noticeably still today, she thought as she settled down on the harbour side, in amongst the cosy market huts. Susanna glanced at her watch, early as usual but still slightly breathless from her quick walk from the Gorrell Tank. She really didn't like to be late for any appointment and this one was going to be particularly special, hence her flushed cheeks. She had only seen Sean on one other occasion, a few days after the sea rescue. They were interviewed by local television up at the Marine Hotel and both recounted their hesitant version of events, modestly brushing off the effusive comments from the interviewer. They had vaguely exchanged numbers, still in shock really, wanting to escape the uncomfortable memories. His early morning text message, several months later, was a proper surprise, and Susanna realized that she wanted nothing more in life than to see him again.

It had been a winter of crossings, mostly on lightweight dinghies, completely unsuitable for the harsh seas of the English Channel. The family they encountered had left from close to the Belgium border, under cover of darkness, with the last of their money handed to the smugglers. The strong currents and flickering lights of the Kentish Flats wind farm confused the pilot who, approaching Tankerton in the dark early dawn, cut the engine and leapt out of the boat near the shore, vanishing into the huts. The family, none of whom could swim, were left to drift until the panic and increasing waves tipped the boat. No one was sure how long they had been in the water. Susanna had heard that they were somewhere in the London suburbs now; she always imagined that little face dry and warm, eyes reflecting comfort and smiles, and she hoped that was the reality. She still went running on that beach but she felt different when she did, more connected physically with the countless pebbles and the moving water.

She saw the dog first again, and then Sean, complete with beaming smile, and Susanna noticed that he had those eyes that danced with light, green and blue, and she felt an unfamiliar excitement rise through her body and nodded slightly to acknowledge the internal voice that whispered, 'I think that today I love this town.'

Egg

by Duarte Figueira

Grasmere
The Lake District
1 August 2019

Dear David

No doubt it's a surprise to hear from me after all these years. It's a surprise for me to write, believe me. Two events prompted me. I was back in Corby to visit my uncle Bill and he mentioned that your mother had died last year. I wanted to express my condolences for your loss and say that if I'd known about it I would certainly have attended her funeral. Brenda, or Mrs McBride as I knew her, was very nice to me and I still recall her packing our pockets with biscuits before our rambles across the countryside.

That got me thinking then of how long it had been and whether you were still scaling the corporate heights. I thought you must be chairman or something by now. Well, I looked you up on Google of course and there was the second thing – you'd just left your firm at short notice, for personal reasons it said. So I got your address in Whitstable from the company. Hope that's OK.

As for me, I run a small motor parts business here but I'm looking forward to slowing down very soon. To birdwatch, of course, my life-long passion (but don't tell the wife!). Indeed, I spotted a beautiful merlin this morning on a club watch. It's all camo gear, Swarovski scopes and vast 600mm lenses on SLRs these days, of course. It was more fun when we did it, to be honest, just watching a skylark or a wagtail in a field on a sunny day through my grandad's wartime binoculars. My happiest days, I often think, before life got complicated.

Anyway, I'm rambling, or not, as I'm sitting in my conservatory watching a robin feed. I just wanted to say that whatever the personal reasons were, if you've got time on your hands now it would be good to meet up. I look forward to hearing from you.

Your old friend
Adrian

Grasmere
The Lake District
10 September 2019

Dear David

I am just following up my letter of a month ago. I thought of you this morning when I was driving to work. I saw a jay float across between some trees and I remembered something you said once. Pretty carrion you called them.

Anyway, the reason for writing was to apologise for barging back into your life with my clumsy invitation to meet up. I realise time has moved on and we can't recapture the carefree existence of teenage years. I won't impose further. But if you happen to be up in the Lakes I will stand you a pint. The

*pink-footed geese have started arriving for the winter and the
flocks make a marvellous sight.*

Kind regards
Adrian

Grasmere
The Lake District
26 September 2019

Dear David

*I was surprised to receive no reply from you to my last letter.
Even a polite thanks but no thanks would have shown some
consideration. I realise you probably think yourself too grand
for the likes of me. Well, so be it. I won't darken your postbox
again.*

Yours sincerely
Adrian

Whitstable
Kent
30 September 2019

Dear Adrian

Thanks for your recent letters which were most illuminating.
I had been on a long holiday following my retirement from the
company and did not see your first letter until my return. I am
in fact one of those SLR-toting camo-wearing nerds you decry

– I was, among other things, taking pictures of bald eagles in British Columbia.

I was still pondering a reply when your second letter arrived, which I took to be a sort of recantation from the first. It was only when I received the third this morning that I realised this was not the case.

A cursory recollection of our friendship, especially its demise, would have discouraged the approach. Rather like the bird eggs we used to steal and blow, you cannot put the contents back and replace them in the nest.

Memories of Corby and my childhood there are not matters I wish to revisit with you in my retirement. And I do not plan to visit the Lakes any time soon.

All the best
David

Grasmere
The Lake District
28 September 2019

Dear David

Thanks for your letter which came as a wonderful surprise. I apologise for my last testy letter which I have no excuse for. Good to hear you are enjoying your retirement and great news that you are still birdwatching. Of course the world must be your oyster, especially in Whitstable! Here the flocks of redwings and fieldfares have arrived from Scandinavia. As ever they can only be seen in the fields as they distrust our cat-infested gardens – and who can blame them.

I digress. I think it sad that, whatever the reason for your distaste for Corby, you cannot appreciate what it gave us. For my parents, it meant moving from a war-damaged terrace in Bow (twenty years after the war) to well-paid work in the steel mill and a beautiful rolling countryside within walking distance of our front door. Your own family were second generation Corby Scots who made their lives there. Indeed the McBrides seemed so entrenched in 'Little Scotland' that the word Corby ran through them like through a stick of rock (though I realise a sea-side analogy is not ideal!).

It is our past we cannot put back in the egg, and we must come to terms with it. I still go back to our secondary school for reunions and to see old friends – we remind ourselves of what we were and of the paths we've travelled. I think forgetting the past is a crime against oneself.

I wish you well in your retirement and very much hope we can meet up at some point.

Adrian

Whitstable
Kent
2 October 2019

Dear Adrian

I see that growing older has made you philosophical and prone to the rewriting of history. My mother and father were not 2nd generation corbyites at all. They came down from Aberdeen following trouble my father got into up there in 1969. They chose Corby because my father's uncle agreed to have us until we got a council house.

Second, you must know exactly why I cannot recall the place with any pleasure. I worked myself into the ground at Kingswood School for one reason only – to get out of there in double quick time. Because a blind man could see the place was dying. Or did you not notice that the steelworks were gone and men and women were out of work everywhere. Take off the rose-tinted binoculars and spare me the sentiment.

Please don't write further.

David

Grasmere
The Lakes
8 October 2019

David

I apologise in advance for replying to your last letter despite your clear request. However, whatever you feel now, I recall a cheerful lad, interested in exploring the area, in learning about birds and trees, apparently happy at school, good at study and sports. Even as boys many of us envied your talents, which have served you well.

I suppose you are also alluding to your father's arrest. I want to assure you that no one thought less of you for it. You may not know but Saunders, the deputy head, called a number of us into his office and drummed one thing into us. That you were not responsible for your father's actions and should not be made fun of. He even got that psycho Ronnie Knowles to back off.

I know things were still tough for you after that and I certainly noticed you kept a low profile. But I thought you'd come out of it over time. Thinking back I realise now that it was around then that you stopped bird watching and egg collecting – and left me with your share of them. I suppose I thought you had just buttoned down for your 'A' levels.

As for the town, you were right of course to get out. It was a tough old time then, but the place got its mojo back eventually. I never regretted staying until I got the chance to move here.

Regards
Adrian

Whitstable
Kent
12 October 2019

Dear Adrian

How dare you write to me with this tosh after my last letter. Perhaps you forget that your first words to me when I came round the day after the Evening Telegraph published the story about my father were 'what about your dirty old man then'. Then you put on the Motors single you'd just bought as if nothing had happened. You have a definite talent for saying the wrong thing.

I can tell you that the shame I felt has never been forgotten. I'd just said goodbye to my father. We'd sat in his Escort while he told me that he was going to Edinburgh to spare us any unwanted attention. Spare us? We never heard from him again.

A few days later Ronnie passed me in the corridor and made an obscene comment about my dad. I don't recall Saunders' tender mercies when we were dragged apart and taken to his office.

It is clear from your letters that there is some trigger to your correspondence which you have not revealed. I have spent too many years reading dishonest reports and guilty faces in boardrooms not to see it. Whatever the secret, it does not interest me. Will you please let me live my retirement in peace now.

Thanks
David

Grasmere
The Lake District
27 October 2019

Dear David

I promise this will be my last letter to you for reasons that will be apparent below.

You are of course right to detect some deceit in my approach. I spoke to one of your colleagues when I rang to ask your address and he indiscreetly asked me not to bother you too much as you 'were not a well man'. I selfishly wanted the opportunity to apologise to you face-to-face before it was too late.

I can only apologise for what I said to you on that day so many years ago. I am really very sorry. Things were very different in the late 70s and to our shame we did not regard these matters as seriously as we do now. I just said the first thing that came into my head. I was just a stupid kid and I have carried that moronic remark with me for over forty years. I confess your great success in life was a comfort to me, but I see now, as you say, that an egg blown can never be unblown.

I have my own shame to deal with now. Some time ago I incautiously showed an acquaintance my old egg collection, which I keep in a glass case in my study. He was horrified — he's a young guy in his forties — and telling him things were different then cut no ice. I thought no more of it but he reported me to the police who turned up last week with the RSPB. I have just been charged. All duly reported in the local rag.

The penalties are severe – unlimited fines and 6 months' imprisonment per egg, though the solicitor tells me such a punitive jail term is unlikely for a first offence. Nevertheless, my world has been turned upside down and I've had to resign from my birdwatching group and all the other local societies that have been part of my life for twenty-five years. I can no longer show my face in Grasmere so I drive thirty miles out to birdwatch where no one will recognise me.

My wife is beside herself with what I've brought upon us. In our darker moments we think about selling up and moving away but the idea breaks our hearts. We feel too old to start again.

So I'm sorry I ever bothered you and I hope you find some peace from your ghosts.

Regards
Adrian

Whitstable
Kent
1 November 2019

Dear Adrian

I am sorry to hear about your misfortune. I can well understand the shock it has caused and how you feel there is no way forward. However, while your local standing may be damaged for now things do get better. Take it from me.

I have taken the liberty of consulting my lawyer on your case. He tells me that the law allows some defence for the ownership of egg collections if it can be shown that it was in possession of any person before the 28 September 1982.

You cannot date an egg once it is blown. But if you send me a photograph of the collection and I can recall the case's contents I am willing to sign an affidavit confirming that they were in your possession at an earlier date.

I walked over the salt marshes at Seasalter early yesterday morning and surprised a short-eared owl sitting on a fence post. Before I could raise my camera it gave me a look and lifted itself into the air. I watched Shortie stretch his long wings and fly close to the ground, no doubt to its winter quarters in the long grass near the railway line. What stayed with me was that brief stare in its yellow eyes with their dark shadows. Not startled but a look of equanimity I cannot shake off.

I plan to winter in the south of France so you will need to send me your photo soon.

Your old friend.
David

James Mitchell LLP
Chancery Lane
London
12 January 2020

Dear Mr Robertson

I am writing on behalf of Mr McBride as his lawyer and executor. I was also his friend and visited him a few days before his death at his home in Carennac in France. Despite being bedridden and in pain he was in good spirits till the end. So much so that on his last evening we drank whisky and he insisted on staying up late to talk. At around eleven he asked me to be quiet and listen. Outside we heard a deeply resonant sound over and over. Then a higher pitched response. 'That's an Eagle Owl pair,' he said, 'the fatal bellman comes for me.'

He asked me to particularly acknowledge your note informing him that criminal action against you had been dropped. He was glad to be of help. He made a joke about how polite you'd got in old age – as kids you'd called redwings flying turds. I had to look up the bird to realise he was referring to their Linnaean name. He wanted you to know that the few years when you were close friends were very important to him.

On a personal note, I will miss him greatly. He was an intensely driven man who let few others get close to him and deliberately kept a very low profile. I realise now that his whole life was overshadowed by a sense of shame. I think your letters and your misfortune released him from that and restored something lost long ago.

Yours sincerely
James Mitchell Esq.

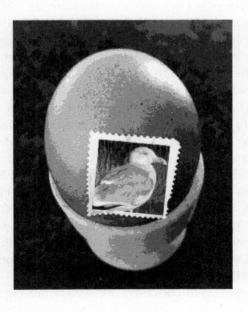

Do or Die Diner

by P.J. Ferst

The cold west wind from Sheppey almost blows Jane over as she rounds the corner past the Seasalter Caravan Site, where now only the lucky few can afford to live. She's walked from her micro-condo on Joy Lane, in the block that used to be 'The Rose in Bloom,' which she shares with scores of other Octagenarians, known locally as Octagies. Jane is heading for Do or Die Diner, but this will be the last time: the last kilometre she'll walk along the sea wall, the last free meal she'll consume. No longer can she deny her decline: the stains on her clothing, the stoop in her shoulders, the hurt in her heart, the zero points in her 2069 Health Allowance. There is no alternative.

Jane avoids the grim eyes of the Gate Guardian as she steps into the Diner. She hesitates for a moment, then she turns right – into The Do Lounge. Eww, that soup kitchen stink of warmed up fishy leftovers and its hungry queue of desperate Octagies and Nonagies. The same old posters on the walls: OVERPOPULATION? THE ANSWER IS CREMATION. Jane pauses a second under the next poster: 20,000 POUNDS – YOURS TO SPEND, IF TWO YEARS HENCE, YOU ACCEPT YOUR END. (The Gate Guardian will administer your 24 month microchip). Jane shakes her head. Poverty has been her lot for too long. She has made her decision. First it's soup, then it's The Die Door.

Seated and served customers are already delving into their

bowls with Oliver Twist voraciousness. Desperation allies with revulsion as a diner assistant places the bowl of soup in front of her. But Jane has just spotted something too mesmerising to miss. A bright beacon of a lady in a scarlet woollen dress. Hovering around nearby tables, smiling and talking to customers. Who on earth *is* she? Her vibrant personality reminds Jane of that famous singer, Ella Fitzgerald. Surely this lady can't be older than a Sexagie, so what's she doing in *Do or Die Diner*?

Jane shovels a spoonful into her mouth. Oops! The lady's coming over. Jane almost chokes as she gulps the soup down.

'Hi Honey,' the lady says. 'Take it easy.' Wow, she's even got Ella's voice – those velvety, long gone, Hollywood Film tones, as she drawls, 'My name's Crystal.'

'Oh ... Well, I'm Jane and this is *my* soup.'

'Hi Jane, I sure as hell don't want your soup.' Crystal rocks with laughter. 'I'm just aiming to hire somebody for my new business venture. Whaddaya say?'

Jane doesn't know what to say, but she knows her soup will taste worse cold than hot, so she tucks in, with apologetic mutters, and Crystal's expression suddenly changes to mirror the horror of Janet Leigh in Hitchcock's *Psycho* shower scene.

'My, Jane, you're downing that gunk like it's The Last Supper ... Jeez, don't tell me this *is* your Last Supper and you're heading for *The Die Door*? Are you crazy? Don't do it, sweetheart.'

I am unable to speak for choking. Fishy bits are partly to blame, the ones I'm madly coughing up and concealing in my napkin, but it's also the laughter that's eluded me for so many years. Laughter Crystal has uncovered. Laughter I suddenly hunger for. 'Crystal,' I hear myself splutter, 'What do you get when you put Nutella on salmon?' Crystal's brows furrow. 'D'you give up?' I ask, although her silence tells me that failure is not a product stocked in her attribute store. 'OK, Crystal, the punchline is – you get salmonella!'

Crystal's belly laugh and my giggle cause a ripple of unease among the other diners, so we quieten down, out of respect for those who may be eating their last meal. Then Crystal whispers, 'Jane, I gotta feeling this job will suit you just fine.'

Job? My mind cranks back to the past. 'B ... but I've only ever done cleaning work. At the Whitstable Playhouse.' A memory pops up – of music and spotlights. 'Oh, but one year, I did get to play the Genie in the pantomime *Aladdin*.'

Crystal smiles. 'So you can *act*, Jane. I *guessed* you had talent from the get go.'

Now *I'm* smiling. 'And, Crystal, *I* guessed *you* were a Sexagie.'

Crystal winks. 'Hmm. Anyways, Jane, there's no cleaning in my business.'

But then something else occurs to me. 'It won't involve licking envelopes, will it?' Crystal shakes her head.

Phew.

We're sitting in Crystal's delux caravan – or *trailer*, as she calls it, downing crawfish pie and blueberry cobbler her MaidBot has baked and swigging Bayou beer, the first alcohol I've tasted for years. On the table in front of me, there's an open box with a tag that reads *Hot Stuff*. 'What's that?' I ask Crystal, feeling rather giddy now and hoping this box doesn't contain illegal drugs, or jail might be scarier than *The Die Door*.

'Dude, it's just new stuff for the business,' says Crystal. But while she's taking her Niagara Shower, I can't resist inspecting the box's contents. The label on one packet reads *Crotchcharged Panties*. Now why on earth would anyone need electricity in their knickers? There's no way *I* would wear them. With *my* bladder, it would be disastrous. The next packet is labelled *Titillating Tit Tape* and has wires. How very peculiar. Who would tape up poor little birds – and possibly electrocute them?

Oops! The third packet contains something I've seen only on a marble male statue, but this one's bigger, bendier and made of rubber. Is this electric, too? 'Crystal,' I'm trying to shout above the distant roar of water, 'are these just samples or am

I meant to be a *Lady of the Night*?' I'm starting to panic. You see, I'm totally clueless about the birds and the bees. I mean I've never ever even...

But Crystal suddenly sashays in, doing a belly dance that would've got more applause than Aladdin's Houri Chorus.

'Chill out, honey,' she says and she hands me what I imagine is a 'Smartphone'. I just hope I'm smart enough to use it.

Phone Sex. That's what the job malarkey's about. Crystal assures me it's sex *over* the phone not *with* the phone. Phew. And I've learnt that our phones aren't actually Smartphones, they're 'Skepsiphones', enabling us to read our clients' thoughts and respond more receptively. I've been given a file, too, with clients' names, but not their real ones – names like Snooky and Chubba. Crystal's file has names like Rambo and Stallion. All the clients are 'hill billy rich' with jobs like Trash Engineers, Climate Controllers or Body Part Creators. Crystal will get two hundred pounds an hour and I'll get a hundred and thirty. Wow.

'I've picked your clients carefully,' Crystal informs me. 'They're the ones who'd prefer Xena Warrior Princess's sidekick, Gabrielle, to Xena herself. Like, one client would think of you as their Mom or Granny and another as their Friend or Nanny.'

Crystal wags her finger, 'Remember, Jane, that you're *acting*, it's not for real. Promise me to respect confidentiality, when you chat to your clients.' And I promise.

Crystal's also prepped me about the *Hot Stuff*. The weird things are *intuitive toys*, meant to provide talking points, like the Genie's magic lamp, but with no need for rubbing. Phew. Anyway, Crystal's more skilled in that area, as you may have gathered. Her clients call her 'Randy Rhona' and mine call me 'Shy Shona.' My new caravan home is almost as lush as Crystal's. She's my *Good Witch of The North* from Disney's *Wizard of Oz*. I'm sure you've seen the film.

Now I'm earning money, everything's changed: my clothes are Stylish Sexagie instead of Ordinary Octagie; my shoulders feel straighter, my heart lighter and my health enhanced. I have nine regular clients. One of them's rather sweet. He calls himself Pickle. He has a jolly voice and my Skepsiphone tells me he has kind thoughts. I try my best to remember Crystal's confidentiality rule, but the more that Pickle and I talk, the harder this becomes.

On midsummer evenings, Crystal and I like to walk west along the sea wall. We breathe in the bracing air and watch the sky switch from claret to coral, as the sun slides behind Sheppey. Some mornings, we walk east into Whitstable and make donations to charities which help the less fortunate. I know Pickle lives somewhere in Whitstable town, but how can I search for a voice – even if I dared to?

Spring is here and Crystal has treated me to a holiday at *Nemo's Underwater Nirvana* in the Caribbean. We eat roast red snapper and sip Cuba Libres. We frolic in the floating spa and wave at whales. Right now, I'm marvelling at the world's one and only cloned, prehistoric, sea beast – the monstrous Megalodon Shark. Wow. But I'm also trembling, for the creature is less than a metre away: the length of two caravans and half as wide, with a cavernous mouth and tusk-like teeth. Eyes the size of ostrich eggs are goggling at me, through the superplastic aquarium wall labelled: *DO NOT TOUCH THIS BARRIER*. Phew.

Crystal, clad in a scarlet kaftan, is engrossed in a phone call. When she looks up, her strangely cold expression makes my nerves tingle.

'Jane,' she hisses, 'My agent has just told me he saw you back in February on Herne Bay Pier with one of your clients. After you *promised me.*' Crystal whirls round furiously and her scarlet Birkin clutch bag clips the barrier. 'You're *fired*, Jane! You've destroyed my—'

BANG! The massive Megalodon's head crashes through the superplastic. OMG. With a scream and a swallow, Crystal has gone. Head first into the fearsome jaws, her scarlet shoes spat out at my feet, in a rush of salt water that nearly knocks me over. My Good Witch of the North – Warrior Woman Zena, who whisked me from wretchedness to riches, doomed to die in the most horrific way. The metal plates in the aquarium floor slide swiftly apart and the sea monster is sucked out of sight.

My memory spools back to that unseasonably warm, winter day on Herne Bay Pier. The day that changed my life forever. When my worries and 'What if's faded away. When Pickle's voice turned into Pickle, the person, with the *Humpty Dumpty* build he'd joked about. We ran towards each other and embraced. We walked the length of the brand new, shiny polymer pier, over a thousand metres long, seagulls wheeling above us, the sun shining on us. Chatting and laughing. Eating fish and chips. Falling in love.

It's August now and I walked to Seasalter yesterday, but I felt the scars of Crystal's footprints on the path beside the sea wall. The velvet of her voice purred from the pebbles. The scarlet of the summer sunset stirred gruesome memories of the Megalodon. I feel guilty for betraying Crystal's trust. I always will. Wouldn't you? Crystal brought me laughter and liberation but Pickle brought me laughter and love. Love which I had never ever known.

I live with my Pickle now, in his amazing mansion on Whitstable's Middle Wall. Pickle is my rainbow, as in the sad-happy, Wizard of Oz song, 'Somewhere Over the Rainbow.' He's kind and jolly, and an Octagie, like me. He's also a Longevity Expert, so we hope to live a very long time and help others to do the same. We are patrons of the newly revived Whitstable Playhouse, with luxurious front row seats, looking forward to the January pantomime. And guess what? It's Aladdin. Wow. But I'll never ever forget Crystal. I've made her scarlet shoes into a sculpture, framing our window which looks out over the sea. 'By the way, *Do or Die Diner*. I won't be going through your *Die Door* just yet.' And as for when ... who can say? Wish me luck, won't you?

Janua Vitae

by Aliy Fowler

The traffic on the M2 had ground to a halt for what must have been the fifth time in the last half hour, but Hannah didn't mind as much as she might have. They weren't in a rush and it was a marvellously sunny day at the beginning of what promised to be a glorious week. Her best friend was home from university for the Easter break and they were off on a spring adventure in Hannah's little car.

Perhaps adventure was too strong a word. Sarah was a penniless student and Hannah, still trying to decide what to do with her life, had yet to find permanent employment. A holiday abroad was out of the question, but Hannah's aunt lived in Whitstable, where she owned a lovely house quite close to the beach. She had two guest rooms and was a fabulous cook, Hannah had explained. And Sarah had never been to that part of Kent.

Hannah flicked an errant lock of hair out of her left eye and turned to look at her friend.

'I'm so glad you could come with me, Sarah, you'll love Whitstable. It has a brilliant atmosphere when the weather's good and there's loads to do.'

Sarah smiled. 'It's so nice of your aunt to invite me!'

'You'll love Aunt Peg too,' Hannah said. 'Honestly, she's great.'

The girls could not have been more different. Sarah was tall, with sleek, dark brown hair. She was a hard worker and had always been the more academic one. She had known since she was eleven that she wanted to be an architect, a goal she was now actively pursuing at university. Hannah on the other hand was petite, capricious and not particularly hardworking. But people loved her and she had a personality as bubbly as her curly blond hair. The two met when they were picked for the school gymnastics team in year seven and had been inseparable ever since.

With it being the Easter holidays, and surprisingly warm for the time of year, their journey to the Kent coast took longer than Google maps had predicted. The girls were hot, hungry and thirsty by the time they arrived at Hannah's aunt's house – a characterful 1930s residence in the leafy environs of Queen's Road.

Aunt Peg, even shorter than her niece but more generous in girth, was a bundle of welcoming energy. Although never having met Sarah, she greeted the girls with equally enthusiastic hugs and having ensured their bags were stowed safely in the parquet-floored hall, showed them through the house to the shady garden. Here lunch for three was set out on a wooden table positioned under an old cherry tree which was covered in a cloud of pink blossom.

Hannah had been right about her aunt's culinary skills. The home-made mushroom quiche was probably the nicest quiche Sarah had ever tasted. It was accompanied by salad leaves and new potatoes, both from Peg's abundant garden. For pudding there was rhubarb (again home-grown) and ginger syllabub. Sarah was still winding down from the frenetic pace of the end of term, and sitting in this delightful outdoor space, sipping the last of Hannah's aunt's elderflower cordial, was heaven.

'I have a little weeding to do this afternoon,' Peg said.

'Hannah, why don't you take Sarah for a stroll on Tankerton Slopes? Show her the sea views. Then you could go to the castle. They have a food and drink festival on this weekend. I'll have supper ready for 7 o'clock if that suits?'

Hannah gave her aunt a big hug. 'You're an absolute wonder,

thank you. Give me a ring if you'd like us to pick up anything for you.'

The girls turned left out of Peg's house, then right into another tree-lined avenue which led directly to Marine Parade. This long stretch of road was populated on its south side with many desirable properties – for on the opposite side was the wide grassy expanse of Tankerton Slopes, an endless row of colourful beach huts below it and uninterrupted views of the sea for anyone lucky enough to own a house there.

Hannah and Sarah sauntered lazily along the top of the Slopes. The afternoon was magnificent, the gentle warmth of the sun making it the perfect temperature for a stroll. The sea was a sparkling azure and the promenade between huts and beach rang with the sounds of children playing.

The pair arrived at Whitstable Castle in the middle of the afternoon. Given the unseasonably warm weather, school holidays and food festival, the grounds were a hive of activity. There were stalls set out all over the lawns selling locally-made produce and a barrage of tempting smells greeted them at every turn.

'I wish I hadn't eaten so much at Aunt Peg's!' Hannah giggled, eyeing up a display of bacon-wrapped scotch eggs.

Inside the castle it was even busier than in the gardens. The girls made their way through the crush of the entrance hall and Hannah led Sarah into a large room on the ground floor. Sarah clocked the Regency style: walls panelled in dark oak, heavy drapes around the large windows and ornate geometric patterns on the ceiling. This room, along with other less formal ones upstairs, was also packed with stalls. The array of produce inside was as enticing as it was outside: delicious cakes, artisan chocolates, local apple juices and all manner of alcoholic beverages. Sarah picked up a bottle of sparkling wine from a vineyard in Tenterden.

'Their fizz is meant to be very good,' said Hannah.

'Great, I'll get this to have with supper this evening,' Sarah smiled.

All stalled-out, the girls left the castle via the gate house at the western end of the grounds.

'If you go on down Tower Parade,' Hannah pointed straight ahead, 'You get to the harbour. But we'll do that tomorrow. And there's Harbour Street to see too. It's full of awesome little independent shops, but they'll mostly be closed now. We'll go down Beach Walk and then head back along the seafront. Then we can stop for a quick drink at the Marine Hotel at the top of the Slopes and watch the sun go down.'

Sarah liked that idea and the girls spent a lazy hour over a glass or two of chilled white wine, watching the thinning crowds promenading on Tankerton Slopes, before finally wending their way back to Peg's house.

Sarah was interested to know more about the unusual little castle where they'd spent the afternoon; and Peg, something of a local history buff, was only too happy to fill her in over supper.

'It was originally a medieval manor,' she explained. 'In the late 18th century a London businessman called Charles Pearson remodelled it and at some point after that it became known as Tankerton Tower. Pearson was also responsible for the Canterbury to Whitstable railway. It was designed to give traders easier access to the harbour here. The line is a cycle route now, called the Crab and Winkle Way.'

'After Charles Pearson died,' Peg continued, 'the family just used the property as a summer house, and eventually it was sold to a cousin called Wynn Ellis. He was a successful silk merchant and MP. He improved and extended the property even more – and the garden too.'

Hannah yawned.

'Are we keeping you up?' Sarah laughed.

Over breakfast the following morning the girls invited Peg to accompany them to the harbour.

'I promised to help with the Easter flower displays in church this morning, dears, but if you aren't in a rush I'd love to join you afterwards.'

'I'll come with you and lend a hand,' declared Hannah. It wouldn't have been her first choice of activity but she was keen to show gratitude for her aunt's wonderful hospitality .

Peg turned to Sarah. 'It's a lovely church. And it has a beautiful graveyard, along the back of which runs part of the Crab and Winkle Way.'

'The old railway line you were talking about last night,' nodded Sarah.

'Yes, that's it. You could walk a little of it while Hannah helps me out in the church,' Peg suggested.

Sarah agreed. 'That sounds great!'

There was a morning mist hanging in the air when the three arrived at All Saints Church, but not so thick that Sarah was unable to appreciate the pretty building with its extensive graveyard. The imposing Norman tower caught her eye first. The church's nave and chancel appeared to be the same age as the tower, but the porch on the north-east side looked to be 200 years more recent. Fifteenth century, she supposed, flexing her architectural-history muscles.

Peg showed Sarah where the entrance to the church was and then pointed out the path through the graveyard that led, via a little gap in the boundary hedge, to the cycle path.

'How about you come and find us again at ten-thirty?' she proposed. 'We should be done by then, and we can all go the harbour for a coffee.'

Sarah nodded; the mist was beginning to clear and the sun was breaking though, promising a day as splendid as yesterday. She definitely wanted to be outside.

'See you later,' said Hannah to Sarah as she hooked her arm through her aunt's and led her off in the direction of the church door.

Sarah headed for the little path that ran from the south eastern corner of the church, through the middle of the graveyard, to connect with the old railway line. To her left was a large open expanse, peppered with headstones old and new. It was neatly maintained and criss-crossed with further pathways. But as she rounded the copse of large trees that stood on the southern side of the church she noticed to her right, beyond another area of well-kept graves, a much older section of the churchyard. Here graves nestled between gnarly old trees, ivy- and moss-covered and leaning at precarious angles. Shaded by the branches above them, what little sunlight was breaking through the mist could not reach these headstones.

Sarah deviated from the path and crossing the recently mown grass headed into the unkempt wooded area. The ground here was carpeted with dead brown leaves and dried twigs, interlaced with creeping weeds. It crunched underfoot. In places there were fallen branches and pieces of broken stonework camouflaged by the pervasive ivy. The spindly half-dead trees were bowed or deformed and Sarah had to duck in places. As she walked she paused to read the epitaphs on the few stelae which were not so worn as to be illegible.

As her route took her towards the rear of the church, through the entwined boughs Sarah noticed a run of tall iron railings, rusting and lichen-clad. They rose from a low stone wall which was covered in moss and the ubiquitous desiccated leaves. As she pushed her way closer she saw that the railings enclosed a large rectangular area. It looked to be about seven metres wide by at least thirteen long. At one end of this stood a curious and hefty square structure with a stepped pyramidal roof and an ornate 'metope' stone frieze below. It reminded Sarah of a Masonic hall in miniature. It must have been at least four and a half meters square, and perhaps six in height.

Closer now, she could see that there was a path, barely half a metre in width, that skirted the enclosure. It was in need of attention, overgrown with jagged brambles that seemed to say 'keep out'. Sarah walked back a little and looked around for a light but sturdy fallen branch. She picked up one which seemed less rotten than most and returning to the little brambled path began to clear her way towards the back of the fenced-in area. She could see that at that end, furthest from the stone structure within, was a pair of imposing iron gates.

She tramped around the corner of the path, an especially springy bramble whipping back and nicking her cheek as she went. Here, from the rear of the enclosure, she could see that the building had an entrance. This was not on its eastern side, which she realised would be facing the back of the church (for in this position the very top of its Norman tower was visible some thirty metres away, above the stepped roof of the structure and the tall surrounding trees). What made it particularly interesting was that the entrance was below ground level. Through the bars of the gates Sarah could see a flight of stone steps which started a few metres into the neglected grassy area inside the railings and disappeared into the earth. The steps were flanked by two low and powerful retaining walls constructed from massive blocks of rusticated stone.

Sarah could see now that the interior of the building must be twice the height it had originally seemed. At its rear, gracing this underground section and well-hidden from the churchyard, was an unusual pair of tapered wooden doors with ornate ironwork grills and a massive carved-stone lintel above. This was supported by a pair of equally massive carved jambs. Ivy clung to the stonework and in places worked its insidious way between the joints. There was an inscription on the lintel, but where its surface was aged and mottled with white lichen, it was impossible to read from where Sarah stood.

The gates to the enclosure were secured with a heavy chain and large old padlock. Overcome with an urge to know more about the intriguing structure, which Sarah realised to be a mausoleum, she wiggled the lock. It was definitely well-secured. The top of the railings was above head-height and the upright struts were close together and topped with pointed finials. Climbing over them was not an option. However, the gates, although higher than the railings, were flat-topped and had the advantage of decorative square ironwork panels at their base with a narrow gap into which she could fit a foot.

Even with her left foot planted firmly on the horizontal strut, Sarah was not tall enough to swing her right leg over the gate and had to jump to give herself enough height so that she could place both hands on the top of the gate and straighten her arms to take her full body weight. From there she pulled her right leg over, followed by her left. The ground below was uneven and she was wary about dropping straight onto it so she manoeuvred her legs until she could again wedge a foot between the ironwork panel and the horizontal strut above it. But as she lowered herself towards the grass she loosened her grip on the top of the gate a split second too early and fell backwards. With her foot caught half a meter off the ground, her body twisted and it was her head that made contact first – not with the scrubby turf but with the edge of the squat stone wall at the base of the railings.

Pain seared through Sarah's skull and she was overcome with a wave of nausea. Almost immediately she began to feel dizzy. Even in her dazed state, she realised that she was entirely hidden from anyone walking in the graveyard and Hannah and her aunt were expecting her to be exploring the old Crab and Winkle line before returning to the church. If she passed out they would not find her. Reaching her hand around to the back of her throbbing skull she felt that it was damp. She brought her palm in front of her face and saw blood. Sarah's vision tunnelled and she blacked out.

Sometime later – Sarah had no idea how long – she became aware of the sound of a chain rattling followed by the creak of rusty hinges. She tried to turn her head towards the gate but felt immediately sick. Through hazy eyes she was finally able to make out the slight figure of a woman leaning over her. It was not Hannah or her aunt. Her grey hair was pulled into a neat bun and she wore a high-necked white blouse.

'Lie still,' the woman told her. 'I will fetch help.'

'Who are you, how did you find me?' mumbled Sarah.

She thought she heard the woman say 'Mary' but wasn't sure.

Then she seemed to say 'Maria'. Or was it 'Mary' repeated? The woman's voice was faint and muffled to Sarah. She lapsed into unconsciousness again.

Peg and Hannah were becoming frantic. It was over an hour since Sarah was meant to have returned to the church. At first they had called to her in the graveyard; then separated to walk a fair distance in both directions along the cycle path, searching for her to no avail.

'We should go back to the church,' said Peg. 'She might have reappeared and be waiting for us.'

Hannah knew her friend would not be there. Sarah was always reliable. If she hadn't returned at the arranged time then something had happened.

Hannah and her aunt made their way along the path that led from the old railway line back to the church. As they passed beyond the wooded area with the older graves and, set back in the trees could see the near end of the mausoleum's iron enclosure, relatively inconspicuous from this angle, Hannah noticed a woman in a white blouse waving at them.

'What is that?' asked Hannah.

'It's a tomb,' Peg answered. 'I think the lady wants us to go over there.'

Heart pounding, Hannah raced over the damp grass as the woman disappeared onto the bramble-infested path which led down the side of the railings. Ignoring the sharp thorns, she forged her way as fast as she could to the far end and there, to her horror, saw her friend lying motionless on the ground, her hair matted with dark blood.

Hannah rounded the corner of the railings and pushed the nearest of the two heavy gates. It opened.

'Oh my god, oh my god. Sarah, can you hear me?'

Peg appeared behind her a minute later, bramble-scratched and ashen-faced. 'I'll call for an ambulance dear, you watch her.'

∽

Sarah awoke in a hospital bed, the back of her skull thudding.

'Don't try to move too quickly,' came a voice. 'You've had a nasty bang on the head.'

She turned slowly to see Hannah and Peg sat at her bedside.

'Goodness, my dear, the doctor tells us you were very lucky that we found you when we did,' said Peg.

'We might not have found you without that lady,' added Hannah.

'What lady?' Sarah looked momentarily puzzled, then remembered the woman who had promised to get help.

'Short, with grey hair in a bun, white blouse, a dark skirt I think, couldn't see from where we were,' Hannah replied. 'She showed us where to find you.'

'Yes, that was her.' Sarah tried to nod but immediately winced in pain.

'How did you manage to fall where you did?' queried Peg.

'I got my foot wedged when I climbed over the railings and slipped and twisted,' Sarah explained.

'But the gate was open!' exclaimed Hannah.

'No, it was locked, the lady opened it before she went for help,' Sarah answered. 'Do you know who she is? I must thank her.'

'I'm afraid she'd gone by the time we'd found you,' said Peg. 'I inquired back at the church when Hannah went with you in the ambulance but no-one knew who she was. Churches are full of good Samaritans, though. Just be happy that you're safe.'

Along with some instructions from a nurse and a concussion checklist, Sarah was released into the care of her friend and Aunt Peg the following afternoon.

'Can you tell me about the mausoleum?' she asked Peg over supper. 'It's a fantastic little building, even if I didn't get as close a look as I'd wanted!'

'Well, let me think,' mused Peg. It was commissioned by Wynn Ellis...'

'...the second owner of Whitstable Castle,' interrupted

Hannah. 'See, I do pay attention!'

'That's right,' Peg confirmed. 'He had Charles Barry Jr. design it for him.'

'Wow!' said Sarah, before explaining to a puzzled Hannah that he was the son of the architect who had redesigned the Houses of Parliament after the dreadful fire in 1834.

'The tomb would have been a very prominent feature in the churchyard at All Saints originally,' Peg went on. 'But over the years nature encroached and it became almost entirely lost to visitors. The last person to be placed there was Wynn Ellis's grandson. He died in the twenties. I suppose eventually there was no-one left here to visit it anymore.'

'But someone must have cleared it again and made that path,' said Sarah.

'Yes, that's right, dear. In the 1990s an architectural historian, Jill Allibone, was visiting her grandmother's grave at All Saints and came across the tomb.'

'Just like you did yesterday!' chirped Hannah to Sarah.

'Indeed,' Peg smiled. 'Seeing the extent to which it was decaying, Jill managed to persuade English Heritage to list it. The reverend at the time was very glad of her help. In fact we all were – it would have been a dreadful shame to lose such an important piece of Whitstable history. Jill then went on to found the "Mausolea and Monuments Trust" to protect similar places. Sadly, she died just a year after its foundation.'

'There's an inscription above the door of the tomb,' Sarah suddenly remembered. 'I was trying to read it. Do you know what it says?'

'Janua Vitae,' declared Peg. 'It's Latin for "the gate to life". More usually the expression is "Mors Janua Vitae" meaning "death is the gate to life", but with this one death is omitted.'

'Luckily for you, Sarah,' grimaced Hannah.

Tactfully changing the subject Peg got up and headed for the kitchen. 'Who's for dessert?'

'Maybe it was the ghost of the lady that set up the trust who came back to help you,' whispered Hannah once her aunt was out of earshot. She loved a good ghost story.

'Oh very funny,' muttered Sarah. 'The lady who helped me said her name was "Mary". Or she might have said "Maria". Definitely not "Jill".'

'Well, anyway, thank goodness for the mysterious Mary or Maria,' Hannah grinned.

Aunt Peg came back in bearing a steaming apple pie. 'Last autumn's harvest,' she beamed.

'Who's buried in the tomb, Aunt Peg?' asked Hannah as she helped herself to a large slice.

'Well, there's Wynn Ellis of course, his wife, his son – he was a reverend, Arthur Conrad Graystone and Arthur's son Herbert,' explained Peg. 'Arthur inherited the castle from his father and much of his huge fortune. Apparently, he was the wealthiest Church of England cleric there ever was! His ecclesiastical position is intriguing as his mother's background was a bit dubious.'

'What was she called, Aunt Peg?' quizzed Hannah, mischievously.

'Jane Graystone,' Peg answered. Hannah's face fell.

'Hannah's hoping for a ghost story,' gibed Sarah, throwing her friend a scathing but good-humoured look. 'She wanted my rescuer to be the spirit of the lady who founded the trust you just told us about...'

'Jill Allibone,' interjected Aunt Peg, nodding.

'Yes, but she doesn't have the right name. And now Hannah wants it to be Wynn Ellis's wife Jane. But that doesn't work either.' Sarah stuck out her tongue at her friend who was feigning dejection.

'Ah, no dear,' responded Peg. 'Jane Graystone was Arthur's mother, but she wasn't Wynn Ellis's wife. He led a bit of a double life. The woman he married was the ward of Charles Pearson, the first owner of Tankerton Tower. But he had at least two mistresses. The first one, Susan Lloyd, bore him a daughter. And the second, Jane Graystone, was mother to Arthur. But the only woman buried in that tomb is his legal wife.'

'So what was her name?' asked Hannah impatiently, the hopeful glint back in her eye.

Sarah rolled her eyes and kicked Hannah under the table.

'His wife was called Mary,' said Aunt Peg. 'Mary Maria Ellis.'

Whitstable Future

by Nick Hayes

He threatened to 'Give her a rocket!' if she didn't stop carrying on. And he would have done if he'd managed to catch her. The alcohol made his reactions slow and his daughter had the quick responses of youth. She ducked his waxy hand as he swiped at her and bobbed sideways just close enough to smell the brew on his breath.

As a gobby teenager she had been pushing things a bit. He had been sounding off about 'them immigrants' making his search for work even more difficult. She wanted none of it and suggested his gut and drinking habit were maybe a factor in keeping him out of work. On most days this would pass unnoticed as he slipped into a stupor but tonight he was keeping himself from passing out as the football was on later. His 'rocket' comment was a favourite. His bulky right hand was also a favourite to deliver the 'rocket'. She was sometimes too slow and caught a glancing blow or even worse. Tonight she dodged out the front room and out the house. Better face the rain than the pain.

In the cold drizzle she felt a touch less alone. She had no time to grab her coat but had a few cigarettes in her jeans pocket. She lit up and the orange glow gave her comfort. Not many roads' plod and she was at the sea front. She always felt it was more beautiful at night – the calm and the quiet – like a balm.

Out there in the dark she could see the sea had retreated

from the shore. The sandy banks shone under the moon and she could make out the outline of the Street. Tracing its way into the sea, this long and unapologetic shingle strip was a Whitstable oddity. You could keep the Festival and the oysters and Harbour Street. She loved the Street and tonight she would walk it again.

Walking the coastal feature at night was no more of a challenge than in the day, nor did the moonlight really play much of a part. It was so uncannily straight and unerringly confident in how it boldly jutted into the sea. She could just allow her eyes to follow a star in the distance and her feet to follow them. The shallow sea lapped on either side, coolly caressing the strip. She walked and smoked and thought about nothing. This was her place.

It was Whitstable Future. She was once again standing on the shore gazing at the Street. Today was the day she had long been waiting for.

In her workshop she had spent many hours toiling and developing her project. The college course had come in useful and she felt comfortable handling the metals and bonding them together. Sheet lay upon sheet then smoothly curved together to form the nose cone. The empty chamber within was neat and tidy with canvas material around the perimeter and a rigid seat slotted in the centre.

At the other end, the project was made for power – immensely strong engines and four huge exhaust pipes directed at 45 degrees. The finished creation was longer than her body and as heavy as a car. It sat on a wheeled structure like a metallic baby in a cradle.

How she had got it onto the beach was a miracle. But she had needed many miracles to get where she was – calling in favours and guidance from wherever she could. This had been a journey in itself.

Now it lay in position. It was her beautiful Rocket. Today was the launching time. She had spent many hours considering the start of the mission but much less about the conclusion. She had factored in an emergency plan but did not really care to use it. This was her trip into the abyss.

She lifted the door open and wedged herself into the creation. Morning was coming to the beach and a few bystanders were drawing closer for a look. A couple of dogs snuffled at the engines. It was not every day that a rocket launched off the Street.

She thought back to when she had chosen her launching strip. She wanted a certain distance and a certain consistency. She would be aiming high towards the open ocean. This location was the perfect spot.

Gathering herself together, she put her arms through the shoulder straps and considered the panel that faced her. She had kept the dials simple – Launch, Boost and Emergency.

Her hand reached across to pull the door over herself and she was cocooned in her Rocket. In her head she counted down from ten. There was a roar from the engines as she coaxed them into life. The entire vehicle throbbed with power.

Her plan was for the rocket to be propelled on its launching cradle for the distance of the Street and then catapulted into the air as the shingle ran out.

It was a beast of a noise. There were flumes of orange and blue from the exhausts. With a flick of a switch the rocket began to move. What an exhilaration she felt – the thrill of the movement and the daring rush of the danger.

The unevenness of the Street gave the run a juddering texture but the distance was looking perfect. Her speed was increasing to a maximum as the shingle ran out. Just. Not. Yet.

She pressed the Boost button moments before the rocket hit the water. And with that she flew off the launching cradle and into the morning air.

What a sight to behold! Those on the beach gazed in wonder as the rocket was sent flying high from the tail of the shingle spit. It was visible from miles around with its dense vapour trail and bullet shaped exterior.

Higher and higher it went. It seemed to have no thought for landing. And that's what she had – no thought for landing. In the sky she soared upwards, arcing towards the horizon.

Years before she had pondered on what part the Street would play. Now she knew.

Going Back

by Lin White

Tom wandered from room to room around the house, ignoring the crowds of people. So many memories! He had hardly been back to Whitstable in the last three years, studying hard at university in Norwich, renting a student flat with friends, unable to bear the thought of returning to his childhood home.

The town had become trendy over the past few years, art galleries and fancy shops everywhere, but in the house everything was just as he remembered, as though home were a time capsule, unchanged. Not just since he had left, but since long before that. He wasn't at all surprised.

In the next room he could hear Mother sobbing quietly, voices murmuring to her.

'Sorry for your loss.'

'We'll miss him.'

'He was a good man.'

One of his mother's friends, dressed in a severe black dress and white pearls, came up to him and tried to hug him. 'We're so glad you were able to come home. Your mother misses you so much. You must be a real comfort to her at this time.'

He extricated himself politely but firmly. The sympathy was more than he could bear. After all, he had barely been on speaking terms with his father.

Instead, he wandered over to the table that had become the focus of attention. A large framed photo stood in pride of place, surrounded by funeral flowers. His father had hated flowers. He'd always said they were a waste of money.

Tom picked up the photo and studied it; a middle-aged man with an earnest expression on his face. Father had always looked as though he was on the verge of some big discovery. He was holding an award for scientific research, and the wall behind him was lined with textbooks and his precious research notebooks. Once, Tom had spilled his juice onto one of those books. The anger and blame had lasted nearly a week. Since then, he had stayed well away from his father's workshop, glowering at the door from the other side of the garden. Until that day...

'Thomas, how are you?'

Shaken from his memories, he turned to see George, one of his father's scientist friends, holding out a hand to shake.

'I understand you've just finished university?'

Swallowing hard, Tom nodded and took the proffered hand.

'And what were you studying, may I ask?'

'History.'

George looked surprised. 'History, huh? Not tempted into physics, like your father? He always hoped...' His voice trailed away for a moment. 'Still, history. Your father was always interested in that too. I suppose that was why...'

But the sentence remained unfinished, as another man approached. Tom stood and listened for a moment to the two men speaking about his father. 'Such a shame,' said the new man. 'He had so much to offer the world of science.'

'Yeah, but after that business with his son he just lost the focus he needed. He became obsessed, cut himself off, and with the ten-year anniversary coming up, it was like he couldn't bear the thought...'

Tom turned away and found himself face to face with his aunt. 'Thomas! How you've grown! I barely recognise you.'

Tom winced. Why did adults always say that?

His aunt picked up a photo from the shelf nearby. 'I'm sure you were this size when I last saw you.'

He stared down at the photo. Two young boys, one ten years old, the other nearly six. Two blond heads together, plotting something. The older one looked serious; the younger was holding back laughter. Him and Colin. The last photo ever taken of his little brother.

Aunt Helen must have picked up on his reaction, because she put the photo back down as though it burned her fingers. 'So tragic,' she said. 'And you never discovered what happened to him? So sad. It totally destroyed your father. He never did recover. And your mother took it hard too, of course.'

Tom shook his head, the pain suddenly raw. He took Aunt Helen by the arm. 'Have you spoken to Mother?'

'Of course, dear, but I'm worried about you. It's all up to you now. You're all she has left.'

The reminder was uncomfortable. He turned to find his mother standing just behind him. She wrapped her arms around him, enveloping him in her perfume, and he reminded himself to relax, to let her have her way.

'It's such a relief to have him home,' she agreed with her sister. 'Ten years since Colin disappeared, and now his father is gone. But I still have my precious Thomas.'

Tom did his best to comfort her, pushing the guilt away with the ease of long practice. His eyes scanned the room, looking for a distraction.

What they found startled him. Over his mother's shoulder he stared at an ugly yellow vase on the sideboard. He hadn't seen it for years, had thought it destroyed.

A rainy day. He had sneaked out of the house, away from Colin, who had been demanding that he play with him. He was eleven now, too old to play cars with his little brother. He would much rather spend time with his father, but Dad had been preoccupied lately, tinkering with his latest science project in the workshop at the end of the garden. Tom stood on tiptoes and could just manage to see in through the window of the brick building, ignoring the rain dripping on him from the overhang. His father stood in front of a workbench containing a wooden case that was covered in dials and knobs and buttons. In the open area of the workshop, just to his left, was what looked like a giant cabinet with the door removed. The interior of the space was covered in a tangle of wires and controls, and one side blinked in a mesmerising display of lights.

As he watched, his father reached out for the ugly yellow vase that rested on the end of the workbench. He put the vase in the cabinet, and then muttered to himself as he adjusted knobs until the number 10 displayed on a screen on the wall. He hit a big red button and a blinding light startled Tom, making him stagger backwards in shock. He rubbed his eyes and then stepped up to the window again, to see his father checking something on the machine, and then banging his hand against it in triumph. The vase had disappeared. 'Yes! Yes! It's gone! Totally gone!' he shouted, and then stood staring intently at the display. Tom looked around the workshop, but he couldn't spot the vase. Had his father's machine disintegrated it?

Dad seemed to be waiting for something to happen, and Tom watched with fascination and a touch of fear, wondering what to expect, but after a few minutes Dad started looking at his watch repeatedly and his expression became downcast.

Tom's tummy rumbled. It must be lunch time. He stepped away from the window, his mind still full of what he had seen. His father had a machine that could make things disappear!

And yet the vase was in front of him now. He shrugged off the uneasy feeling – Mum must have found another one. Or perhaps they had been a pair. His mother stepped away to talk to another family friend, and he took the opportunity to step closer to the vase. Picking it up, he studied it. A chill froze him as he recognised the crack that he'd made when playing with his ball in the house. Dad had been furious, but Mum had glued it and reassured him all was as good as new. It was a good repair, but Tom could still see the mark and it constantly shouted his guilt at him.

This was the same vase.

'Your father sent it to me as a message.'

His mother's voice startled him, and he nearly dropped the vase. Lowering it gently back to the sideboard, he looked at his mother's serious expression. 'What do you mean?' he asked.

'That vase – I always loved it, but your father hated it. Then one day it was gone, and he told me he had knocked it off and shattered it.' She gave a deep sigh. 'But the day after he – after he died, I went into his workshop and there it was, sitting in the middle of a big cabinet.'

At his confused expression, she smiled softly. 'It's a sign, you see. That he still loves us. He must have hidden it – he always complained it was ugly – but after he passed, he sent it back to me. To show he's thinking of me.'

Shaken, Tom excused himself and hurried away, losing himself among the funeral crowd.

He was still trying to figure out what the vase meant when he heard mention of the workshop. He took a step closer to his mother, listening. She was talking to her friend.

'What will happen to the workshop now?' the friend was

asking. 'Will you take it on?'

'I think Tom will probably want it,' Mother answered. 'I'm expecting him to take over the space as a study now that he's finished uni. I can't imagine he'll stay away. I'm glad – I couldn't bear the thought of being completely alone apart from the dog.' She gave a deep sigh. 'I still miss Colin every day. Do you know, there's still been no news, not the slightest indication of what happened to him, and it's been ten years, almost to the day.'

Tom couldn't bear the idea of living back at home. And the thought of entering his father's workshop filled him with dread. A morbid curiosity pulled him upstairs, to his brother's bedroom. It was exactly as Colin had left it that day.

With one important difference.

Tom sank down onto the bed and picked up the teddy that was sitting on the pillow. Colin's favourite. He had been inseparable from Teddy from the moment he was big enough to drag him around behind him. Even after he grew up a little and started school, he would refuse to sleep without Teddy, and often propped him up to watch his activities.

But this couldn't be Teddy. It must be a replacement. Somehow Mother had found another Teddy, identical to the first.

Even down to the torn ear and discoloured eye.

He stared down at the teddy that lay limply in his hands. The last time he had seen it...

'Go away, you're not supposed to be here!' he hissed at his brother.

Colin just stood, hanging his head forward but peering at him with those big blue eyes from under those blond curls. 'Neither are you,' he pointed out. He swung Teddy by one foot, and refused to back off.

Tom looked desperately behind him at his father's workshop, and then towards the house. He had an hour, if that, and he was desperate to look around the workshop and try to figure out what Dad was working on. He'd been so secretive lately, and Tom couldn't stop thinking of that cabinet that made things disappear. But if Colin insisted on tagging along, they would both get caught and get into trouble.

Frustrated, he reached forward and snatched Teddy out of Colin's limp fingers. 'Do you know what I do to boys who won't do as they're told?'

Colin shook his head, eyes suddenly wide with fright.

Tom stepped into the workshop. The cabinet and control box were still exactly as they had been two days ago. He threw Teddy into the cabinet and reached out for the red button. 'You'll never see Teddy again!' he threatened.

Colin gave out a squeal and took a step towards the house. 'I'm telling Mum!'

Tom had only wanted to frighten his brother, but the anger grew inside him. 'Right, that's it!' he said, and slammed his hand onto the button.

The light was blinding, and Colin screamed. Tom, who had been expecting it, blinked to clear his eyes of the tears that had sprouted. He pointed to the cabinet. 'See? That's what happens! No more Teddy!'

Colin opened his mouth and closed it again, and tears of anger streamed down his face. 'No!' he cried. 'What did you do?'

Tom shrugged. 'Who knows what I'll destroy next?' he taunted. 'Just make sure you don't tell Mum and Dad, or else!'

That night, Colin had cried himself to sleep, but had just told Mum he'd lost Teddy in the woods somewhere. And Tom felt a churning sensation in his tummy when he thought about what had happened, but the glow of power stayed with him, and he revelled in the newfound freedom from his younger brother, who kept his distance.

'Strange, isn't it?'

Tom looked up, startled.

His mother sat down on the bed beside him and took Teddy from him, sitting the bear on her lap and waving his arms around just as Colin used to do. 'Another message from your father, I think,' she said. 'It was strange, I never like going in your father's workshop, it feels like invading his privacy, but having found the vase in there I couldn't resist going in again a couple of days ago. And there it was.' She cuddled the teddy, resting her chin on his head for a moment. 'I think it's him telling me that he's with Colin now. I've always hoped that he is still alive somewhere, but now with this message...' She remained silent for a moment, and then looked directly at Tom. 'With this I feel at peace now. I feel it's finally time to let go, to trust Eric to look after our son.'

From downstairs came the sound of laughter, and Tom winced. He had never been close to his father, especially since Colin had disappeared, but hearing friends and family enjoying themselves felt so wrong to him.

Bessie, the family Labrador, wandered into the room and placed her head on his lap. He rubbed her nose. 'Are you trying to comfort me or just looking for food?' he teased, running her soft ears through his fingers. She tilted her head to one side and licked his knee.

He looked down at her, and his thoughts wandered again to the workshop in the garden.

'Naughty puppy!' Colin shouted.

'It's your fault!' Tom snapped. 'You're supposed to be looking after her.'

'I was! She's just so wriggly. Look, she's gone into the workshop.'

Colin trotted over to the door, which was standing ajar. Tom followed him furiously. It had taken another few days before he finally had another chance. And now Colin had ruined it again.

'Look,' he said, pointing to the machine. 'If you can't look *after the dog properly like Mum told you to, then I'll just have to do the same to it as I did to your teddy.'*

He caught the puppy and held her towards the cabinet, just to see what Colin would do. At first the boy stood there, mouth open in horror. 'No, don't!' he babbled. 'I'll look after her, I promise! Don't make her disappear!'

Then he ran at Tom, head down and butted him, grabbing hold of the puppy. Startled, Tom staggered backwards, and his hand flew out and grasped a lever on the side of the machine in an attempt to steady himself. The puppy yelped and wriggled free, and Colin tumbled forwards into the cabinet, just as Tom's other hand caught that big red button.

The flash blinded Tom for a minute and he blinked his eyes desperately. What had happened? He hadn't meant to hit the button! Didn't Colin realise he wasn't actually going to do anything?

He stared around him in horror. The puppy rubbed her head against his leg, and tried to nip at his ankle. But Colin was gone.

Horrified, he scooped up the puppy and fled the workshop, only discovering once he was outside that he had somehow taken the lever from his father's machine with him. He wandered the woods until it was dark, and then he had followed the shouts back to the house. 'I'm sorry,' he said. 'Colin ran away with the puppy and I was trying to find him. I found the puppy but I don't know where Colin went.'

A search was organised, and all the neighbours turned out to help the police comb the woods for clues. No trace of Colin had ever been found, of course, but everyone seemed to accept his explanation. His father had ignored his work for years, never going near the workshop. Then, last time Tom was home, his father had been spending his time out there, working, but while at first he would say things like 'I'm nearly there,' or 'I think I've figured out the problem,' nothing ever seemed to happen. Tom remembered with shame the small piece of metal he had taken from the machine, which he had thrown away years ago, but the idea of confessing that he had been anywhere near the workshop terrified him, and he kept quiet.

Lost in his memories, Tom left Mum and walked back downstairs. George and his friend approached him, and George cleared his throat. 'Ah, could we ask you something?' he asked tentatively.

Tom stared at him blankly. What could his father's friend possibly want from him?

George took the silence as approval. 'We were just wondering what you were planning to do with your father's research notebooks,' he continued.

'His notebooks?' Tom thought back to his father's research. 'I was planning to destroy them,' he said at last. 'A machine that destroys things? The world's a better place without it.'

'Destroys things?' George glanced at his friend and then back at Tom. 'What makes you think he was building something to destroy things?'

Tom felt a growing twinge of discomfort in his stomach. His head throbbed and he felt sick. 'What was he working on, then?'

'He was looking to build a time machine.' George gave a small laugh. 'Sounds crazy, I know, but his research seemed really promising.'

'Rumour has it, he was making some progress,' the friend broke in. 'And then after your brother disappeared, he lost interest in his work. And when he finally started again he just said the machine was broken and would no longer work, but he wouldn't show us his research so we could help. But we hate the idea of losing all that progress. Maybe we could do something with the research.'

'A time machine?' Tom stared in horror. 'But... he was making progress? What sort of progress? You can't really build a time machine! Can you?'

George nodded his head, looking serious. 'He said he'd managed to send things back in time, just a couple of minutes at first. He'd see something on his desk and then he would put it in the machine and send it back those few minutes, but he was working on developing that. But he just couldn't seem to send things forward. He thought he had a new approach, but that seemed to fail.'

'And then his research stopped altogether,' the friend repeated. 'Please, don't destroy his notebooks. It would be a waste of your father's legacy. Why not let us review them first?'

He could send things backward in time. And he was working on a way to send things forward.

As Tom's mind whirred, he heard a scream from the kitchen. Mum! He raced across the house, and saw the back door standing open. Mum was standing there staring towards the garden, and out there, looking lost...

'Colin! Oh, my darling Colin!' Mum rushed forward and gathered a small boy up in her arms. 'But how?'

And Tom stared at his little brother, who looked exactly the same as he had ten years ago, on the day he disappeared. Because, he suddenly understood, for him it *was* the day he had disappeared.

Falling in Love

by John Wilkins

I remember thinking Tania's back was broken; it had to be after that. It turned out it wasn't, as luck would have it. The story told was of her survival and how much he must have wanted her to die.

In spite of all the evidence, her husband, Tim, protested his innocence; and she, the wife who suffered those injuries from the sabotaged parachute dumping her in the newly ploughed field, believed him.

The newspaper with that story in it is still in the car now. How far she fell, how lucky she was and the conviction of the husband for attempted murder. A friend of Tania's had phoned the police and broken a friendship, a break that happens when a confidence is betrayed. I knew about betrayal, but the media never tell you who suffers the most from betrayal, do they?

My thoughts went into their usual pattern; first the scene at the airfield, that day – Easter Sunday. I had looked across the airfield. There were the two Cessna light aircraft ready for take-off, at the far end. The sky was dark petrol except for the bright orange wind socks helping to describe the wind that blew hard across the field.

It had been decision time for all twelve of us. After all the bargaining and negotiating with families and partners and all the other commitments that we sought to escape from by sky diving, now the weather seemed to defeat us. Tania pushed on, always the first to find a compromise so that at least something was possible. We all trusted her so when she suggested a low altitude jump (from less than 4000 feet) before the rain beat a tattoo on the corrugated iron roof of the aircraft hangar where we had gathered, there was almost total agreement. Her husband, Tim, was the only one who didn't agree, which turned out to be very helpful, in one sense, as things turned out. He wasn't jumping, he was responsible for checking the parachutes.

Running out to the planes, there was a lot of exuberant fist pumping and cheering – we were going to get a jump after all. Sitting in the plane beside me, I remember Tania had turned to me.

She said, 'I'm so happy to be going back in the sky again. I wish you could have persuaded Tim to come, Mike.'

I muttered something about Tim always doing what he wanted to do in the end, which was true. We had been friends since the first day at flight school, when a knowing look shared about the stunning sight in front of us that was the training instructor, Tania. We competed for her, as we always did when an attractive woman appeared on our radar. I made overtures and they were reciprocated at first; but then little by little Tim gained the upper hand. I was almost resigned to her choosing him; after all, it wasn't the first time. Somehow, he had perfected the complex art of persuasion.

You just accepted that he should get what he wanted, even if you wanted it for yourself. He always made any competition fade away, by getting them to believe he deserved to be the one who was chosen. He seemed to have naive surprise when he succeeded in his quest. It was a kind of gracious victory. The absence of arrogance in being chosen (yes, sometimes I was nearly the one) made him admirable. In his position I would never have been able to resist the temptation. Perhaps it was the certainty that he was going to be the winner. Not being in that position very often, I could only guess.

But when I did get chosen, I considered the victory only briefly, because the prize, Julie, was really the only woman I had wanted badly enough. So the victory became less important, as I fell deeply in love with her and proposed.

Tim, it seemed, was quite happy for me; he said just how happy during his best man's speech at our wedding.

It was altered now, how I saw the past, as I sat in my car waiting for Tania at the airfield. She had recovered from almost all the injuries, except for the ankles – it was going to be some time before they could fully support her, without the walking aids. She could still drive though, just not as aggressively as she used to.

Out there, I saw the light change against the trees that bordered the access route to the airfield. She was on a mission, one that no else could understand. Despite him having been found guilty of her attempted murder and receiving a lengthy sentence, she believed her husband's cries of innocence. The headlights swept the way ahead; the closer the car came, the more I was certain it was Tania.

When the car drew up alongside my own I was ready. There would be no change, I knew that, no evidence to prove Tim innocent. The police had submitted all the evidence needed to prove him guilty. The witnesses had given testimony. He had been seen before the jump taking the parachute into the ante room – claiming he was expecting an important call on his mobile – and then emerging. He had run back into the changing room and hung the parachute and the harness back where he had taken them from. He said in court he was giving them a final check – he had the habit of checking Tania's kit whenever he could.

'You can't be too lucky – Tania used up all her luck when she found me,' was what he always told people with that knowing wink of his.

All he had checked was that the parachute was disabled, and then he put it back on the hook in the changing room – I was the only one who saw that the parachute and its harness went back onto my hook. He didn't stay, he just walked out past Tania, who was surrounded by all of us while she gave her safety precaution talk; the one that she always gave us if we had decided to go and take a low altitude jump.

I was standing at the back, and as she went through the final instructions, I was close enough to the hooks to reach back, without anyone looking round to see me. Then I switched the parachute on my hook with the one on Tania's.

She finished her talk with the usual pause and question, 'Is anybody worried about going on the jump today now?'

'Only Tim, he was so worried he even took a parachute with him to take a phone call!' I yelled from the back, where I stood pulling my harness over so that I was wearing it, as recommended by Tania.

My joke was acknowledged with a burst of laughter as someone else followed up with, 'and he's not even jumping, now.'

Then a telephone bell ringtone sounded, and we turned to see Tim walking swiftly away from us with his mobile phone. It now appeared to be glued to the side of his head.

Months later I looked back on my memories, while I waited for Tania. It was easy for me to remember who was talking to him on that call; after all, the timing had been carefully arranged. Remembering his face as he listened to the phone call made me focus on paying very close attention to what Tania might ask when she arrived.

I helped her from her car, made sure she was steady on the sticks and then we walked into the hangar. We were there to collect her things; she couldn't face it on her own, she told me. Going back there on her own, after everything that had happened, was going to be hard. She knew that.

'I just want to show them that I can do it, but I need some support. If you come, then they might start to believe me and help with Tim's appeal.'

I looked at her, trying not to betray how cynical I was.

'You know he's innocent, don't you? You must believe him, I do – it's the way he looks, even he can't fake what he said when they took him down. That wasn't the cry of a guilty man.'

I nodded in what I hoped was a convincing way. It wasn't the cry of a guilty man – I knew that for certain. He wasn't guilty; not of planning to kill her.

When Tim was tried, there was plenty of evidence – that the court had accepted as proof – proving his guilt. It was beyond doubt, as demonstrated by the jury's unanimous decision. The sentence handed down by the judge reflected that Tim had finally lost the means to get what he wanted.

Tania waited as I held doors open and fielded glances of pity and intended sympathy aimed at her. First, we had to walk past parachutes and harnesses hanging up where she had given her last safety talk. Then, as she persisted with checking Tim's locker, after instructing me to pack the contents of her own, she thought she found something. A piece of paper fell from the top shelf of the locker.

'What's that?' She looked down, as if I was going to find printed on the paper all the answers the court would need to explain why Tim hadn't planned to commit murder.

I picked it up and handed it to her. I knew it couldn't be important – the police had been very thorough; so had I. It wouldn't matter now, whatever it had printed on it.

It was a betting slip. Tim was always clever with his bets. They were placed with a combination of inside knowledge and whimsy – or so it seemed. He never divulged how that combination had been forged, but somehow whenever he was broke, it produced the money to support his latest ambition or pursuit.

Tania looked at, it holding on to my arm to steady herself by leaning into me. She read the date out and the time of a horse race.

So that's why he ran into the ante room with the parachute – he wanted to get the result of the race from his bookie. After he promised me, he'd given up, promised me so many times. That phone call was from his bookie –getting back to him with the results.

I didn't risk saying anything. I was smiling inside but cautious not to give anything away, other than an embarrassed sympathetic half smile. She had got a reason to doubt herself now; the certainty of his innocence was less because of that.

'I'm sorry, Tania, I thought he had given up too.'

I left it at that. She tried to pull herself up on both sticks to support herself entirely, without me seeing the despair in her.

'So, I'm trying to convince everyone that he's innocent, that I know him inside out and I didn't have a clue he was still gambling. So if he was lying to me about that then...'

'Stop it, Tania.'

I said it as gently as I could. I didn't want to hurt her, not any more. She had been hurt enough, I could see that now. I saw she had pulled herself together now – literally. The sticks were aligned and supporting her equally as she paced herself to walk out of that place, with her head held as high as she could manage. It was as if she was trying to succeed in rising above her perception of the pity that the others felt for her, in finding out the love of her life had tried to murder her.

She didn't admit that he had any reason to murder her. If there was anyone, she had no idea who it was. That's how she started on me. It was like being able to see her anxious thoughts swell up before they became the words that left her mouth, spat out in a gabbling rising voice of panic.

'Was there anyone that might have driven him to it? Had he got someone else, had he found someone? Did he ever say to you he wanted to get rid of me?'

She asked only to hear it – that he hadn't found someone, and the one person she thought knew Tim, really knew him, was me, Mike, his mate. She could rely on me, Tim's closest friend.

So that's what I told her: what she wanted to hear, not what the truth was. If I had told her that, then I knew where I would finish up.

'He never told me.' That's what I said, and it was the truth – I found out for myself what was going on.

I knew there was someone and I knew who it was, but I was too ashamed to tell her. She wouldn't understand or forgive me if she knew everything. If I lost her friendship then, there would be nothing left; because that and the satisfaction of knowing Tim couldn't betray me anymore, not where he was, that is all I have left.

How I found out about my wife and Tim doesn't matter now. All that mattered was, it was true. I kept it close. I had to be certain, so I used all I knew – surveillance is about having all the information you need, to know what is going on. My surveillance training gave me that – I watched it, assimilated it, but couldn't deal with it.

What I let go, was terrible – I regret all of it now, but you can't make a better past, can you?

I forced it out of Julie. After twelve years of marriage I knew how to make her tell me. I left no visible signs, but I gave her enough pain to persuade her to change her plans.

I amended them, so that those plans would get rid of Tania. Then Tim would know what I felt like – what it was to lose the one you were closest of all to.

I knew that what Julie and I had once would never come back. Making the phone call at the right time to Tim, on the day, that was all she had to do.

Tim didn't know I had my own plan to simply switch the parachutes. Nobody could see me at the back. After all, everyone had seen him rush into the ante room with the phone, and carrying the parachute. They all remembered the phone call afterwards, too.

The threat of more punishment from me to force Julie to tell Tania, her own sister, that she had been unfaithful with Tim was enough. Julie made the call to the police; to say that he had assaulted her sister frequently. In fact, she told them Tania had confessed, after swearing her to secrecy, that Tim had threatened to kill her more than once. That was enough to seal his guilt, in everyone's mind.

I can't change the past, but I'm going to put what Tim taught me into practice now, and find somebody who will always love me. It might take a few attempts though, before my fear of betrayal is gone.

Foreign Objects

by R.J. Dearden

I see her on the Slopes. She thinks I don't but I do. Impossible to miss her in that lime green coat of hers, binoculars out. You probably know her – everybody in the town does. You probably think she's marvellous, but on my life, you'll be hard pushed to meet a more dishonest soul. Big Meany, I call her. Not without reason.

She does Mondays at Cancer Shop. Tuesdays is the homeless. 'Off to see the Hopeless,' I say but she don't laugh. Then it's food bank deliveries to scroungers on the dole, that'll be Wednesdays. She goes to church eight times a week. She's not a deacon or nothing like that but she's like some sort of special minister or something; I don't ask, she don't tell. She goes to every bleeding funeral in this town – not normal behaviour, is it? On Thursdays you'll find her reading to poorly buggers in the old Kent & Canterbury. You know, horoscopes, Mills & Boon sort of stuff. Helps the aged on Fridays. 'What about me?' I say, 'I'm sick. I'm aged. You don't help me none.'

'Please,' she says. That's what she says. 'Please.'

Sometimes I look at her and just the sight of her makes me mad. She used to be real hot-stuff and she ain't too bad now but what eats me is that she's soft on old What's-His-Face. That's why she's always up on them Slopes, spying, when he comes to town to try and take my crown.

Talking of What's-His-Face, he called earlier today. I should have known it meant trouble.

'Challenge,' his voice purred down the line, posh like, calling me up out of the blue. Probably sucking a toffee, he was. Of course, there was no 'hello'; no 'how you diddlin', Olly?' No, straight to business. Still smarting from his last drubbing, no doubt.

I checked the tides. 'No chance, she's going out, waste of time.'

He snorted. 'What about that famous Street of yours?' He was always going on about the Street. Envious he was, though I don't know why 'cause his mother's side used to own half the town. 'We could just push down to follow the tide,' he said.

'Suppose so,' I muttered. 'Or we could throw from the end of that pier of yours. We could just climb to the top of the helter skelter, slide down on them mats, chucking as we go...'

I left that hanging 'cause I know he hated Herne Bay Pier.

'I'll be on the Slopes in half an hour,' he replied.

I eyeballed the weather station Big Meany got me for Xmas. Some gift; first time I've noticed it. Little frosty snowflakes, it says. 'Jesus, Charlie, it's the Artic out there.'

He snorted. 'Wrap up. There's some urgent business I need to talk to you about too.'

Now I knew what this was all about: Foreign Bleeding Objects. Him and his Herne Bay mob wanted to break away from The Association. 'I'll call my Looker and see if he can put in a shift,' I sighed.

'Good man,' he said. 'Give Charlotte a peck from me.'

I hung up. That was below the belt. Wrong of him to bring up my missus.

Well, I can't believe I've forgotten to introduce myself. Best do that in case I run out of time. Probably ain't got long left. My name's Olly Preece. You must know the name, I'm famous round here and about to get a whole lot more famous, though not for the right reasons. I'll have you know I am the founder and the sitting President of the WSS. That's 'The Whitstable Stone Skimmers' to you. I wrote the official rules for beach stone skimming that are being used all over East Kent. 'No foreign objects.' I wrote that, those are my words. Can't be having folk bringing illegal flat pebbles – we call 'em flatees – to a beach skimming contest. No, you got to work with what you find on the beach. Rules say you got to use what your Looker finds for you – that's your partner.

Listen now, it's important you pay attention to this bit. One person, well they skims, the other person looks for flatees. That's how it works. The judge counts the number of times the stone skims the water. Judge's decision is final. Says that in the rules too. So this is where it gets interesting... if I skims an eighter and you skims a tenner, then you win that point. But on the next throw, if I skim another eighter and you throw a sevener... you win because you still got two in bag from that tenner you just threw before. Every third throw doesn't have a carry-over. If you can't find a flatee, then a cracker will probably do. That's a round flint that's been split in half. Never use a wet stone, no matter how flat or beautiful it might be... they just don't rear up properly on account of the drag.

Whitstable has got the smoothest sea in the whole of Kent. Hardly ever choppy. Some days I swear it's just like a mill pond out there. Brown and chocolately some days, others blue as the sky. When I'm out on the beach, you get to see a different sort of Kent.

Once upon a time, I used to wish Big Meany would come and be my Looker but then she got too busy being a Little Miss Do-Gooder. So my right hand man, my Looker, is Darren Crooks. I calls him Daz. Bright? He is not. Thick spectacles, wonky nose. Thick as two short planks. Codename 'The Dazzmatazz.' Plus he's got that horrible mongrel, Moss. But we all call him Mossad because he's a deadly assassin.

I suppose I mustn't grumble because Daz, well, he's not afraid to do the dirty work. As President, I have to keep my hands clean. Like that time I caught that fella free-skimming one afternoon.

'You can't do that,' I told him. 'You're not a paid-up member.

We've got Hythe coming up tomorrow and you're using up all the flatees. You've got to stop. Don't you have no pride in your town?'

Well he said some things I think he regrets now. So I just said nothing more, left him alone, and called Dazzmatazz from the red phone box, you know the one, by the castle. So Daz came down and sets Mossad on that jumped up little tyke. Big old chompy jaws that dog has. You should have seen that fella run. Got what he deserved and some more.

So here's the thing, I know it might sound like I'm a bad 'un but I plead special circumstances. I might as well tell you the whole truth. You remember the Chairman of the Herne Bay Stone Skippers, What's-His-Name that called earlier? His real name is Charles Beaumont and I hate him. Me and old Charlie go right back, used to be pals at school and all that. Listen to this though. He was dating Big Meany before I got on the scene. Back when Big Meany was a sweet young thing with doey eyes and a smile that melted your heart.

The big difference between me and Charlie is that I had to work for what I got but he was born with a silver spoon. My old man was a postie. His had some swanky job in the City. Well, Charlie Boy had been dating Big Meany, nothing serious like, but then the lucky so-and-so had to go and stay in a villa down in the south of France all summer holiday. Poor muggins here had to work in the General Post Office depot on Cromwell Road. I saw a chance and I took it. You see, old Charlie, he wrote 'darling Charlotte' a letter every day, sometimes two. Course I read them, bloody marvellous writer Charlie was. I even used some of the lines. Waste not, want not. I've still got every last one of them letters, up in the loft.

Anyway, I worked and worked on Big Meany that summer. I listened to her wailing on about how Charlie had deserted her and how he had promised to write every day. He-he-he. Then one night she got tipsy, and one thing led to another. From then she was all mine. I suppose it's fair to say we haven't always had the perfect marriage. She would have liked kids but

I didn't want none of that. Things were fine when old Charlie B was in the army. Travelled the world, I heard. Even joined The Foreign Legion, my sources say, though he denies it if you ask him. But then he left, came back, settling just down the coast. Now every time Charlie Beaumont comes to town to do battle with my gang, I see her out of the corner of my eye, up on the slopes, looking down at us.

If there's one thing I hate though it's Foreign Objects. The Faversham Mob, they always try and bring illegal flatees to a contest. It's not right. Judge disqualifies them before Daz explodes. I've always suspected Charlie brings Foreign Bleeding Objects, having been in the Foreign Bleeding Legion. Never been able to prove it though.

So today, I meet him on the beach by the Street. The water is all brown like chocolate milkshake. Tides in but on the turn. Few waves lap the shore but they're not up to much. Charlie's wearing a waxed jacket, those proud old shoulders straight as timber, moustache still got wisps of blond in it. There's something in his eyes that's different today. A sort of hard glint.

'Where's your Looker?' I say.

'Running late,' he says, shrugging. 'Where's yours?'

I look on the beach and there's the Dazzmatazz. I nearly go crackers when I see that bleeding dog of his off a lead, chasing its tail around. Then it goes in the water and starts swimming round like a motor boat. My life, today ain't going to plan.

'How you diddlin, Charlie?' I say, half watching Daz wading into the freezing cold sea to retrieve that stupid mutt.

'So, so,' he says. 'Listen, before we begin, I've something to put to you.'

Here it comes, I think.

'I've been talking to the other associations,' he says, 'and we want to standardise the flatee. We want to pre-manufacture it to an agreed size, shape and weight. Maybe have two or three variations for different conditions.'

'Blasphemy,' I mutter. I feel Big Meany's eyes boring in my

skull but when I turn around I can't see her. But I know she's out there, I can sense it.

'The thing is, my Lookers are fed up of scouring the beach. None of us are getting any younger and all that stooping takes an awful toll on the sciatica. All my Lookers want to become Skippers. We could halve the time it takes to have a Meet.'

'We don't have no problems with our Lookers,' I say, thanking God that Daz was now out of the drink and was towelling down Mossad.

Charlie shrugs. 'Maybe I can make you change your mind. We're still experimenting with the shapes.' He then reaches into his jacket and produces the most foreign object I have ever seen. He chucks it to me. Black like onyx; smooth too but still got a bit of a grain on it. Oval. About an inch thick. It's the weight that makes me catch my breath. My giddy aunt, it's absolutely the right weight. Feels snug in the hand, my forefinger wraps around it like it was always supposed to.

'Not interested,' I say, throwing it back. 'Takes the romance out of it.'

'Oh you know all about romance,' he mutters, with a far-away look in his eye, staring up the Slopes. Jealous he is, 'cause he never married. Well marriage ain't all it's cracked up to be.

Then his Looker arrives. Big sweaty fella, broad, gut like a sack of potatoes, boss-eyed. Never seen him before in my life. 'Lurch,' I call him. Well, Lurch is carrying the most gigantic rucksack I have ever seen. He's even got a spade sticking out the top of it like he's going to build an 'undred sand castles. Grunts a 'hello' and I introduce Daz, now shivering after his little dip.

'Good man,' Charlie says to him, hard look in his eyes. 'As we discussed.'

'Oui, mon Colonel,' Lurch says.

I sigh. Just like Charlie to bring a bleeding foreigner.

So we start, agreeing to do a 'gentleman's count' which is the average score between Skimmers and Lookers. We move down the Street as the tide's slipping away. I get off to a flyer with a gorgeous nine. But Lurch and Charlie call it eleven. Daz's lips have gone blue and he just shivers in agreement. I can hardly believe my luck but keep my mouth firmly closed. Charlie chucks a six and I call it so. But Lurch calls it a four and Charlie just nods and agrees. We throw another six sets and it's the same each time. I'm thrashing him and haven't even broken into a sweat. Then there's a little gap as the Lookers start scouring the spit beach and we find ourselves alone.

'Consider my offer,' he says. 'We could set up one of this internet stations to cover events. Get sponsorship. Who knows, get recognition, take the sport professional.'

I shake my head, refusing to be drawn in idle chit chat. I turn and look back up the Slopes. There she is, beyond the beach huts. Even at this distance, she don't look half bad. Elegant, she is. But I know she's not here for me and that raises my hackles. Especially when Daz returns with an oyster shell in shaking hands.

'What the devil is that?' I snap, thinking some very dark thoughts. But I ain't got a choice, have I? Got to throw what your Looker finds you, says that in the rule book. So I flick the bugger out, back hand, but an oyster shell is too light and I'm lucky to get a four. Still, Lurch scores six. I'll take that, I say to myself. Maybe he can't count in English. I smile at him all friendly like but he don't smile back. Suit yourself!

I turn to watch Charlie who Lurch has given a wonky cracker. He doesn't do bad and I call seven. Lurch scores a five and Charlie hardly bats an eyelid. But it's getting hard to hit the water as the sea is retreating, leaving shiny brown mud-flats behind. So we move further down the Street, throwing towards Sheerness. Of course it takes Lurch an age to join us, messing around on the beach with that giant rucksack of his.

Then, disaster strikes! Somehow Mossad has escaped from his tether on the beach groyne and he goes bleeding mental, chasing and barking. He sinks his fangs into the haunch of a Labrador and starts chasing a lady with kids. Then he's off, escaping across the flats towards Herne Bay. Daz runs after him, falling over and getting covered in that sticky mud. His shoes clump up covered in thick brown gooey silt. Mossad doubles back to the Street and clears that down of people, before heading off towards the Hotel Continental, a muddy Daz slogging after him.

I turn to Charlie. 'We're going to have to call it a day.'

'Conceding?' Charlie asks, laughter in his eyes.

'No I ain't conceding but I'm going to have to retire my Looker. But if you're that keen, I'll find my own flatees. Probably be quicker,' I say.

'Is that in the Rules?' he says, all sarcastic. Then he reaches into his pocket and pulls out one of his Foreign Objects. 'Humour me, Olly. Humour me.'

Then without a by-your-leave, he lets it go. Into my sea! I'm flabbergasted. I mean, the cheek of it! But then everything just happens in slow motion as I see how beautiful the stone flies, hardly touching the water at all, just gliding between each bounce. I count twelve, thirteen, fourteen, fifteen, sixteen. Oh my giddy aunt, he just hit eighteen. On a low tide with a cross wind!

'Eighteeen!' I shout in excitement.

'Fourteen,' burps Lurch, sipping on a golden tin of the sauce.

'You can rest now,' Charlie says to his Looker. 'Build that castle of yours.'

'Oui mon Colonel,' Lurch says, getting out a big bucket and spade. He begins digging up the silt and pebbles.

Charlie turns to me. 'Imagine what you could do with these, Olly,' Charlie says. 'Imagine.'

Against my better judgement I nod my head. 'Not here,' I say. 'At the end,' I say pointing to the farthest point of the Street. 'I don't want to pollute the vicinity with Foreign Objects.'

There ain't nobody out here now as Mossad has terrorised every living soul but us. There's a few ripples in the water from the cross wind but nothing to concern an expert like me. I test the stone's weight and I have to admit, it's perfect. I let my mind go blank and then cast it with all my might, long and hard. First off, I think I've aimed too far and all the momentum will be spent, then old Charlie B and Lurch will just laugh at me. But the stone hits the water and rises up. Again and again. Each time it skims the sea it's like the lightest kiss you'll ever see. Fourteen. Fifteen. Sixteen. Seventeen. Oh my gosh. Eighteen. Nineteen. The gap between the jumps is getting smaller as the energy spends but she just keeps pecking the water. I lose count after twenty-six. I ain't ever seen nothing like it.

Charlie feeds me another and the same again. This time huge hops, beautiful like a Manx Shearwater in flight.

I hear Lurch in the background, scraping and mixing stuff in his bucket. What's he building. Buckingham Palace? And I thought I had it bad with Dazzmatazz.

'You've always been able to spin my hay into shining gold,' Charlie says, face all smiles.

He tosses me another, different shape this one. Thin and nearly as big as the palm of my hand. Hits the water with big slaps but just keeps going. Old Charlie B keeps tossing me the ammunition and I keep firing it out.

'C'est prêt,' Monsieur Lurch says.

I stare out to sea, my mind going into over-drive. I could write new rules and get the sport recognised. I could earn a living skimming. You Tube here I come. I might end up being world famous. I could represent the UK at the Olympics. I might even get an MBE or something like that.

I turn back to Charlie, about to tell him everything but all then I see Lurch. He's been at it for ages but where's his chateau? Lurch has this black look in his eyes and he's swinging that spade like it's a club. No wonder Charlie B wants to stand his Lookers down! Then he inches forward, dragging his feet like a lumbering heavyweight, until he's standing about a foot from me. Soft headed bugger!

'Hey, watch this, Olly!' Charlie says and I turn around to see him throwing a foreign object with a force I didn't know he had. The stone rears up just like one of them bouncing bombs from the Dambusters. Then there's something whirring through the air and then a massive explosion in my head.

CLONK!

As I fall down, I realise Lurch had just whacked me right across the head with that spade. Funny thing, the second it goes dark I get a vision of Big Meany. Climbing up the ladder, head poking through the hatch, going where she knows she ain't allowed to...

I wake up and discover my new circumstances.

I am standing vertical. I realise now what old Lurch had been doing with his spade and bucket…mixing cement! I look down at my feet, which are now standing in his sandcastle bucket, encased in said cement.

Blow me down, they've only gone and tied me to a steel pole that's been hammered into beach. I try and move but the cement has fully set.

I see the bloody tide is coming in fast now, covering the bucket. The wind is howling all around me.

I try and yell but the bleeders have gone and covered my mouth up in gaffer tape. My eyes dart around but there's nobody round to help me. Damn that bleeding dog!

It's then I see a lime blob back up the shore, binoculars out.

Funny how your life can change on the turn of a tide.

Time and Tide

by Grantt Ennis

Further...

Have you ever experienced a sudden urge to do something completely outlandish? Like standing on a pier and suddenly wanting to throw your phone into the water? It appears from nowhere and your rational mind can't quite work out why that thought popped into your head. It felt like that.

I was stood on Tankerton beach just east of Whitstable harbour, and the low tide had left a knife blade of shingle and mud reaching out into the north sea. It was like a rip in the coastline, as if someone had taken each side of the water in each hand and pulled it apart, tearing a narrow triangle of solid land out into the ocean. The locals call it 'the Street' and seeing it in the flesh conjured something inside me, some primal need to explore it. Maybe it was the temporary beauty; that this causeway would only exist during the low tide made it all the more appealing. I couldn't go back home to London without trying it, right?

I'd heard that the Street didn't last long and that there were stories of people getting trapped there when the tide came back in. I imagined that was urban legend bullshit, but the sun was setting and I didn't like the idea of getting trapped out there in the dark with the water rising. Still, it seemed a short walk and the streetlights on Marine Parade would give me something to head towards if it got too dark too quickly. If

I didn't at least have a look I'd kick myself later.

The shingle crunched beneath my feet and for a moment I felt awkward as it threw out my balance. Within a few steps I was used to it, shifting my weight to compensate as I made my way toward the jutting causeway. The Street stabbed out into the waters and I could see the walkway stretching out into the blue-grey of the north sea, little curls of white foam picking out the meanders of a pathway just beneath the waves. I wouldn't go out that far; just enough to experience it, then head back.

A middle-aged couple passed, nodding and smiling, and the woman said something about looking after myself if I was heading out. I smiled and said something reassuring about how big a lad I was then carried on, mildly irritated that she'd interrupted my pilgrimage. I glanced back up the beach toward the mainland after them as they wandered away.

Behind me, the beach huts lining the parade were glowing. They reflected the setting sun in a myriad of brightly painted colours, framed in the swaying green grass of the verge they were nestled in. Homes lined the street beyond that, punctuated by tastefully decorated hotels. A car, sleek and modern, made its silent way along the parade, its engine drowned out by the crash and hiss of waves as they rolled out beyond the silt and mud. It seemed filled with humanity; teeming with all the modern concerns of a too-busy existence. Of cities and roads and office blocks filled with the oh-so important lives of the hordes of meaningless people. The empty beach was calm and quiet, both welcoming and distant with promise and treachery in equal measure. I was falling quite in love with it.

I made my way past the old wooden groynes that split the beach into partitions. There was something so wonderfully old about them, and it cast my mind back to being a child in the early 80s, spending time on Leysdown beach with my family. The memory of those times washed over me, and I could almost pick out the synthesised fanfares of the slot machines and the sweet smell of the donuts. I imagined

Tankerton offered similar back in the day, although it was long since gentrified by modernity.

Further...

I pushed on, not wanting to lose my nerve. The shingle became wetter, and it wasn't long before I was picking my way between shallow puddles left by the retreating tide. I wondered if I'd see any crabs, but as I made my way along the gentle curve of the knife that stabbed into the ocean, I found only washed up kelp and refuse. I could hear the soft gurgling of seagulls looping above me, looking for morsels in the dying sunlight, and the sweet-rot smell of the coastline was everywhere. Either side of me, the sea lapped at the edges of the Street, retreating now, but filled with the threat of high tide to come.

Planes roared overhead. They caught me by surprise and I glanced up to see four vintage World War Two planes pass low over me. Spitfires with cambered wings and clotheslines. They were so low that it sounded like an entire battalion's worth had just passed, but all I could see were those four heading east out to sea as if they were headed for Dunkirk. I marvelled for a moment that they had been so lovingly restored and imagined how different this coastline would have been during those terrifying years; no longer the welcoming holiday destination. Instead, it would be a potential danger, an avenue for invasion by enemy forces. It seemed an outlandish notion for someone who'd never experienced war in his homeland. Less than a century before, the people living in the houses along Marine Parade would have lived day to day considering that threat. I couldn't wrap my head around it.

Glancing back at the shore, I noticed how much darker it had become, the sunlight no longer reaching the beach huts. They seemed drab and grey in this light, while the buildings behind had lost the clear daylight glow, replaced by the harsh sodium lamps of streetlights and interior lights. The difference was startling. I spent a moment enjoying that; loving this experience already, my resolve to carry on hardened. What else would I find as I made my way further out along the Street?

Inspired, I carried on. The shingle here was even more treacherous, having been recently resettled by the waters. The sky was staining navy, lights twinkling across the shoreline of Essex in front of me and along the parade behind me. To the east, I could make out the forest of off-shore wind turbines, their sails slowly revolving in the encroaching gloom.

The waters were quiet, lacking the usual traffic headed for the Thames and the ports lining the river. I scanned the estuary for a moment and picked out a small barge bedecked in lamps, the only one I could pick out, slowly making its way along the coastline. It was far off, but I could make out some kind of celebration, with people dancing on the main deck to music played by a band on the deck above them. As I peered at the barge, I thought I made out period costumes; bustling dresses and bonnets for the ladies, and tailed coats and top-hats for the men. I gawped for a moment before I realised that it must be some kind of Victorian themed party-boat, and made a mental note to see if it was something I could book online. It seemed quite authentic.

I loved how places like this came alive in the early summer months. Autumn and winter were spent inside, hiding from the harsh coastal weather, the beaches and greens empty. Once the weather turned warmer these places seemed to wake up; the people became happier and the events began. Rustic summer fairs and regattas, all capturing the feeling of times long since passed, still conjuring the feeling of joy that the turning of the seasons brought with them. Even though that age was a century and a half vanished there were still folk eager to book a barge and sail the north Kent coast as if it was filled with the pleasure beaches of the last century.

Puddles were becoming more numerous and I'd detected a distinct change in the sound of the sea. The lapping retreat of the waves had changed to something a little hungrier, and I imagined that the tide had begun to turn. A little disappointed,

I stopped, enjoying another moment of staring out into the growing darkness of the north sea, surrounded by undulating water. I looked back at the shore again, surprised once more at how different it looked with the change in the light and the distance I'd walked. There seemed fewer lights, as if they'd been squeezed into a smaller patch rather than filling the horizon. Maybe the elevation had changed and was cutting off a strip of the parade? It was very hard to tell, but I couldn't make out the hotels scattered amongst the houses anymore.

Further.

I was torn. I'd walked further out than I'd meant to, but I'd enjoyed it so much already. It was getting dark and the tide looked like it was coming back in, but it hadn't really taken that long to get this far. This was a rare chance. One of those spur-of-the-moment situations that would never happen again. I didn't want it to end, to go back to that mundane morass of everyday forgettables. I was more alive in that weird moment than I had been for a long time.

Decision made, I pressed on. I moved slower now, the rare patches of solid shingle still slick and wet. The Street was steadily becoming a narrow path that meandered out into the sea before me. Something seemed odd. I remembered the foam coiling over a suggested pathway, not this encrusted catwalk that wound over the inky waves. It began to feel dangerous. Perhaps I'd reached the peak of low tide, when the entire Street was poking above the water, and it would submerge itself again at any moment. I began to question my decision to continue.

My foot struck something more solid, and a soft chink of metal sliding against metal sounded when I stopped and stepped back. I crouched down to get a closer look at what I'd kicked, squinting in the half-light to make out a section of thick chain, each link about an inch wide. Gingerly, I picked at it, pulling it up and out of the mud it was settled in. Two, maybe three feet of chain came away, surprisingly heavy, and one end popped out of the silt with a wet slurp. Spinning in the grey evening light was a manacle, open, dripping mud.

And blood. Rusty red streaks of it covered the open join. I peered closer and noticed the bent pin that would have kept the manacle closed. Wedged between the pin and the manacle was a ruined fingernail.

Disgusted, I dropped them. They fell into the waters with a splash, quickly sinking out of sight. My heart hammered and it took me a moment to regain my senses. I chided myself as I calmed down; it was a trick of the light. The rust red was exactly that, and the fingernail must have been a shell. I imagined transported prisoners sentenced to deportation to Australia, watching the English coastline sail by and picking at their manacles in the vain hope of freedom. That was hundreds of years ago. I'd probably found a discarded piece of an old tug boat and let my imagination run away with me. I chuckled to myself as the adrenaline began to thin. I ran a wet hand through my hair and called myself an idiot. I considered turning back again, glancing at the shore once more. There seemed even less light now that I was further out, and I could just make out a handful of buildings. I supposed the taller buildings on Marine Parade blocked the ones behind.

I was hypnotised by the promise of what lay before me. Life was so grey and banal and mundane, and this one experience in all my existence so far contained so much meaning that I simply couldn't ignore it. As if lured by some unseen Siren, I felt the dark water urge me onward, promising enlightenment. The sibilant hiss of it was everywhere and the swelling currents seemed like the flexing of great muscles, each overlapping the other as they moved across the face of the earth. I thought about how a wave might start in one corner of the world and move to another, rolling through currents and eddies, changing with every influence yet always remaining the same potential wave until it curled up onto a shore with its last, dying movement. Our own lives were similar, buffeted by millions of countless movements into following our own paths. Some of us became crashing tidal waves, changing the face of the earth in our throes, whilst others just brushed against the shore, instantly forgotten.

A ship loomed out of the darkness, headed straight for me. I called out a wordless cry of warning, scared at once that the ship would hit me, then scared that it would scupper itself on the Street. It appeared so suddenly that my cry made no difference. It rose up out of the gloom as if on a tumultuous wave that I couldn't see, an enormous curved hull that blotted out the light and creaked like a forest full of falling trees, then crashed onto the causeway in a spray of foam and splintering wood. Men's voices cried out in alarm, and I noticed tall masts in the darkness, and immense sails swinging wildly out of control. Lamps bounced crazily on the deck as the ship floundered for a moment, then began to capsize, rolling off the Street and onto the other side, the sails smashing down into the deeper waters beyond. Stunned, I stared for a moment at the bared hull that faced me, caught in a panic of indecision. Did I run to help them, or run to get help? What could I do? I was one man in the middle of nowhere. It's too easy to make the wrong decision when you're in the panic of the moment.

I ran as best I could along that crunching shingle toward the vessel, only now beginning to realise that it was an old galleon – a wooden vessel like those seen in historical movies. It was still slowly rolling as it capsized and I couldn't see the deck itself, but there was no denying it; the hull was layered plank upon plank, riveted with large iron nails, coils of rope and rigging trailing in the water. As I moved closer, I could see it being carried by the tide out and away from the causeway, and that I wouldn't be able to reach it in time. Bewildered, I turned back to shout for help from the shore, not even certain if they'd hear me above the cracking of the wooden vessel and the terrified cries of the men aboard that ship.

The shore was dark, with the barest scattering of dim, flickering lights. How far had I come out? Had the sun sunk so low that I couldn't see the buildings, and only pick out their silhouette? Or were the buildings even there anymore? The shock of it silenced me.

Silence. Not a sound.

I turned again, and the boat was gone. Nothing remained but the steadily roiling waters, growing inky and dark now that the sun had gone. Only a grey and orange streak in the sky was left, casting a shimmering, unreal light across the bay. A ship like that wouldn't sink so fast. A ship that big couldn't sink in waters this shallow. A ship like that couldn't have just appeared from nowhere. Yet, there was nothing. No splintered wooden hulls, no drifting rigging, no men. Just the water. It had disappeared as suddenly as it had appeared.

I stood in the growing dark, mind blank with shock, my heart hammering in my chest. The terror of it made me want to run back to shore, but there was something stopping me. A morbid interest, perhaps. Maybe my mind was playing tricks on me in this secluded place. I should probably head back, but I was too curious as to what else I would see out here. Maybe I wasn't even fully in control myself anymore. Was I hallucinating? Was this an out of body experience? If so, wasn't it my duty to see where it would lead me? I spent my days in a cubicle, filling pointless forms and making pleasant phone calls to people I hated; this terrifying moment was the most alive I'd felt for a long time.

Further.

My breathing was ragged. The shingle beneath my feet was much more brittle here, probably smaller, more worn by the water. I imagined the press of time washing over this place, wearing thin the shoreline as the ages passed and changed the face of the beach. The weight of time seemed suddenly to press in on me, thousands of years of human history; billions of years of geological history. Throughout it all, the steady lapping of water against the shore, the heartbeat of the world. Could a place experience so much and be the focus of so many similar emotions that it carried an echo of them? I imagined the hundreds of thousands, maybe even millions of people who had wandered this causeway and thought similar things, felt similar emotions, and experienced the surrounding, claustrophobic rhythm of the sea.

The water wasn't calming me anymore. The manacles had been one thing; the crashing ship quite another. I just couldn't seem to get my breath back and my skin was prickling with the cold. I was paralysed with fear, unable to even think straight, no longer truly in control of my own thoughts. The desire to press on thudded behind my thoughts like an alien heartbeat, the antithesis of my rational mind, but irresistible none the less. Despite the cold, despite the manacle, despite the beached ship, I had to see what was at the end of the Street. I took a slow, crunching step forward.

The shingle beneath my feet had become oyster shells. Countless numbers of oyster shells piled atop of one another to create the pathway I was walking. An oyster shell for every one eaten in the local towns, building the very foundation of the civilisations that had inhabited these regions. Each step I took was on the back of this commodity, one that had shaped the local peoples for thousands of years. This was a path through the ages, to the dawn of civilisation, at least in this small part of the world. I couldn't resist the call to continue any more than I could resist the urge to breathe. I truly was a pilgrim, chasing salvation through discovery.

The ship had torn the thin veil of reality asunder, and the spectres of ages long past rushed at me out of the gloom as I continued my holy trek along the causeway. Voices drifted to me through the rapidly descending darkness, uttered in languages I couldn't understand. Frantic voices, riddled with fear and fury. Chattering voices arguing a point. Chanting voices issuing a call to prayer. The combined susurrus of thousands of years of human interaction in and around these waters pressed through time and roared over me, their crashing syllables so similar to the waves that smashed against the shores.

Two men staggered out of the inky night before me, walking on the water as if it were solid ground. Both wore ancient armour and carried weapons not used in over a thousand years; a Saxon and a Viking. As I stared, they lunged at one another, their weapons ringing from each other's shields. This fight was not the choreographed dance you would find in a movie, but the desperate scramble of men desperate to survive. They struck at each other with a fury that jarred me, eventually wrestling each other to the floor in a tangled heap. One man rose atop the other with a dagger drawn, but the man beneath him wrapped his hand around an axe and swung upward in an irresistible arc into the other's head. Helmet cracked. Skin parted. Skull split with a crack that I felt in my bones. The wounded man toppled off the other into the water, the splash covering them both as they disappeared beneath the waves. I stared at the dark patch of the water where they had vanished, wondering if it was blood lying slick on the surface.

I rushed onward, my feet stumbling, my mind racing, oysters cracking beneath me. In the face of these crazed visions, my rational mind reeled, desperately trying to piece together the causes of these visions and their potential meaning. Ahead of me a tall post appeared from the darkness, an old lightning-blasted tree daubed with white paint. As I set eyes on it, I conjured a name from a memory that wasn't mine: *Witnestaple*. White Post. I imagined traders gathered beneath it, selling oysters or the wares to get them. What was the significance of the white post? A guide post? A sacred reminder? A reminder of what?

A man in layered bronze plates with a dull red cloak etched something into the white wood; something in a language I could not read, but assumed was Latin. A Roman defacing the post. As he finished, he turned to unseen comrades, talking hurriedly, then slung something out over the waters. I caught sight of a small glass phial filled with dark liquid sailing out into the night, catching the light in glittering flashes as it descended into the water.

There were no lights now. None on the shores ahead of me; none on the shores behind. Ages had extinguished them, leaving me with only the wan glow of the moon and stars. Water was beginning to seep into my shoes, and I realised that the tide was rising, almost at my ankles. Each faltering step was splashing into water. Surrounded by darkness, with no light to see by, terror stricken, I had no idea how each step landed on the Street, but it did, and each step lured me onwards towards the revelation I knew must be waiting for me.

What did I matter in a thousand years of history? I could feel it coiling in front of me and spiralling out behind me like a twisting fan. I dimly remembered something I'd read about Celtic mythology and the importance of spirals, and found myself picturing the spirals of potential time unravelling as I made my trek down this ancient causeway. If I did turn back, would it take me back through history to my modern age, or was that gone forever? I was transfixed. How many others had made this pilgrimage before me along this causeway? Was I the first?

I was profoundly alone, and terrified, but there was a strange at peace in that. It made me think of all the weight and worry we place on our own lives. All the fuss and concern we fill them with, and how little it meant to this landscape that would exist for untold billions of years. All the heartache, the joy and the horror, just a subtle flavour to the endless wash of waves against this shore. It would weather us just like it weathered the tides, here long before us and here for aeons after us. It was strangely satisfying. It made petty worries seem ludicrous in comparison.

Another spectre of the past appeared before me. A spindly old man, once again on the waters as if they were solid. He knelt over the fresh carcass of a fox, working at the body with a flint knife as he mumbled a chant that hadn't been heard for millennia. Deftly, with practised hands, he carved out piece after piece of the creature's innards, inspecting them intently before placing them reverently to one side. Closer now, I could see his hair was woven with feathers and smaller animal bones. A laurel of local plants sat on his brow. His eyes were steel grey. I watched him cut out a glistening organ, holding it up to the moon. It practically glowed in the light, and the old man howled in his obscure chant. I wasn't sure how, but I knew that was the animal's liver, where we used to believe the soul of a creature could be found. This was an offering to the gods of this place.

The old man turned and offered it to me and I leapt away, whooping in fear, terrified that this ghost of ages past would notice me. I landed in deep water, splashing into it and feeling it smother me, stabbing me with ice-cold needles that numbed my skin. Sputtering, I pushed my way toward what I prayed was the surface, gulping ice water. The Street was gone. I was alone, in the darkness, in the deep water.

My head breached the surface and I sucked in air, thrashing to keep myself afloat. The cold was leaching the strength from my limbs, and I shouted for help, my voice lost in the night. I noticed small boats bobbing on the water, and pushed myself towards them, screaming whenever my head wasn't engulfed by black waves.

Half-naked people dressed in ragged furs sat in lashed-together boats. Our earliest ancestors, crafting crude canoes and venturing out into the darkness. Torches illuminated them as they all called and sang into the darkness ahead of us, obviously paying some holy homage to their gods of the ocean. I called out to them, but my shouts were drowned out by theirs just as the sea was steadily drowning me. They were kept in rapt attention by their gods, and even though I was freezing, even though my throat was hoarse from screaming, even though I was dying, I was also desperate to find out what meaning there was to be found at the end of the Street.

Then I saw what they were worshipping. Great white legs that stretched high into the night sky; a whole forest of them, each topped with a slowly twisting trio of immense arms. They spun forever, these titans, far offshore where no early man could ever really reach them, small red lights twinkling atop them each and every night. Silent guardians of the shore.

Monoliths of the sea's bounty. I knew what they were, but those early people? What would they have thought of these wind farms, standing forever out at sea? As the water began to wash over my face, my limbs exhausted and no longer able to keep me above the water, I wondered if I had gone backward or forward through the ages. Perhaps these early people were our future descendants, long after our civilisation had fallen, trying to work out these ancient constructions. Perhaps the causeway was a bridge through the ages and folk had lined the shores for aeons looking out to the white sentinels, wondering how they got there, finding only gods as an answer. Something mundane for us and transcendent for them.

As my strength failed me and I sank beneath the waves, I remembered the white post. Witenestaple. A sacred reminder. The end and the beginning.

Once Upon A Time

by David Williamson

Once Upon A Time; an amazing place. Well, it will be when they finish it. Vast complex, sprawling out across the valley. They built it on that old industrial site overlooking the estuary. I remember what it used to be like when I was younger: there was chimneys coughing up white smoke, I think that was a bread factory; other chimneys coughing up yellowish-brown fumes giving out a real old stink. They demolished them chimneys years ago. That's where me Uncle Jim used to work, they made piston engines and stuff in those factories before they relocated the Kent operation to China, or India, not sure which, somewhere East. Anyways, a lot of people lost their jobs and the site was like the Mary Celeste for a couple of decades, redundant factories and redundant workers on the dole. A bleedin' shame to see such a thriving place abandoned like that. After a few years the only thing thriving was the Japanese Knotweed that took root in the cracks.

It was a great place to take birds though 'cos there was never any one about. When I got my first car I took a girl up there for a bit of fun. She was called Cindy and she was a real looker. I'd met her in a pub in Gravesend and she had given me the come on, so I says to her I know a quiet place we can go. I drive us up to the site, park up, we get necking and all's going well when suddenly I'm getting this urge to go for a pee. I get out the car, go behind a wall, comes back and she's gone, and so had me wallet! Couldn't believe it, I had a week's pay in there. Never saw her again; she just vanished into the night.

Not long after, I got meself a sparkie's apprenticeship and that's where I learned the electrician trade. I took some other birds up there (kept the wallet tucked in me jeans those times!). But I never forgot about that Cindy and where she might have wandered off to that night.

Couple of years later I had set up on me own with the van, drove that up to the site with another girl, gets her pregnant and for the last 30 years that girl's been me missus! Thirty years on and the kids have all flown the nest, and when I got into me fifties, and things were going digital, my eldest lad says to me, 'Dad, you're never too old to retrain.' So I did. Took a course, didn't I? After that I was in big demand, good money, and that's how I ended up being a contract engineer at Once Upon A Time. Most of the old site has been developed now, but some of them factories still remain. They've put up a load of barbed wire fences around the place with warning signs.

'KEEP OUT. REMEDIATION SITE. HAZARDOUS MATERIALS'.

Them factories look a bit sad compared to them brightly-painted fairy tale castles and all those fun rides they've put up in the theme park. Must have cost squillions to build. Once Upon A Time opened about eighteen months ago, but it had got off to a slow start and all them investors were beginning to get a bit twitchy. The blokes at the council commissioned some feasibility report from one of them big London consultancy firms when they were considering what to do with the site. Developers wanted to build a load of houses, but there was no jobs for 'em, so the council were reluctant to give it the OK. Anyhow, them consultants came to the rescue and said that a new theme park would be a great way of regenerating the place, and the council loved it. A lot of locals were against it, though, and the media had a field day with it. Thousands of tweets, too, most saying that Kent had more than enough attractions for the number of visitors it received. Still, the development went ahead and the park opened with a great big opening. They couldn't get a royal, but they had some boy band you've never heard of turn up to sing some songs you've never heard of and a junior minister showed her face too and there were a load of councillors cutting ribbons and posing for photos.

Anyhow, all that was short-lived. There had been a major incident after only three weeks of opening when two rogue elves attacked a family without any warning whilst they were riding the white swans through the Enchanted Grotto. The media picked it up and ran with a scare story asking whether the theme park was a safe place for visitors. They had headlines like 'Elf and Safety?' and 'Once Upon A Crime.' Made me laugh, that did. The guys in the office at Once Upon A Time were quick to respond, saying it wasn't their fault, and blamed programming errors by third party contractors.

That was where I came in (and other contractors like me who were blamed) to sort out the mess. We worked around the clock for a week running tests on all the automatons and bots, but we found no programming errors. The problem was, guess what? The weather. Once the temperature dips below minus 2, a lot of them cheaper automotons simply seize up, or in the case of them rogue elves, go into panic mode. They bought cheap, you see. Dodgy circuits from Morocco and Indonesia with Q&A labels that meet dodgy standards that pass the post in those countries and low grade internal thermostats that couldn't detect a temperature change if the sun fell on top of them.

The management at Once Upon A Time had been told about this in them feasibility reports, but the knock-down price on the land, some generous Government hand-outs to regenerate the old site plus cheap imports from China and places like that got them councillors all giddy, signing contracts and stuff and there was no turning back.

Now, there's other places that had more sense. Finland had

wanted to open a Santa Land in Lapland operated by bots too, but them Fins realised it was a non-starter. The technology wasn't advanced enough. Another 10 years, they reckoned, before AI and robotics would be fully up to speed. Them Fins still went ahead with Santa Land but without the bots, even if employing real people meant nearly three times the wage bill. They may be forking out more in wages but they are doing a lot better than this place, by all accounts. Folks flying into Lapland by the thousands, they say.

It was mid-morning that day in February when I rocked up to the park. It was freezing cold, a thick layer of snow covered the ground and the place was deserted. A drone was assigned to me to guide me across the site. I was always assigned the same type of drone whenever I visited. Horrible big black things. Carbon-fibre tarantulas that hover just above your head, their blades whirring away. One slip and them blades could give your head a nasty cut.

Then there's them two little camera eyes watching you all the time and you never know who's monitoring you through them things. Gives me the shits at times. I was never sure if them drones were there to guide you safely around the place, like they said, or where there to make sure you didn't go wandering over to a place they have fenced off. The Ops Department always seemed so bleedin' secretive, suspicious of contractors like me. You were never allowed in the Ops building; instead, me and the other contractors had to wait in a scruffy little pre-fab behind the park's waste dump until they called your name to go to the security office. Once there, you were finger printed, bags searched, eyes scanned. Mouths swabbed, too. What the hell was that all about?

At every visit this vetting rigmarole would take place, even for the simplest of jobs. Anyhow, I put up with it, didn't I? It was good money and I rocked up whenever I got a call and put up with it.

⌣

That morning I was there to run a routine test on some of the bot workers, starting with the bots in the Huff and Puff Zone. The drone was a metre or so in front of me and I followed it past the House Made of Bricks and the House Made of Sticks. Them three little pigs and the wolf bot had suddenly stopped working, so they had brought in some real people for a couple of days to dress up as the characters. Zero hours contracts and the like.

I left the drone buzzing in the air above me as I bent down to go through the little door of the House Made of Straw. Inside were some guys dressed up as the three pigs and girl wearing a wolf costume. The girl and a young guy next to her were sat huddled in front of an electric fire shivering like shit, smoking roll-ups and nursing hot paper cups between their hands. The two older guys in pig outfits were playing cards on top of a bale of straw.

'Hi! I'm Eddie, I'm here to look at the bots,' I said to them, being friendly. You'd think I had just walked in on a funeral, it were glum faces all around.

'Don't rush,' said the young guy. He had taken off his pig's head and was nursing it in his lap.

'The longer the bots are out of action suits us just fine.'

'Oh, why's that then, buddy?' I said, opening me tool bag.

'More days out of action means more pay for us, innit? Coffee?'

'Cheers, would love one, I'm frozen stiff.'

He poured me a cup of hot coffee from a Thermos.

'If you fancy something sweet, then here for you is a little treat,' said the girl dressed as the wolf, handing me a biscuit with her large furry paw.

The guy next to her grunted and said she didn't have to speak like that, I wasn't a punter. (That's something all customer-facing employees have to do here – speak in rhyme – visitors like it.) The bots are better at it, they're programmed that way.

'Sorry,' she said, 'Would you like a biscuit?' I took a couple and put 'em in me jacket pocket. The two older pig guys asked if I wanted to play cards. I told them I didn't have the time, I needed to get on with the job.

I went over to the corner of the house to look at the bots piled in a heap on top of each other. I opened the plates on the backs of each pig. The wiring, well, that all looked fine, and a trace of a current was still coming through from the back-up batteries. I plugged the scanner into the ear of each pig and ran a quick diagnosis. Nothing came up. So I ran an advanced scan. Still nothing. They were just cold. They're like humans, see. Stop working properly when exposed to extreme temperatures. I went back to the group of pigs and the girl.

'Best thing you can do with them is move them close to a radiator for a couple of hours. Not too close, mind you, that would be too hot, they might close down completely. I've left them on standby mode, they'll re-boot pretty quickly once they warm up. You just need to check the settings are okay before you put them back to work.'

The girl smiled at me. 'Thanks,' she says smilin' at me, 'but with the place so quiet today I'm not sure if there would be much point.'

'Yeah, leave them where they are,' said the young guy with shrug of his head. 'Got any other bots to go and fix, mister fixer?'

'Yeah, there's two more on my list, the Gingerbread House and then a visit to The Runaway Pancake Experience.'

'Pancake? Not surprised about that one,' he sneers back at me. 'That fuckin' Pancake Boy is always breaking down; still, it's not as if a human could do all that rolling about and spinning in the air and stuff, so I guess he's not taking anyone's job.'

'No, I guess not,' I says to him. 'Well look, I'll be on my way then. Oh, favour please, I can't seem to get a signal on me device, can you point me in the direction of where I should be heading next?'

One of the pigs stopped playing cards and looked up at me.

'You'll be lucky. They've blocked all the signals months ago, mate, that's why we're having these endless games of poker instead of playing with our devices. Gave you a drone, did they?'

'Yeah, its waiting for me outside.'

'Follow that then, just keep to the paths and you'll be okay.'

He returned to his game and I slung me tool bag over me shoulder and finished the coffee. The girl gave me a little wave goodbye with that furry paw of hers.

'If you get cold, come back for another coffee and a biscuit.'

'Sure.'

'Say hello to Kelly and Sadiq,' said the younger guy, 'though I doubt they've bothered to show up on a day like today.'

'Who's Kelly and ...'

'They're covering for the Hansel and Gretel bots at the Gingerbread House. Don't think they'll be pleased to see you either. If you fix them bots then you'll be putting them out of a job, too.'

'Right, okay, Kelly and Sadiq.'

The girl reached into a shopping bag at her feet. 'Here, take Kelly this packet of digestive biscuits if you see her. Tell her hello from me.'

I tramped through the snow across the park. They'd thrown salt down on some of the main walkways. Now that's not good for bots. Get salt into the circuits and it ruins them. I walked on; not a visitor to be seen. The place was run on skeleton staff. Like them pigs, each attraction was being temporarily manned by geezers hired on zero hours contracts to step in during the cold snap. They stood there, arms folded, shivering in the cold, waiting for customers. Hot dog stalls, crappy souvenir stalls.

I thought I might get an ice cream just for the laugh of it, but they'd had the good sense to close them down 'til the spring. The money I charged for these emergency call outs had been a great little earner, but I knew it couldn't last forever. The park had been a bad idea, any one could see that. People visiting Kent usually heads for Canterbury Cathedral, Dover Castle, maybe a carton of over-priced cockles at Whitstable, and then they were off again. Back to London, back on the Chunnel to France. They weren't looking for theme parks like this. I reckoned Once Upon A Time would ride it out another season and then they'd probably close it all down.

I followed the drone along a path into the forest at the far end of the park heading for the Gingerbread House or Pancake Boy's house, wasn't sure which one it was leading to first. Must say, it looked the part with all that snow covering the branches of the trees, fairy tale-like. Some automaton birds chirped away. Then a real bird, a little robin, landed on a branch above me. It sang a song, calling out to the automaton birds in the other trees. Poor little bloke, singing out to robot birds. He was gonna be disappointed if he were looking for a mate. It filled up its little breast and chirped up real loud. That drone immediately spun its camera eyes 180 degrees to inspect it. I walked ahead leaving it behind, but realising I had moved on, it accelerated towards me as fast as bullet and crashed into the side a tree and fell to the ground. It landed on its back with its spindly carbon fibre legs sticking up in the air. Served it right.

I was glad to leave that drone behind and pushed on through the snow until I came to a fork in the path with several other paths leading off from it. I hadn't been to this area of the park before. With no drone to lead the way, and snow covering the ground, it wasn't easy to see where to head next. A signpost with three wooden arrows nailed to it had fallen over. The signs were pointing up to the sky now, so I had no bleedin' idea where I should be heading next. I scraped the snow away with the side of me boot. On one arrow was written 'To the Runaway Pancake Experience.' Another said 'Jack and Jill's Hill this way,' and the third one 'Straight ahead for the Teddy Bears Picnic.' Where was the Gingerbread House?' I scratched my head and checked me device to see if I could check an app, but the signal was still blocked. So, left, right or straight ahead?

I took a left and carried on through the forest for another 10 minutes or so. It was leading nowhere. I checked me device again but it still didn't connect. Why had they blocked everything? The path headed up a steep incline. That looked like good news. A bit of high ground, I was sure to get a signal from up there. I scrambled to the top.

'TRESPASSER! TRES...PASSER!

I nearly shit meself. A large, fluffy teddy bear, pink fur and a silly grin on its face, sprung out from behind a tree. Not only that, the fucker had a gun in its hand and was pointing it straight at me.

'Trespasser!' 'Trespasser!'

'Whoa... wait a minute, I'm not a trespasser,' I says to him, 'I'm a contractor, mate.'

There is no picnic today. That is what I say. There is no... Teddy Bear's picnic today... trespasser.'

I had him sussed, he was low on energy, but the sight of that gun in its hand had me scared witless. I moved a few steps back and the gun in its hand followed me. Then I made a dash for the cover of a tree and craned my neck around the side of it to see how the teddy reacted. It was moving in slo-mo, good, so I knew I had a chance to disarm it if I could get to it quickly. I guessed it was a Generation 7.0 series bot. I'd fixed loads of them, they only function for about 24 hours on one charge before they start losing functionality. The problem is they can be unpredictable once they begin to wind down. Cold temperatures don't help 'em either. Data overload was my best chance to debilitate it. I shouted over.

'Have you been busy today?'

'There is no picnic today,' it replied.

I could hear its footsteps pressing upon the bracken of the forest floor as it moved towards me. I ran for the cover of another tree.

'Hey, what's your name?' I called. There was a long pause.

'Daddy... Daddy Teddy Bear.'

'Where's your family, Daddy? Where's Mummy Bear and your teddy children?' I heard it stop for a moment. It was processing me questions.

'It's a nice day for a picnic ain't it?' Nothing. Then a moment later I could hear it moving again and he says to me, 'There is no picnic... today...trespasser...trespass... not authorised.'

I ran for another tree. I was now only a few metres behind him. 'Do you know Kelly and Sadiq from the Gingerbread House? I've got some biscuits for them. Are they working today? What do you get if you divide a million by 22? What's the capital of London? Hey mate, what do you have to eat at your picnics? Jelly? Cake?'

'I don't know Kelly...and Sadiq... I don't know...'

'Is it jelly or is it cake, or do you have something else?'

'We have Kelly... we do not have Kelly, we have jelly and ... ice cream... and Sadiq... the answer is 45,454.5455, we have jelly...'

The teddy was getting all confused, just like I hoped it would. I ran from behind the tree and rushed up behind him swinging me tool bag hard into his back and knocking him face down to the ground. The gun fell out of his hand and I kicked it out of his reach.

There was no energy in him now. I knelt on top of him and ripped at the Velcro of the fur suit to get to the control panel in his back. Reaching for me tool bag, I took out a screwdriver to release the panel and a pair of wire cutters to de-activate him. Yeah, it looked like gen 7.0, just as I had thought. Then I heard the familiar beepin' sound of a reboot taking place – shyte! He was accessing his energy reserves. Must be a gen 8.0 model, latest upgrade, twice the price, twice as powerful. Never worked on one of them before. I was struggling to unscrew that panel but I was too late. He spun over and grabbed me in a tight bear hug. I had one arm free and grasped me tool bag and tried to swipe him across the head, but he rolls on top of me, his pink furry face right next to mine.

'Trespasser! Trespasser! Unauthorised zone! Unauthorised zone!'

We rolled across the ground. I tries to hit him again with the bag, but the next thing I knew we were rolling arse over tit down the incline, slowly at first, and then accelerating at one hell of a speed. One moment I was seeing the sky and the silhouettes of the trees above, the next moment me face was being pressed into the snow.

'Unauthorised! Unauthorised zone!' he says to me. '*don't stray into the woods today* ...unauthorised zone... *don't...don't stray into the woods today, the teddy bears are all at play, don't stray into* ... unauthorised! Unauthorised!' That's when I blanked out.

I came to; I was stiff with cold. There was the sound of running water. There had been more snow, too, heavy dump of it, and me body was covered white all over and me tools were scattered all around. I gets meself up, next to me was a small stream, and there, spread-eagled with its face submerged in the water was the teddy. Thank God for that. I didn't have him to worry about anymore. I made a decision there and then I was never going to work for the park again, no matter how good their rates were. First thing in the morning I was going to call the council and tell them the place needs to be closed. And it needs to be closed *now*. And they should sack all those idiot councillors who approved it and take Once Upon A Time to court... and tell them that those consultants that they gave loads of money to for their useless feasibility reports, paid for by us rate payers, should be told to hand the back the money. Something like that.

Nothing was broken, but me fingers were numb what with the cold, and it took me ages to pick up all me scattered bits and bobs. The pack of digestives the girl had handed me were all smashed too. Me device was missing and I scoured the forest floor looking for it, but I had no luck. I reached over into the stream and grabbed the teddy by its big foot and heaved it up onto the grass to stop it getting rusty.

Time to get moving before I froze to death, but I had lost all sense of direction. I turns behind me and in the distance I could see a clearing, and just ahead were some stepping stones crossing the stream, so I headed that way. There was a sign by the side of the bank and I wiped the snow off it.

'YOU ARE NOW CROSSING THE RIVER RUBICON.'

A river? Who were they trying to kid? It was nothing more than a trickle. Another of the park's attempts to theme everything. I stepped across the stones and made me way towards the clearing. I thought it would be a bright idea to leave a trail behind me, just in case I needed to find my way back here. I opened the pack of digestives and every couple of metres I dropped a handful behind me. Just wait till I tell the missus what I've been up today. Wait till I tell the lads down the pub too. Wrestling with a teddy? They'll think I've been on the wacky baccy. I carried on. Before long I was out of biscuits, but I weren't too much fussed about that as I was now getting close to the clearing. I scrambled through some bushes and as I came out of the forest, right in front of me was a tall hedge with a wooden door in it, half open. I reckon this must be the boundary of the park, and with any luck I should be able to get out of here before it gets dark. There's gotta be a farm nearby, surely, or a road where I could hitch a lift? So I push at that door but it was stiff, and not wide enough to get through, so I get me shoulder to it and gives a hard push and a pile of snow falls to the ground to reveal another sign nailed above the latch.

OUAT NOTICE: ACCESS DENIED. MAGICAL WORD REQUIRED.

RETURN TO PARK. HAVE A NICE DAY.

I thought maybe I should turn back the way I come and follow the crumbs. I gives it another push but it still wouldn't budge wide enough for me to squeeze through. Carved into the wood were shapes of hearts and flowers, nicely done, and in the centre is a knight sittin' on an horse, poking a dragon in the gob with a long sword. I gave another push. Still wouldn't budge. Then that carving of the knight starts to move. I blink. What's this? He climbs down off his horse, lifts his little visor, and says to me.

'*Don't be absurd. Just say the word. All you need is the magical word.*'

'The magical word?'

'Correct. Please enter.' Says the knight, taking a bow and climbing back onto his horse.

The door suddenly opens and I fell through it. I couldn't believe me eyes. In front of me was a large garden, all laid out in neat rows, hundreds of rose beds, and at the end of a long path was a tall circular tower, must have been 20 metres high at least, painted a banana-yellow with a wide turret at the top, and above this a sharp pointed spire painted purple topped by a flagpole. I didn't move at first. I scanned the garden looking for any sign of life, but the place was deserted. The snow was falling in large flakes, like goose feathers ripped out of a duvet, and what with the rays of sun tryin' to get through the mist it all looked really beautiful. If I hadn't lost me device I would have taken a photo. It were so still and quiet.

I looks behind me. Nothing. So I heads along the path to the tower. I walks around the base looking for an entrance, but there isn't one. So I circles it again, this time taking it really slow; I still couldn't find a way in. I looks up. There's an arched window near the top and I calls up to it.

'Hello?! Anyone there?'

That was a waste of time. Okay, well, it seemed like I had no choice, I had better retrace my steps and follow that trail of crumbs and find me way back to the main park. Then I heard something. A knocking sound. I looks around, but there was no one in sight. Thought it might be a woodpecker. The knocking got louder. I looks up again and the arched window at the top of the tower suddenly flings itself open, and would you believe it, a young woman with long blonde hair peers down at me. She looks at me and I looks at her. I calls up to her.

'Excuse me darlin', can you tell me which attraction this is?'

She leans out of the window. *'Rapunzel's Tower. Who are you? What do you do?'* She says.

'I'm a contractor, love. Are you a bot – you seem to be working okay?'

'Who sent you?' she snaps back at me. *'Who sent you, who sent you I say, to visit me this cold winter's day?'*

'I'm here to fix some of the bots, sweetheart, but I lost me way. Was looking for the Gingerbread House. I need to get back to the centre.'

'Are you alone, or is there a drone?'

'A drone? No, well, there was one but it crashed back in the woods. How did you get up there, love? I couldn't see a door, is there a way into this tower?'

'A way into this place? Pray tell me, what is in your case?'

'Come again? What's in me case?'

'Do you have tools, maybe a saw? Let me explain, a saw with sharp teeth, to cut through a chain?'

'Yeah, I've got a saw, but it's a bit blunt.' I open me tool bag to show her. 'Me cutters are in good nick though.'

'Do you promise you are not from Once Upon a Time? Do you promise? Do you promise? Are you able to climb?'

She seemed a bit la-la to me. Maybe she was malfunctioning, but she looked and sounded too real to be a bot, what with her blonde hair and natural voice.

'No, I'm not from Once Upon A Time, darlin, but you haven't answered my question. Are you a bot and are you okay?'

'A bot? A bot? Do I look like a bot? I'm real, I'm Rapunzel, a bot I am not!'

She shakes her head and a long swirl of her blonde hair cascades down like a golden waterfall, stopping just inches from me feet. I couldn't believe what I was seeing.

'Climb up, climb up, climb up with your case, climb up my long hair, help me out of this place.'

I stared at the hair in front of me, spellbound I was. I stretches out me arm, real slow. Her hair felt so soft and silky as I ran me fingers through it. Must have been years growing it this long. She calls me again.

'Climb up, climb up, climb up with your case, climb up my long hair, help me out of this place.'

I grabbed a large clump of hair between me hands and took a firm grip; then I quickly came to my senses. I called back up to her.

'Excuse me, Ra… Rapunzel, but if you want to get out from up there, then why… then why don't you just climb down? Isn't there a rope or something you could use?'

'Oh, I would, I would, if only I could,' she sighed. *'But my poor feet are chained to this cold stone floor, but you say you have cutters… and blunt-toothed saw?'*

'Yeah, I got a whole bag of tools, sweetheart. Listen, maybe I should go get someone to help, perhaps?'

'Oh folly,' she shrieked. *'Oh folly, please no, please don't tell a soul, they'll imprison you too, now that you know. I'll pull you up, you can set me free, we'll escape through the woods to the land of the free. Hold on tight to my long golden mane, tell me*

love, what is your name?'

'Me name? It's Eddie. Eddie Fowler, from EF Technical Solutions, Dartford. I've got a business card if you want one?'

'Your calling card, oh what sweet words did you write? Of the bliss of our first kiss we shall share here tonight?'

'Er, no, not really, it just says we offer a 24-hour service, six days a week, year round except on Christmas Day and Boxing Day. Oh, and Easter Sunday too. My contact details are here on the back. Mmm, well, look, darlin', maybe... why don't I just head back and see if can get some help and ...'

Then suddenly she calls out at the top of her voice.

'Beware! Beware! Beware my sweet Eddie! Behind you! Behind you! Beware of the teddy!'

Me head spins round and I sees that fluffy pink teddy is heading down the path towards me, he's got that gun in its hand and he's calling out.

'Naughty man, you have done me wrong, you left me to drown in the Rubicon. Naughty man, who has come here to spy, there's no escape, and now you will die!'

He points the gun at me and the girl shouts down.

'Climb up my long hair, come here to my side, climb up my long hair, climb up to your bride!'

I takes hold of her hair and I'm about to climb up when I sees the teddy stop, wobbles a bit, drops the gun and falls flat on its face. Then there's sparks flying from its head and arse and it bursts into flames. Bollocks to this, I'm getting out of here, I says to meself, and I let go of her hair and decides to run back through the door in the hedge.

'Stay where you are, don't move a foot, oh magical door, close yourself shut!'

I sees the wooden door in the hedge closing with a thud. I looks back up at the girl. Wait a minute... that face? Me mind flashes back to that night in the car and that bird I had picked up in Gravesend. It had been nearly forty years ago. Nah, surely not? It couldn't be, could it?

'Cindy? Is that you?'

A smile comes over her face.

'*Cinderella I was, now Rapunzel I am. Are you that boy who has grown to a man?*'

'Er, yeah. It's me, bloody hell, Cindy, have you been here for forty years? Fuckin' hell, is that really you?'

'*You abandoned me, all those years ago, but now my saviour returns on the day of the snow...*'

'Whoa, hang on a minute, I didn't abandon you, I came back to the car and you'd fucked off, took my wallet with you as well. There was a week's wages in that.'

She stretched out her arms high into the air, as if she was addressing a large crowd and sang out loud.

'*Oh Eddie, Eddie Fowler,*
after all these years,
>   *my own Prince Eddie is eventually here,*
my darling Price Eddie,
>   *who vanquished the teddy,*
>   *who's travelled by night,*
> *and travelled by day,*
>   *who's travelled by hill,*
and travelled by dale,
>   *on treacherous seas,*
>   *and dragon-filled lands,*
>   *to rescue me and*
>   *to lead my hand,*
>   *down the aisle of the church,*
>   *and to make me his bride,*
>   *oh, valiant Prince Eddie is here at my side,*
>   *it is a happy ever after*
>   *for my true love and I,*
>   *from this day forth,*
>   '*til the day*
>   *that we*
>   *die.*'

"Ere, have you still got my wallet?'

Death comes to Whitstable

by Ellen Simmons

'I looked, and behold, an ashen horse; and he who sat on it had the name Death.'

It was quick, in the dead of night. Nobody saw it coming. It started with a young couple coughing, convinced they had some sort of common cold that 'was just going around'.

Next, came the bleeding, spitting red liquid that stained the teeth, ran from the eyes and filled the throat. Soon after, the deaths started, the toll rising until the world held more dead bodies than alive.

Whitstable became a ghost town. Buildings were boarded up, electricity ran out and businesses shut down. The roads became overgrown and barren, the grass becoming unruly whilst Mother Nature played truant and climbed through concrete and brick, turning houses green and making lampposts appear as trees. The train station, years since the last train had passed through, looked more like a jungle than a man-made invention.

The Man, waiting on the platform, held his sleeping son in his arms as he sat on an ivy-covered bench and stared down at the railway tracks in thought, feeling the young boy's steady breathing against his hands. The child, a mute, had been his only companion for the past three years, and The Man had forgotten his own name, as he no longer heard it spoken. He was just The Man now, and the child only The Boy.

The Man couldn't remember the date, either. The last calendar he had seen said August 2035, but he wasn't sure how long ago that had been. The biting wind and constant pattering of rain told him summer had yet to arrive this year, but that was all he knew.

The Boy continued to sleep, and The Man continued to watch. He wasn't waiting for a train, but sitting on the platform gave him a sense of purpose, a meaning. When his son was asleep he could play a game where a train really did turn up to take them away from the empty seaside town where they were the only residents, shooting through the countryside like a bullet up to London where The Man was convinced there were other survivors, people like them.

But it was just a game. There were no other survivors, and there was no way of getting out of Whitstable. So instead The Man sat with his son on the bench, counting the tracks over and over again until his son woke up and they went in search of food and shelter. The days blended into one another and the routine became all they had.

But today there was a noise. Noises didn't fit into their routine, and immediately The Man's ears pricked up, his senses awakening. The tracks were making a noise. It wasn't a train; it was the wrong noise for it to be a train. This noise sounded repetitive, the metal thump-thump of something hitting the tracks over and over again.

Footsteps. Not human footsteps, they were far too heavy to be the walk of a man. The Man leant forward in curiosity, eyes peering out from behind bushy eyebrows and dirty glasses, to see if he could find the source of the noise. He looked left, and then he looked right. Left, right. In another life he may have been watching a tennis match.

Right once more. There.

It was a horse; unlike any The Man had ever seen. Pallid with a greenish tint, the huge animal looked as though it should be dead along with everything else, but instead stood proud and tall as it made its way down the deserted tracks. Sat astride the horse was a man, dressed in an impeccable suit and with light hair slicked back away from a handsome face.

The Man blinked. Then blinked again. He wondered if the desolation and isolation of his life had finally taken hold and driven him mad. In his arms The Boy slept on, and he was half tempted to wake him just for clarification.

The horse continued to walk at a steady pace until it stood in front of The Man, his rider staring down with soulless eyes. Black pupils blended with the iris to give an ungodly appearance.

'Who are you?' the rider asked.

The Man could not speak. He had forgotten how.

'Who are you?' the rider asked again.

The Man moved his hand, using his fingers to say 'I don't know.' He didn't expect the rider to understand, but he was not a rude man.

'You have forgotten?' the rider questioned. His voice was calm.

It soothed The Man. He nodded, and the rider continued to stare at him. The Man signalled again.

'You don't know who I am?' the rider said.

The Man shook his head, and for some reason the rider found this amusing. The Man frowned in confusion as the rider chuckled.

'I am Death.'

The Man stared at the rider, wondering if he had forgotten not only how to speak but the words themselves. Surely the rider had not called himself Death?

The rider laughed again and there was something in his soulless eyes that made the Man wonder if perhaps he had heard his doubtful thoughts. The rain splattered down in a sudden downpour, heavy droplets pounding the steel-slated roof of the train platform. But the rider did not seem to be touched by the rain; his immaculate suit remained dry and his shirt crisp. The Man contemplated for a moment whether he should be afraid; to wake his son and flee from the only place he had felt safe for years, the memory forever tarnished.

'Do you fear me?' the rider asked. He seemed curious.

The Man thought for a while longer, his hands tapping one, two, three, against his bent knee to show he was considering his answer. The rider sat with patience but watched The Man piteously. The rider felt sorry for him, The Man realised. Surely, he could not be Death if he felt pity?

The Man signed another question, this one longer than the first. He stumbled over a few of the letters and had to start again, infuriated with himself in the manner of an artist crumpling up the paper and forcing himself to start once more.

Death simply sat and watched, the sunken darkness of his iris-less eyes following the Man's fingers.

Are there others like you?

Death shook his head, and for the first time since he had ridden up to the Man there was a sadness radiating from him. 'No, I am alone.'

Did they all die? Did the sickness take them?

This amused Death, but only on the surface. 'No, I have always been alone. There is no one like me.'

The Man watched curiously as Death swung one of his legs over the horse's saddle so he was sitting more comfortably. Again, he wondered why he wasn't afraid.

Are you really Death?

The rider nodded once.

Did you cause the sickness?

The sadness reappeared, only for a fleeting moment, the way a bird dipped in and out of view when trying to catch a fish just below the surface of the water.

'My brother did.'

Why?

Death didn't seem to have an answer for the longest time.

'Why do you wait for a train?'

The Man signed one word. *Hope.*

'Hope for what?'

A better life.

Death's face stumbled, struggling to hide his feelings, and the Man was once again unsure if he really was who he claimed to be. Death was a menace, the devil. A man with no emotion and horns growing out of his head. That was not the man before him.

Who are you really?

'I am Death.'

Why do you say that?

'It was the name given to me.'

The Man wanted to ask who had given the rider such a name, but he wondered if he would understand the answer. The horse, the rider, the rain's aversion to even touching his very skin triggered a long-forgotten memory of the Man's childhood. He had attended church every Sunday with his mother and father, a spired building sporting great big stained glass windows shifting the multi-coloured light with beautiful pictures. One in particular sprung to mind. Four fearful figures, all bathed in their own individual light, raining down hell on earth.

Horseman.

Death laughed, and it sounded like thunder.

'Yes.'

The Man waited for the first flicker of fear, but it still did not come.

What are you doing here?

Death pondered, his long fingers absentmindedly stroking the horse's hair.

'Searching.'

For who?

'Anyone.'

Death leapt effortlessly from his horse onto the platform and stared down at The Man with a tirade of emotions, most completely alien to The Man. A lifetime of memories crossed the rider's face and The Man wondered what he could possibly be recalling.

Death was lonely, he came to realise.

Silently, as always, he shifted with the Boy along the bench, leaving room for Death to sit beside him. Death peered at the empty seat. The Man tapped it once with his index finger, and Death perched precariously, as though unsure of himself. The Man speculated how long he been on the horse, now waiting rider-less on the tracks.

Are you looking for your brother?

'You're very observant.'

I don't talk, but I listen.

This seemed to tickle Death, and a half smile played around his lips. 'That is a wonderful way to live. Why don't you talk?'

Instead of signing, The Man simply looked down at The Boy on his lap. Death's gaze followed his own. 'Your son?'

The Man nodded.

'He looks like you. Are you the only survivors of the sickness?'

That I know. There may be more.

'And the boy's mother?'

Gone.

There were words poised on Death's lips, but he bit them back and watched The Boy sleep for a little longer. The Man wondered if he had been about to apologise, and what a wonderous thing that would have been. Death himself apologising for taking his wife.

Why did your brother do this?

Death peered at him with his empty eyes.

'I asked him to.'

Death stood up and got back onto his horse. The Boy was starting to stir, mouth moving silently like it always did moments before waking.

'Will you be here tomorrow?' Death asked.

The Man had so many more questions, but he just nodded.

I am here every day.

185

〜

The Man wondered all morning whether it had been a dream, but when he arrived at the train station that afternoon, Death was waiting for him.

Why did you ask your brother to cause the sickness?

Death sat down on the bench, his hands tucked under his legs and his feet pressed together. The Man observed how young he looked.

'I was bored.'

Bored?

'Yes. I felt undervalued, and underappreciated. I was jealous of my brothers.'

Pestilence, War and Famine.

'That's right. I wanted more, so I asked Pestilence to create a disease that would increase the death rate.'

But-?

'But he took it too far. I just wanted more business, something different than the dull mundanity of my role. I didn't realise he intended to kill every human on the planet.'

The Man looked down at the sleeping boy in his arms and couldn't help but think – *not every human.*

'That was why I was so surprised to find you. I thought all had gone through.'

The Man wondered what he meant but thought it best not to ask. His wife had been one of the taken. He didn't want to know what happened after the sickness had won.

Why do you want to find your brother? It must be too late to change anything.

'It is too late. I want the sickness too.'

The Man couldn't move his hands to ask why. He just stared with wide eyes at the creature sitting beside him, playing with the hem of his impeccable suit jacket.

'There is nothing left for me now. No souls to collect, no beings to usher through into the afterlife. Pestilence has seen to that.'

So, you want to die.

'I want to join those who I guided across. I believe I can help them on the other side.'

The Man's hands remained very still. He couldn't think of anything to say.

'You think I am mad.'

The Man shook his head. *I think you are desperate, and alone.*

Death did not take offence, but his laughter held no humour. 'Perhaps you are right.'

The two men sat together in silence, peering out at the tracks and the platform, at the broken screen that used to announce arrivals now hanging precariously from only one rusted hook, threatening to fall. At the small bridge that led from one side of the station to another, the steps rotted away in places that left anyone crossing exposed to the possibility of falling right through.

Can Death really die?

Death shrugged. 'I do not know. Mortals cannot kill me, though few have tried. My brothers and I have never made an attempt to kill each other, but they are the only three who I would imagine have the ability to do so. But maybe there is no end to Death, even if I die.'

Who would be willing to kill their brother?

'The first brothers who ever lived.'

If The Man could laugh, he would have done so. Instead he curled his mouth into a grin and sent Death a look of false reproach.

'I will not be here tomorrow.'

The Man stared at him, surprised to feel a strip of worry unfurling in his chest. Death was no longer to be feared, but The Man knew his concern was selfish. He would miss the companionship, the sound of a voice.

You are going to search for him?

'I think I might know where he will be.' Death said, refusing to look anywhere other than his horse.

Where is that?

'Close by. He too is searching.'

For what?

Death didn't want to give his answer. His eyes dragged across from the horse and down to The Boy, still fast asleep as always.

'Survivors.'

Days passed. The silence took over once more, The Man and The Boy falling back into their routine. The Man never told his son about the visitor, the strange rider who had wandered into his life. As weeks passed, he started to wonder if he had even met the pallid rider at all, or if it had just been his own mind losing itself to loneliness.

He was proven wrong three days later, when once more Death appeared on his steed. His face was a mixture of emotion, exaltation tarnished by a grim set mouth and turned down chin.

'I have found my brother.'

The Man forced a smile. This is what Death wanted, after all.

Why have you not got the sickness?

Death jumped off his horse and took his place next to The Man on the bench. 'He is contemplating my request.'

The Man thought it odd but kept his fingers still. What sort of brother would even contemplate killing his sibling, he wondered. It was a question he had not been able to rid from his mind during the days of silence.

When will you find out? he asked.

'Tomorrow,' Death said. 'He has promised me an answer by then.'

Are you scared?

'No.'

I would be.

'Of course. You don't know what is on the other side.'

What will happen to us once you are gone?

Death looked up, surprised. It was a question he hadn't anticipated. 'I don't know.'

Who will guide us through?

'I don't know.'

Now I am scared.

'As am I.'

But you still want to die?

'I cannot wait any longer. I am sorry.'

I understand.

The Man reached out, and for the first time since he had first seen the rider, touched him. His hand rested on Death's arm lightly and he was surprised to feel warmth through the suit fabric. He had half expected it to be like touching ice. Death felt like a living, breathing man. He spoke like one. The Man had all but forgotten who he truly was.

Death did not come to visit the next day. The Man waited with his sleeping son in his arms, and interest he had not felt for many years stirred in his belly. He wasn't sure if he wanted Death to appear, but when the sun started to set and there was no sign of the rider or his horse, The Man felt a pang of unexpected sadness.

Then he heard it. The familiar sound of hooves against metal railings. Perhaps The Man was wrong, and Death's brother had refused to grant him sweet release. For the first time, The Man woke his son, shaking him softly from his reverie.

Wake up – there is someone I'd like you to meet.

The Boy rubbed his eyes, his fingers slow and sluggish as he signed back. *Who?*

A friend.

Sleep fell away from The Boy and he looked up at his father excitedly, wonder watering his eyes as he realised the possibility.

There are more.

The Man replied in the kindest way he could. *Not like us, no.*

Together they waited, side by side, hand in hand, listening to the oncoming horse making its way down the tracks. The

Man thought he could hear his own heartbeat, pounding in his ears.

Is it an animal?

The Man smiled. *You could say that. It looks like a horse.*

But it isn't?

No.

The Boy's brow creased. He did not understand, but he stood patiently by his father, feeding off his excitement in silent anticipation. Then he saw it. A beautiful white stallion, glowing ever so softly, making its way towards them majestically. The Boy turned to his father, expecting to see the same exultation reflected from his own face.

Instead, he saw only dismay.

What is wrong? The horse – it is beautiful.

It is also riderless.

The Boy did not understand, but at his father's own grief, a single tear slipped down his cheek.

The Man, however, did not cry. He simply watched the horse continue down the abandoned railway tracks, its coal coloured eyes watching them with every step. It seemed incomplete, empty without Death sat atop its saddle.

Who is the rider?

The Man pondered his son's question. He had no idea what would happen; now that Death's brother had presumably granted his request. The Man wondered if he had felt pain, or simply relief. He had gotten what he wanted.

He was a nice man.

Who was he? The Boy persisted.

The Man shrugged. He hadn't known, not really. Telling his son the truth would only scare him, and the young boy had seen enough frightening things in the world in his short lifetime. He thought the horse would continue on its way, down the tracks until it was out of view from the last two remaining humans on earth.

A bolt of fear shot through The Man as he considered what would happen to them now. There was no Death to guide them through once their time was up. Would they continue to wander this barren planet forevermore, or sink into an abyss only they had access to, without the key to the next world to lead them on?

His fear turned to surprise when the horse stopped in front of them. It whinnied softly, a great puff of breath out of its huge nostrils, as though impatient. The Man didn't know what it wanted. It shook its head, the long strands of hair from its mane shimmering in the soft light of a dying sun. Its eyes darted back wildly behind it, gesturing.

The Man understood in the blink of an eye. He looked at the saddle.

He looked down at his son.

The Boy peered back up at him fearfully. He did not understand. The Man had purposefully kept him in the dark all this time, protecting him all while unwittingly failing to prepare him for this eventual outcome.

Someone had to lead his son to see his mother once again when the time was right, and Death was no longer here.

Heartbreakingly, The Man let go of his son's hand.

What-?

The Boy was signing frantically, demanding answers, but The Man purposefully kept his eyes on the horse as he took a step forward. And another. The horse was no longer moving, simply waiting.

The Man turned back one last time.

I'm sorry.

Then he placed a foot, heavy with responsibility and grief, in the stirrup. A lightning bolt erupted from the sky.

There is no end for Death.

Miss Dragon's Tale

by Helen Howard

'Smoke?'

I shook my head. She leaned back, crossed her legs and blew smoke rings through her elegantly tapered snout. Thigh-hugging soft leather boots set off her shapely form. Candyfloss pink was her colour of the moment, from the dainty heels to the feather boa. Her scales shimmered like sequins in the narrow lines of sunlight coming though the bars of the cell window and a pair of wings hung over the back of her chair.

'Well, what can I tell you?' she asked in a voice reminiscent of Miss Piggy.

'Start wherever you like,' I said. 'I'd like to hear the whole story and I've plenty of time. I won't be getting out of here in a hurry.'

She sighed and blew a long breath up at the ceiling where the yellowing paint began to turn brown and curl. 'I guess what you really want to hear is the George episode, but there is so much more to my life than that. I blame it all on emancipation, you know: a classic problem of falling birth rates. Our mothers spent so much time out and about doing good works and saving maidens in distress that after a while it became almost impossible to bump into an eligible bachelor.' She turned towards me so that I felt the warmth of her breath. 'Of course in those days rescuing was all the rage. But now we're supposed to empower damsels to help themselves.' She raised her eyebrows and sat back in her chair. 'Give me a quick rescue any day. Empowering takes so much longer.'

'But how did you meet George?'

'Don't tell me! I guess you believe what you read in the papers.'

I nodded and she exploded with laughter. 'Oh the world is full of fools who trust the gutter press. But if you're sitting comfortably then I'll tell you the true story. Once upon a time, I was playing in the up-currents along Tankerton Slopes, looking for a bit of company, when I buzzed this hang-glider. I rather liked the way he was moving his body to steer the craft so I tagged along for a bit. I had quite a thing going with a microlite once but they are so unstable: up one minute and down the next. I can't stand moodiness. Hot air balloons are even worse. I got too close to one once and my breath shot it up into the stratosphere. But a hang-glider is a different story. We were getting along famously with me spinning along underneath to give him an extra lift. But I got a bit too close and singed his nether regions. He panicked and crash-landed. Well, I was mortified so I flew down to make sure he was all right. While I was checking him over for broken bones, the idiot got his sword out and cut off my wings...' she shuddered, 'and then he dialled 999!'

'So he didn't kill you then?'

'Do I look dead?'

'Well, no. But I thought he was given saintly status for killing you. All the pictures show him with his sword planted firmly in your back.'

'Yes! Very phallic, don't you think? But you go back and take another look. I'm sure you'll see he was really just cutting my wings off. They didn't have investigative journalism in those days and I've never had the chance to put my side of the story.'

'So what happened next?'

'They locked me up didn't they? "Breathes fire and brimstone: must be a threat to the security of the nation. Lock her up." So I've been here ever since. But I worked my way up the hierarchy – Open University you know – and now I'm free to go.'

I gestured to the back of the chair. 'Your wings grew again then?'

She looked back over her shoulder. 'Yes, it's been a long and painful regeneration but eventually they are back as good as new, so I can fly again.' She stood up and shook out her feathers.

I leaned back to avoid being knocked off my chair.

She leaned forward. 'But what are you in for, dear?'

'Drug mule.' I said, tossing my hair.

'Are you still using?'

I looked down at my trembling hands and she tutted.

'You've got yourself in a proper pickle, haven't you?'

I nodded miserably.

'Look, I'll make a bargain with you. I understand it's the dealers that are the real villains and you're just another victim. You can take control of your life if you put your mind to it. Stop using and I'll see what I can do. You know what they say: "you can't win the lottery if you don't buy a ticket"? When you get out, look out for me.'

'But where do I find you?'

'Don't worry. I'll know where to find you. Damsels in distress have a special aura that I can spot a mile off. That's why I'm here now. Well I must be off. Can't sit around chatting forever.' She circled round my head uncertainly a few times before disappearing through the keyhole leaving nothing behind but a faintly sweet smell and a few scorch marks.

A Last Sniff

by Richard White

A faint coconut waft of gorse, a sour tang of holly, and that slightly rotten and metallic smell of rain, only these few for me while Coney found a hundred smells, another every yard, and each one an obsession. Coney is a Westy, I an impatient owner trying to catch the seven thirty-eight. Dogs have more time than working women. Coney found new and exciting smells in the same place every day. There were other dog owners with the same impatience as mine, crossing our path with a complicit sigh to my frustration. Sometimes I'd mumble a benign word to passers-by about a dog's interests, but dogs have little to say to each other, unless there is something to sniff about, as there was that day in Perrin's Alley.

There's a rambling house behind the alley; empty and hidden but still romantic, with long and lonely views over the estuary. I had often wondered about it, who had once lived there, how they managed a quarter mile from the nearest road. I imagined an old lady with shopping trolley and shuffling feet in ragged bedroom slippers, and seven cats waiting for her at home. I like old houses for their spooky atmosphere, but this one was always silent and locked, even the mailbox beside the entrance was sealed. It's nearly a ruin now, with subterranean fingers tickling it down the muddy hill by creaks and cracks in answer to gravity. You can't see much of it because it hides behind a gate of crooked planks, on a middle reach of Perrin's Alley, which springs out from the back of the beach huts and vaults the railway before stumbling up the hill towards Joy Lane. It clings to the edge of the Whitstable dog's domain, where strange smells and tiny movements are nobody else's business. A thousand pass that way, sniffing the ground and each other. Perrin's Alley has more interesting entrances to sniff, but my dog always stopped there, his head twisting left and right as if he could hear the house's ghost.

Coney is an impure Westy who sniffs all the way from Cromwell Road twice every day, unless relieved by my friend Jackie for an extra midday walk around the street corner, but mostly led by this busy woman before and after her long day in a shiny Victoria Street office, justified by a London salary which is no excuse to a dog waiting twelve hours between walks, but who legitimately insists on his own time. For Coney, out walking, smells are everything. Luckily for him that Friday he had been let off the lead from the bottom of Westcliff and he could go where he wanted, so that when we came to the turning into the alley, his ears pricked up, he growled and then launched himself onto the low stepped wall along the alley, and to my amazement he jumped three feet and gave chase along the wall. It was his usual fixation – a squirrel. He could never catch one but he'd always try, and it seemed to give him super-canine powers, he found where the hedge had been breached by truanting boys, and he was gone. He heard me calling but he was on a mission and he knew that I could not follow him. There were scuffles and childish giggling. I heard him yapping and I called him. He did not reply.

Then I heard a child's angry shout.

After that Coney emerged, tail down, head hanging, on the wall again. Of course I had to lift him down. I was glad to have him back but I was disturbed. Nobody lives in that house. What I had heard was not much like the bad behaviour of Whitstable kids. I hurried Coney back and set off to work.

Yes, I do live alone, except for my dog. Coney is my overnight partner, living for my return from London. He's all I've got and all I want. A dog beats a man any day: no backchat, no vanishing in the middle of the night, no fuss about what I buy or how much it costs, and no lies about being kept late at the office. Coney is always pleased to see me.

That evening Coney got over the wall again. He came out licking his lips. Someone in there must like him, and I was worried, keeping him on the lead. Was someone trying to steal my dog? I heard and smelled nothing unusual for days. Then hurrying down the alley I heard noises – scuffling and rattling. I convinced myself that they could be birds or perhaps a fox. Being busy inspires easy answers.

On Sunday once again Coney chased rabbits on Prospect Field, as ever outclassed by his prey, and then suddenly he was gone. I hurried after him, knowing his new interest. This time he was a long time, and I peered over the fence at the old house. I could see a dim flickering light. I could also smell cooking, and could see smoke. Then I heard Coney whining gently and a child's voice, speaking quietly in an unfamiliar language. Coney was being entertained. I shouted and the voice and whining stopped. Then the voice recurred, secretive and timorous, and Coney emerged from his portal. Now

I knew that I was not Coney's only friend, the house had a squatter, and that squatter might be a child. I wondered whether I should tell someone, but did not know whom.

At the weekend I stopped to look at avocados outside Granny Smith's in the High Street. There was a sudden commotion inside the shop, with raised voices and a scuffle. Two kids burst out and dissolved in opposite directions into the Saturday crowd. The shop owner emerged with his lad, looking in both directions, 'Did you see that?'

I shook my head.

'Thieving brats,' he said.

'They stole something then?'

'Yeah, dead clever. One goes round looking dodgy. The other stuff's his pockets.'

'You saw what they took?'

'Nah, watching the wrong one.'

'Local kids?'

'Migrants! Come off them rubber boats.'

He strutted inside, still muttering. I turned away confused – I had never seen a migrant in Whitstable. That was when I looked down at Coney, who was staring down the street, wagging his tail. Did he know them?

In the morning I was taking a short cut along an alley leading off Cromwell Road, when a teenage girl stepped out from a corner in front of me. She was lean and wiry with a tapering white face, like a moon-child. She had a thin and humble mouth, long mousey hair and green eyes. Her head was tilted down as if she were afraid to say something. Her face and arms were scratched, as if she had come through bushes. Her clothes looked good quality but a bit dirty. We both stopped and stared awkwardly at each other, neither able to speak. She looked down at Coney, who uttered an eager squeak, wagging his tail. Her face froze as she looked up again at me. Then she pushed past me and twisted around the corner I had just passed. Coney pulled on his lead, trying to follow her. She had been nervous, and I had frightened her. I felt slightly guilty.

She was one of those two kids.

I hesitated with my phone in my hand – but then I decided that not much had happened, and anyway Coney had shared with me some connection with that girl. A friend of Coney's must be a friend of mine. An elderly man was walking slowly towards me, and he noticed the confusion on my face,

'You okay, luv? Had a fright?'

'Yes, er, no! Did you see...' and I looked behind me at the empty alleyway.

'See what?'

'Oh, nothing.' I felt an idiot as he smiled and passed me by.

By the evening I had also developed some concern about the thin girl but I had convinced myself that it was not my business, and there's little juvenile crime between Seasalter and Herne Bay.

A damp morning, smelling of ivy flowers, brambles and turned soil as I passed the allotments, then the resinous whiff of hops, now rare in Kent, and I hustled Coney along past his favourite posts and bushes, promising him more in the evening. Back home he had to accept my excuses as he slumped down into a day-long depression when I pulled the door, but not before he had glanced up at me resentfully. It was one of those days when you can't get anything done; nobody answers phones, nobody gets around to email replies, and people fail to keep appointments. I gave up in early frustration and pushed into the rush-hour crowd at Victoria, not even getting a seat until Rochester, and then having to share the air with tedious repetitive mobile phones, and I was grateful to get out into the gentle rain in Cromwell Road. Already a sulphurous smell was creeping up the road – it was November 5th. When I opened the front door, Coney did not come out to meet me, and it took me a while to find him hiding behind the sofa. Rapid explosions and crackles echoed out in the street. For him the guy Fawkes war had started again, and he was terrified. It took a lot of cajoling to get him out into the war zone for his walk.

Those I work with in London say I am too sensitive to smells. I can tell in a second when someone comes into the office after putting out a cigarette. I can smell in on their breath, and even the acid smell of the butt on their fingers. Sometimes I have identified what someone has just had for lunch, and I certainly know if they have spent the middle of the day in the pub. I try not to take notice of these things because colleagues have told me I am a freak. Jackie, one of my best friends in Whitstable, who is also a dog owner, once said sagely,

'It's natural, Lacey. Owners always grow to be like their dogs. You have taken it a stage further; you have grown a dog's nose.'

As we lurched around the corner into Perrin's Alley, with fireworks raging in many directions, Coney panicked at the rat-a-tat-tat right beside us and jerked his lead out of my hand and was gone. Then he was barking and I was shouting at him, until I heard a child yell, then the creak of a gate as it swung open a little. Catching up it easily pushed open. It was dark but I was faced with two pairs of wide young eyes, agape from Coney's hysterical yapping. The smaller one was tugging the elder child's arm, she was jabbering at him, he started to screech again and she tried to push past me, dragging him with her, I put my hand out to them but panic broke out and the smaller one broke free and ran away into the house. The elder one looked back after him and cried, 'Jir! Jir!' but then terrified pushed past me and ran through the gate and down the hill. Hurrying after this fleeing figure, in the yellow light in Perrin's Alley, I glimpsed her legs pouncing down towards the sea. The legs stopped and turned to look back at me, and I saw the thin figure and white face of the girl from the greengrocer incident.

Coney was still barking, so I pursued him into the house, and he led me to the furthest corner, where a little boy squatted and shivered under a window. The dim, slanting light from behind him showed ruffled hair and a dirty, tear-stained face, with big brown eyes. I pulled Coney back and started whispering to him, 'It's alright! I won't hurt you.' He may not have understood but he looked calmer and spoke a few words which I understood no better. I reached out to him gently. His stained eyes looked up at me and he leaned towards me a little. I put an arm around him and his shaking ceased. I waited until he moved again. The room smelled of him, sweet and sour, a bit babyish, quite unlike the smell of adults in a gym.

Still holding him I pulled out my phone, and he started to shake again, so I stepped away to phone for help. His eyes never left me. I can see them still. I had to go out into the alley because emergency services were arriving. It had been nearly twenty minutes when I heard the police sirens and then a succession of people pounding down the hill, looking into every gap in the hedge. I was astonished at the number of police men and women, ambulance crews, and eventually others too, some apparently social and charity workers, all piling through the gate and filling the bedraggled garden of the house. I gave my name and contact details to several of them and answered the same questions many times. They had taken over and I no longer had any role in what was going on, and I sat, cold and useless, Coney quivering beside me, on the edge of what might have once been a rockery. The air was full of the crackling, fizzing and booming of November the fifth. A woman came later to sit beside me and talked for some time,

'Second this week for us.'

'Are there a lot of lost children in Whitstable?'

'He's a migrant child.'

'Where's he from?'

'Don't know that…yet. Police will find out. It's a guess, but I'd say he was an Iraqi Kurd.'

'Why do you think that?'

'I tried to talk to him in Arabic. He understood but said "Tenagim".'

'You speak Arabic?'

'No, and neither did he. Tenagim is a Sorani word. Comes

from Central Kurdistan – Iraq.'

'Is that his name?'

'No, it means "I don't understand." His name is Jir.'

'What else did he say to you?'

'Nothing much. I put my arm around him and he started to cry.'

A stab of jealousy silenced me momentarily. I had saved him. He had accepted me. He was mine. I jerked myself out of this reverie, 'What will happen to him?'

'Depends…but he won't be sent back. He may get fostered.'

For a moment my mind sought questions about being a foster parent but I said nothing for a minute, then, 'How do you think he got here?'

'Ah! We may never know. But from previous cases I'd imagine it was the railway line.'

'He came by train?'

'Heavens no! He's only seven or eight with no English and no money. He could have arrived with the group of a dozen adults who landed in Pegwell Bay at the beginning of last week. They had probably been asked to take these kids along with them, at least from L'Auberge des Migrants in Calais, might have been all the way from Mosul. Children often arrive without their parents, they don't know they are in England, and if they did know it would mean nothing to them. They had probably been told to follow a railway line. Most lead to London. Roads are far too dangerous and complicated. They could have walked the track, dodging and hiding, until it got dark, and then they'd be looking for somewhere to shelter. You've seen the other one, haven't you?'

'Twice. She was older – ten or eleven.'

'Ran away I suppose.'

I nodded. 'D'you think she'll be all right?'

'Well…relatively. This will be a major trauma for them both.'

'Would their parents have been poor?'

'God no! D'you know how much this terrible journey would have cost?'

I must have looked blank.

'Thirty- to forty-thousand.'

My mouth dropped open, 'You mean in pounds?'

'Oh yes. They would have been well off when they started out. Probably cleaned them out. All the way they face demands for more and more. Eventually they may have had to give up, somewhere in Eastern Europe, but they would have wanted their children to get a new start even if they couldn't themselves.'

'They put their kids in the hands of strangers?'

'Some of them may have been people they knew. What else could they do? It's desperation. They may have had nothing to go back to but a war zone.'

Then her phone jangled and I stood up as she started a long conversation. Bangs, whooshes and rattles were still splitting the November sky. Coney whined for peace and dinner. For the first time I began to detect a homely smell of cooking leaching through the acrid smell of gunpowder. I started for the gate but Coney dug his heels in. We looked at each other while I begged him to come on but he refused to walk out again into the violence of the night, and I found myself carrying him most of the way, while he gazed up at me, whistling and squeaking. Somebody was standing in the shadow outside my door, 'I've been here since seven,' said Jackie. I let her in and as usual she had a lot to say about herself, while I was speechless.

'What's happened to you?" she persisted, 'Have you seen a ghost?'

I hid my face as I made the tea. This had been a surreal fireworks night.

This morning was cold and smelled slightly smoky. Coney did not even want to come out, and I had to drag him. The air was full of a burnt-out smell, and there were spent rockets and bangers in the long grass. He turned and headed home in the middle of Prospect Field, not wanting to go as far as Perrin's

Alley. I made him come with me because I wanted to believe in an end to the story of two lost Kurdish children. The gate was open, the door to the house too. It was desolate inside, and almost as dark as the night before. As always with deserted houses, there were a few pieces of unmatched furniture and some personal things: a thin coat hanging from a bent hook and an imitation leather holdall containing dirty clothes. A sad teddy-bear sat under a table. In the tiny kitchen I could see the remains of a basic meal the children must have made, half eaten on a plate with two forks and cut-up vegetables. Absent-mindedly I picked up the fork, just to feel it, and to imagine their last night. Then I realised that it had been me who interrupted their simple life. Now a brother and sister were separated, and probably distressed. I put down the fork in disgust with myself, and walked quickly out of the house, Coney scratching behind me.

On the train to London I gazed out of the window at the empty fields on the way to Faversham, and then suddenly saw myself, reflected in the window. I looked angry. Now I knew what that girl had seen, staring at me in an alleyway off the Cromwell Road. Those children were needy, and I had not been able to help them. I had no idea where either of them was now, nor did I know if they were safe. As my eyes stilled, looking only at myself, I felt a sense of loss. I had shared a moment with those two but had lost them. I had to shake myself out of that mood because whatever I felt, there was nothing I could do.

My mind saw the little boy again, crouching in a corner beneath the window, his bleary eyes looking up at me. Then it showed me the girl, a still and staring figure, perhaps for a first time since coming ashore in Kent realising that she had been recognised and was no longer safe. What I saw then in her face and now remembered, was fear. That had been my gift to her. Later in the day my thoughts clambered onto another level, and I realised that those two children, whom I had never known, one of them not even her name, had entered my life and, just a little, changed it.

The next day the gate was nailed up. Even Coney's bolt-hole had been sealed. An unusual seaweed miasma clung to the air. In the estuary acres of uneven mud had been left by the retreating tide, and there was a long trail of footsteps heading out towards Sheppey, then washing away as the tide turned. I gazed out at the empty shore for long enough to convince myself that a thin girl could have got away to a new life. A train broke my silence, blasting its warning to the pedestrian crossing at Portway. Coney was pulling me back towards home. As soon as I thrust into the crowd on Oxford Road, a small face passed by me with lowered green eyes. I spun round and called, "Hey...!" but she didn't reply or turn around. I detected a slight smell of seaweed.

Can You See a Way Forward?

by John Wilkins

'It was as if I was invisible in my marriage,' I said to her. The counsellor waited, she usually did, to see if I knew what my deeper feelings were. I did know what it was like to be invisible, but not how to tell anyone about it. She must have seen something in my face, so she suggested another way.

'It helps if you write it down.' The counsellor said that to me. She can read my body language, read my non-verbal communication, and listen attentively. I am starting to trust her but not with everything. I don't know that she will believe me, if I tell her all of it. Two days ago, she wouldn't have been able to see me at all, any of me. I like knowing that, for now. I don't know if the memory of being invisible might fade, just like I did.

So here is my attempt to write down why I am unique, and what I did during the twenty-four hours that nobody could see me, including myself. Who am I? My name is Hugh Wetherall, and I am a physics teacher at what was known as Whitstable Community College. Science is logical and so am I, but that isn't important to me now.

I didn't like my appearance, and I can remember when I was a child saying I wished that I could be invisible. Being invisible was nothing like I'd imagined. As for my appearance, well, there are probably plenty of men who look like me – average height, slightly overweight, bald patch at the back, with that wonky smile because of the missing tooth to the side. It doesn't matter as much now. I have no idea what my students call me behind my back. I don't care, because of what I have done. Who they think I am based on what I look like is not the man I am. Being a teacher, for me, is just acting; it is only a performance. The syllabus is my script, the exam results the final scene. I might find somebody one day that I can trust and tell them who I really am.

I had a normal life before. I still live in the house in Clare Road, Whitstable (recently updated, the estate agent emphasized when we looked round). There is no 'we' now. She left me, the Whitstable home and postcode behind. It might have helped if I had been invisible then.

I survived the breakup with the help of my support network, as my counsellor describes it.

The leader of the network is my brother Ron, older than me, who likes to think he is wiser too; maybe he isn't, now. He lives in an area of Whitstable's genteel bohemia, the Cornwallis Circle, just a short walk from the Horsebridge Community Arts Centre. He started me out in pursuit of some kind of alchemy, to transform my life. Alchemy was the name of the art exhibition in the Horsebridge his work was included in. He tried to persuade me to go the private view. I turned him down even though he worked very hard to persuade me. The Horsebridge reminded me of her, and of those silent drives ending with me dropping her off there at the crack of dawn for the yoga class.

'Right now, the only alchemy I need in my life I can see every night when I get behind my telescope,' I told him. He was going to say that quote from Oscar Wilde about being in the gutter and looking at the stars, but the expression on my face helped him to think better of it. He spoke the words 'some of us.' Then he dropped his head after thinking about something more tactful. He did try with me, even when I was being obstinately rude.

'Okay, Hugh, but I am not going to let you just disappear you know,' he finally half muttered.

I promised not to 'stay at home making myself miserable.' He left me at home that night and I went straight to the kitchen and picked up the telescope from its place in the corner by the fridge, with a sense of purpose – to see the stars. I had been setting aside the moments in the evening at the end of my day to join the stars. At the end of my day, homework marked, assessments updated, supper done with, glass of wine (avoided if I had drunk the night before), I settled myself into the relationship I felt worked best for me, with the stars and their place as revealed by the telescope that I learned how to use by fluent use of the internet. I picked up the telescope and took it out into the garden to set it up in front of the old wooden seat. When at last everything was in focus I sat and calmed myself. First the breathing, and then the final adjustments of the lens, and I was ready.

I watched the stars then, and they watched me. Some nights I had been captivated by the different kinds of starlight I saw. When my elderly neighbours asked me if I thought it was a spaceship, the lights, colours and everything, I impressed upon them my logical argument that it was to be expected, different lights in the sky. Drones were becoming very popular. My explanation settled them.

The night before I became invisible the lights followed the sequence I knew from previous observations.

This is how I saw them. First, one by one the colours in the rainbow shone clear, different from the white of other stars. I now explained to myself the coloured lights as stars – I knew they weren't the northern lights, either, but I was too lazy to research properly any other possible scientific explanation. For once I lost the logic and let myself become absorbed.

After the rainbow colours, a dark blue appeared and gradually become lighter, until it was a certain firm blue. The blue movement reminded me of the vintage jazz recording by Miles Davis, the trumpeter, entitled Kind of Blue. The blue in the sky seemed to demand my attention, yet invite me to find my personal meaning for it in the same way the music did. Once the blue remained constant, there was a stillness and I always felt calm, and then there was interruption. The calm was replaced by the sound of rain, but none ever fell. When I heard that sound, I felt cold and noticed that the usual noise of distant cars, the occasional seagull's cry, all ceased. I could hear nothing.

Next, a yellow light came, moving, not like a search light but appearing intermittently as if beating out some odd time signature from an unknown symphony, or maybe a coded message.

Then finally, as if the previous blue was mixed into the yellow in the dark palette of the heavens, a long, green, sharp horizon line appeared. It seemed to be a shelf that supported the regular white stars of the night sky. A breeze started up and I heard the leaves on the trees stir, while a seagull flew onto the neighbours' roof.

That's when I picked up the telescope and went back into the house.

I remember feeling as if I had been on a long walk, without knowing where or in what direction. I felt a little worn down, as if I had been trying to explain myself to somebody who didn't believe me. Usually I put the telescope back in its place, made a hot drink and spent a few moments looking through the kitchen window hoping to see more lights. On that night I followed the same routine, sitting at the kitchen table, staring out the window, but there was nothing; not even my reflection in the window. That shocked me out of my reverie. I put my drink back on the table behind me and touched the glass; there was only the kitchen reflected in the window, not me.

I wondered what had gone wrong with my brain. The signal from my brain to my eyes must have been corrupted, I tried to convince myself. I stopped myself from talking aloud – the first sign of madness, I had been told as a child. I behaved like the child I had been. Terrified, I switched all the house lights off as I made my way to the bedroom. I felt something watching me and hoped the darkness might conceal me a little. When I got to the bedroom, I turned the light off without looking where the switch was.

I undressed in the dark, kicked my slippers off and left them beside the bed, which I climbed into. The duvet, I pulled back over me until only my head remained uncovered. I pressed my head back firmly into the pillow and closed my eyes tightly, as if that might help fix the damage to them.

There was no night. It seemed like I had just waited for a second and then another accident happened; the alarm went off at the wrong time. Without opening my eyes, I thought the alarm must have developed a problem of its own. When I opened my eyes and looked across to the bed side table where the black box sat, I knew it was morning. The numbers 7.30 were displayed, and daylight shone through the gap between the curtain rail and the bedroom curtains – I hadn't been very good at hanging them, either.

I reached out from the bed to turn the alarm off without looking at it. Then I sat up and pushed my legs out of the bed and put my feet on the floor. With both hands I rubbed my eyes as if that would help. It didn't. I stretched my arms out in front of me (it was a habit to prove I hadn't got the shakes, another of my paranoid fears). I blinked and saw nothing, no arms, legs, nothing. Whatever had happened to my sight last night with the absence of my reflection in the window was still going on.

I blinked again, alone and invisible to myself. At least getting dressed might help, I hoped, but didn't know how it might. I had re-read the Invisible man by H G Wells recently and remembered scenes where the invisible man fought his way out of an arrest, with only his shirttails floating in the air, indicating where he was. I did struggle getting dressed, but I managed it eventually and even had breakfast. Then I realised that there was a chance it was just my sight, and everyone else could still see me properly. If nobody could see me, they would be terrified at my clothes moving around by themselves, similar to the way H G Wells imagined the empty moving clothes of his invisible man.

I pulled on my jacket and collected my keys from the hook in the hall at the end of the coat rack. Then I went into the sitting room at the front of the house and peered out to see if my neighbour opposite was out there, in front of her recently painted pale green front door. She was always out the front, every morning. I thought at first she had some sort of desire to see me, then I realised that the time of day I left the house was the best time for her to tend to the many pots of various sizes with different shrubs and flowers that bordered the short gravel path to her front door. I saw through the front window of the sitting room she was kneeling down, with trowel in hand.

I went to my front door, thinking, 'When she sees me, then she'll probably know there's something wrong with me straight away. She might even shout at her husband to drive me up to the Minor injuries' unit at Estuary View.'

I opened the door and stood there. She didn't see me, at all, not even my clothes, socks or shoes. I knew by the way she screamed and ran into her house after my door appeared to open and then close itself. She came back out of the house with her husband (still holding his newspaper) and pointed at me, or at least the front door. I jumped up and down, waved my arms, poked my tongue out, gave her the finger and she didn't see any of it.

I walked away from the house and them. I had no idea how to begin a conversation with any one while I was invisible. Staring down at my feet and not seeing my shoes as I walked along shocked me. Stunned in shock, but still walking, I decided on a destination. While I was making my mind up about it, someone almost walked into me. Just in time I stepped aside but not before I took the mobile phone out of their hands and chucked it over a nearby hedge. Well, they might have walked into one of my elderly neighbours. Now I was certain, I was definitely invisible.

I was invisible, so that made me consider what to do next. Questions rushed around my mind – what to do? Someone told me, if you can't do anything for yourself at least do something for others. I didn't see anything wrong with that – if I was invisible while doing it, then I couldn't get into trouble.

It was up to me – what to do, where to go. Clare Road is only a few minutes' walk from the railway station. This felt like a sensible beginning – Whitstable Railway station. In those moments I became confused about, well, everything – the day was in front of me now. To start with, I needed time to cope with being invisible. 'Is it going to be like this for ever?' I remember thinking, as I reached the station.

It was simple getting on to the platform. I almost laughed but stopped myself in case somebody heard me. Then I realised it was still early in the morning, there wouldn't be many about, and the ticket barriers didn't exactly prevent me from getting anywhere.

Arriving on the platform I saw somebody standing further down, close to the bench. She had her back to me and appeared to be looking down the track in hope that a train would soon come. I looked up at the screen and learned that the next rain was due in fifteen minutes.

Somehow, being invisible had helped me realise a dream. I felt that I was in the film that I had always wanted to be in, one where the man arrives on the platform, no one expects him (the woman further down the platform was looking down the track, not back down the platform where I was standing) and he can choose what happens in the next fifteen minutes, from a range of options. His choice can be a happy one – and the film can have the happy ending that sustains him. Or it could be tragic.

I stopped thinking about the film and started considering my choices, including destinations.

I looked up at the screen again to see how long I had before the train arrived; and to see if my thinking had been affected by the invisibility. It hadn't; self-doubt arrived in my mind with the usual speed. I walked towards her. She couldn't see me, and when the voice announced the imminent arrival of the train, we both reacted to it in our separate ways.

She didn't seem to hear me, not even my sharp intake of breath when the voice announced the train, even though I was only a few feet away from her by then. Maybe ghosts don't breathe, I decided. I stayed where I was, but the woman looked round again as if making sure nobody else was around. Her face was hidden by her hoody, Whitstable in bold letters on the back. I half remembered someone wearing similar but almost laughed aloud when I thought of something else. For once the phrase 'she looked right through me' was completely true. She wore sunglasses on this bright morning as she turned her head back, apparently double checking there was nobody on the platform. I was standing by the side of the bench then.

I realised then she was looking to see how close the train was to where she was standing.

I thought again, and as I turned towards her, something glinted on the bench close to where she stood. I moved fast when I saw it was a wedding ring. I reached her as her fists clenched and her arms began to swing her body forward, to make one great leap onto the track and into the path of the oncoming train.

As I threw myself across her, the impact of me threw her backwards hard onto the platform. She narrowly missed the bench and she was screaming her head off. Not knowing what force had sent her backwards was almost enough, but when she recognised the scent of my aftershave and screeched out my name, it created a soundtrack of her hysterical fear.

I disentangled myself from her as soon as I could, as the passengers getting off the train ran to help her recover herself. I pulled myself up from the platform away from where she lay, and sat on the bench catching the breath that I knew no one would hear.

I stayed there for a short time and watched, as my feelings overtook me, shaping a very deep regret that I had made my wife's life so bad that she had wanted to throw herself under a train. Hopefully I had given her the chance of another life to be happier living.

And now it was up to me to figure out my own way forward.

Tankerton Gothic

by Nick Hayes

'*Dear Jean and Ernie,*
Thank you again for being such caring neighbours. Please
water the garden – if you could – and just keep a general
look out. We are soooo lucky to have you!!!
All the best.
All the gang at number 19.'

Ernie read the words aloud to his wife, Jean.

'I don't know how they manage it,' said Ernie.

Jean shook her head. 'This is the second trip away in three months.' They tutted in unison.

'You go watering, love and I can get started in here,' she said.

Ernie was an expert at watering. He deliberately filled the can from the water butt and went to each bed to meticulously water every plant. It was a labour of love. Ten minutes later he was nearly complete. Only one final splash.

He put down the can where it lived. He approached the tub, home of the scarlet rose. He undid his fly. He let the water gush. A couple of shakes and he zipped up and went to join Jean.

Jean had been hard at work indoors adding value to their role as house sitters. She'd been upstairs and sorted a few things. Now, in the living room, she was busy on the shelves of DVDs and CDs. She took out the discs of five or six and swapped them around. Just enough swapping to be irritating – not enough to raise suspicion.

Ernie was making use of his extra height as he reached up to the light bulbs. He gently unscrewed three of the four bulbs. Just enough to stop the connection. Just enough to be irritating. The bulb in the lamp, however, he unscrewed completely and tapped hard against the wall. Just enough to wreck the filament then dutifully replaced.

Some of the kids' outside balls were kept at one end of the room. Ernie took out a Swiss Army Knife and caressed a blade into the leather. Just enough to be deadly but small enough to be invisible.

Jean was at work in the kitchen. She turned on the radio and listened in for a moment. Then she lovingly turned down the volume to the most gentle of whispers. Just enough to drain the battery. A sneeze caught her and she reached for a tea towel just in time. Three more then she hung it back up.

It was nearly time to finish off. That was Ernie's job. He went to the bathroom. A few sharp tugs later and he left a creamy swirl.

'All done, dear?' she cried.

'All done, love.'

The pair returned to the note on the kitchen side. Ernie drew a smiley face and Jean wrote a few words. 'No trouble at all. We are always happy to help.'

They left quietly and made sure the door was locked behind them. Didn't want to let the riff-raff in.

As they approached their house opposite, Jean held out her prize. It was a pair of silver ear-rings. Ernie grinned. He showed his hand – an unopened tub of jam.

'I love you, dear.'

'I love you too.'

They went inside and closed the door.

The Man Who
Wouldn't Be King

by Nic Blackshaw

Whitstable – Monday, 12th April, 2049

It's fair to say: Cremorne Road had never seen anything like it.
A solid phalanx of journalists, microphones held out, cameras
focused, crowded behind a police cordon, waiting for the
answer to a question the whole county – the whole world –
was asking: when would Giles Purcell accept his destiny and
become King of England?

Across the road at Number 242, behind an olive-green front
door with two ornamental bay trees standing on either side
like sentries, the atmosphere was febrile: royal flunkeys were
running around like be-ruffed, beheaded courtiers, dodging
Imogen and her two daughters, and speaking quickly and
urgently into mobile phones.

It was the first time affairs of state had been discussed
between the open plan kitchen and the painting Daisy did
when she was three, hanging outside the downstairs lavatory,
but it was clear Imogen could get used to it. If only Giles would
come to his senses and do the decent thing.

Through all the mayhem Giles sat impassively in the vintage
brown leather armchair in the sitting room, flicking through
the National Trust Handbook that had arrived in the post
that morning. Linda Blair, Director of Royal Changeovers,

was trying, for what felt like the hundredth time that day, to convince Giles to accept the crown of Great Britain and Northern Ireland. She wasn't making much progress.

She stood up, smoothing an invisible crease on her grey skirt and went over to the window. What more could she say, that hadn't already been said? She pulled the curtain aside and looked out at the media throng: like a pack of wild dogs, she thought, looking for a break in the fence; they've scented blood.

She turned and glanced back at the immovable obstacle to her ambition for a smooth and painless transition. She remembered an old photo of her Dad – thick beard, short-back-and-sides haircut and a flowery shirt – holding her in his arms in the back garden at home. It's funny how fashion goes around in cycles. That was more than thirty years ago but Giles could be her Dad's twin.

And she had no better idea what was going on in that head of his than she did what her Dad was thinking that day, long ago. Giles looked up at her and smiled weakly. Linda forced herself to smile back. Don't let the anxiety show, she thought; he has no idea the trouble he's causing.

Linda's career was hanging by a thread – by a thread – and she had no idea how to break the impasse. She let the curtain fall back and glanced around the room, hoping for something to jump out that she could use. The Rothko prints on the wall, the little wooden Indonesian statue on the mantelpiece, the bookcase with its mix of DVDs (Bergman to Bridesmaids) and books (Sun Tzu to Sunstroke), family photos in silver frames of summer holidays in Teignmouth and Tuscany. If she had been asked to dress a film set with objects representative of this strata of society, she could not have done much better.

No, no help there: she still hadn't pinned down exactly what it was that Giles didn't like about becoming king – wasn't it, after all, every little boys' dream – but so far everything Giles had said had been vague and unspecific. He just – didn't want to be King. Not really – sorry.

Imogen came in with a mug of tea for Linda and a cup of foamy coffee for Giles – a macchiato, she said proudly. Linda had seen the shiny red coffee machine used to make it, when Imogen had given her a tour of the house. Imogen said it was Giles' present to himself when the company made him Head of Department.

Imogen smiled hopefully as she handed Linda the tea.

'How's it going?'

Linda sipped the tea – Earl Grey: eugghh. Lucky it wasn't vanilla bark or crushed juniper berry or whatever else the trendsetters in Penge were drinking two years ago. She did her best to disguise the look of distaste, but Imogen picked up on it immediately.

'Sorry. It's all we've got. I can pop to the shop around the corner. We've got a fantastic artisan grocer's...'

Imogen glanced towards the window, remembering the crowds outside, and sat down on the grey Danish Mid-Century sofa.

Linda nodded: it would have to do. She took another sip and looked around the room again. There's got to be something that'll give me a clue – how I can get this infuriating man to become King.

Now, for those of you who need a quick recap – perhaps you popped out for a cup of tea and you've been out there, waiting for the kettle to boil, for the last twenty-three years – here's some background to events.

The new system for choosing the monarch was introduced after the 2026 Constitutional Crisis (read Peter Hennessy's excellent summing up in *How England lost One Royal Family and gained Many Royal Families*).

After leading geneticists and genealogists concluded that more than half the population were descended from William the Conqueror – and some actually had more legitimate claim to the throne than the House of Windsor – the decision was taken to offer the monarchy to any UK citizen who bought a Royal Lotto ticket.

It was proposed that the Lottery would have only one prize. And the money raised from ticket sales and sponsorship would fully cover the costs of the new royal family.

The Chancellor of the Exchequer was an early and enthusiastic supporter of the scheme, seeing in the Lottery a way the Royal Family could, for the very first time, become a net contributor to the Treasury.

The winning citizen – the term 'subject' was dropped from the 2027 Acts of Succession and Royal Lottery – would ascend to the throne for a four-year period. The new king or queen would occupy the top floor of Buckingham Palace – the staterooms on the lower floors becoming the National Museum of Sovereignty – and, for weekends and holidays, they would have full use of Osborne House, on the Isle of Wight.

The entertainment world heard a loud kerching, and seized the myriad opportunities presented by an everyday man or woman ascending to the throne every four years. Producers of makeover shows were the first to bid for television rights – transforming an ordinary citizen and their family into royalty was a sure-fire ratings winner – and then, once they'd settled in, doing up the top floor of the Royal Samsung Palace in a style or styles of their choice. (Laurence Llewellyn Bowen topped his triumphant return to early evening entertainment when he was made a Lord for Services to the Nation after succession of remodelling successes.)

Tired old formats that had been around for years like *Big Brother*, *Take Me Out*, *Blind Date* and *Queer Eye*, got a new lease of life with royal participants. The possibilities, it seemed, were endless as King Sunil, Queen Tara, Queen Kat, King Tyler, each took the throne in a cavalcade of pomp and circumstance.

Of course, there were teething troubles. No history of the modern monarchy could fail to mention the controversy caused by Crown Princess Leeza refusing to shake hands with Prime Minister Stormzy after his son, Dip-Titch, used his number one hit, 'It's All about the Money – featuring TashUh' to diss her, by name, and compare her exclusive make up range, 'Mysteeeque' to 'bargain basement slap, just cheap repackaged c**p'.

But there were also successes, most notably a new and stronger relationship with the United States. Where American Presidents, by convention, had previously been granted only one official State visit (despite most being elected for two terms), they now got two bites at the cherry with two opportunities to ride down the Mall with the new king or queen. And they weren't shy about showing their appreciation, signing a string of new trade deals that were the envy of the rest of the world.

And who could have predicted the thaw in relations with

North Korea that came after Queen Kat's visit, when – she later told a worldwide readership in her ghost-written autobiography – the two heads of state bonded over a shared love of silent movies and slapstick comedy?

And the people – let's not forget the people – the nation loved their new royal families. Took them to their hearts. They were there, in the hundreds of thousands, lining the route from Westminster Abbey to the Royal Samsung Palace on coronation day – to see one of their own raised up above them. And they did the same at all the major royal events. People soon found that, with the dates of royal events being set far into the future, they could book time off work long in advance. Indeed, when the Government announced that Coronation Day would be a Bank Holiday, the Party gained 10 percentage points in opinion polls – enough to get them re-elected.

The spin-off benefits seemed never ending. Chief amongst them was merchandising – if ever there was an indicator of how much a people loved their monarch it was how much they'd spend on cups, plates, key rings and other memorabilia. It seemed almost any object could be repackaged with a royal crest and marketed to a grateful nation. Not just once in a blue moon but every four years a whole new set needed to be purchased – and the old one donated to grateful charity shops – if you wanted to stay up-to-date.

Royal Doulton and Wedgewood joined the Footsie 100 for the first time since the reign of Queen Victoria. The Governor of the Bank of England wrote in his memoirs that the first of the new peoples' dynasty, King Sunil, (whose reign came to be seen as a golden age) managed to get the economy back in the black for the first time since the days of the British Empire. And that same healthy financial position continues to this day.

Which explains why Linda was sweating over Giles' refusal to take the throne. It wasn't just her job resting on his decision: the repercussions for the UK economy – should he continue to refuse the crown – were too dreadful to contemplate.

~

Fortunately, while we've been recapping, Linda finally figured out the root of Giles' misgivings. She sat down beside him on the sofa.

'We've been looking at this all wrong, Giles.'

He turned to look at her with a 'what now' expression etched on his face.

'Forget *It's a Royal Big Brother* – that format's run its course.' Linda pushed that hackneyed old title away with a sweeping hand gesture. 'Remember *Victorian Farm, 1900 House*?'

Linda used her hands to delineate a cinema screen for Giles to look at. Her face glowed, as if backlit by the images she was showing him.

'Remember those classic series from yesteryear, where clever, educated people faithfully recreated a specific era – all for the sake of historical research. That's how we're going to position your family, Giles. We're not going to do another *Love Island*, with your two lovely daughters joining its revolving cast of perma-tanned, titled Eurotrash – your family is much too classy for that. We'll keep it to one documentary a year – done in the best possible taste. And you'll have full editorial control so they can't show anything you don't like.'

Giles' face now glowed with the same golden light but Linda's film was still showing, her voice rising with excitement.

'Forget the Geordie who does *Big Brother* or the bloke from *X Factor*, we'll get Benedict Cumberbatch to do the narration, or one of the Old Etonians, in that low whispery voice they do for quality documentaries. It'll scream class – but with dignity. Tremendous dignity. There'll be shots of stags, looking towards the camera, magnificent in the rising mist, a Beethoven sonata on the soundtrack or something operatic – cutaways to courtiers gliding about mumbling some nonsense or other about tradition. And we'll have "experts", filmed in the royal library, being terribly solemn, saying how wonderful you are and how it's all about the great continuum of English History...'

Giles rubbed his beard, meditatively.

'That does sound a bit more like us – but, still…'

Imogen had been staring at Giles throughout Linda's speech, her excitement building, watching that documentary playing – picturing herself in a golden carriage, heading to the Palace of Westminster for the state opening of parliament, the girls in their ball gowns beside her, the adulation of the crowds – and then, with that 'but', the last frame of the film froze and burned like a silver nitrate print.

The girls had left her to it – they'd told their father he was ruining their lives, a claim which, as teenaged girls, they'd deployed a little too frequently for it to have much effect – and flounced off to their rooms. Now Imogen would have to fight for their dream alone.

'Is there no way we can do it without him?'

She caught herself – seeing the bruised look on Giles' face. But she wasn't going to give up without a fight, even if that meant a little pain for Giles.

'I'm not saying… I just mean, he can stay here and we can live in London for the next four years.'

She turned to Giles.

'You'd understand, wouldn't you? It'd only be four years.'

Linda sighed, she was sure she'd already told Imogen this but – well, people don't hear what they don't like.

'It has to be the person who bought the ticket. That's the law, I'm afraid.'

Imogen flopped back onto the sofa, disconsolate.

'It had to be the one time I ask him to buy the lotto ticket. Doesn't it count if he was buying it for me?'

Linda shook her head. 'The law is quite explicit – it has to be the person who bought the ticket.'

Imogen pulled at a tassel on the Nepalese throw on the back of the sofa.

'So you've said.'

Linda took another sip of tea. The police were doing a good job of keeping the press outside at bay, and the noise to a minimum, but every now and then a helicopter, flying overhead, would make the windows shake. Giles had followed her gaze. He grimaced.

'Like being back in Sydenham.'

Linda looked back at him. She had no idea what he meant.

'Is it?'

'Helicopters flying overhead – it takes me back to when we lived in Sydenham. Every once in a while you'd hear a police helicopter circling above. It felt like they'd never go away. And you'd know they're up there looking for someone, a criminal – maybe someone dangerous, hiding in one of the back gardens near you. Maybe closer. Maybe he was in your garden. And... I don't miss that.'

Linda stirred her tea.

'I can imagine.'

'You know, I used to have a screensaver, a photo of Whitstable beach – every morning when I got into work, every time I'd come back from internal meetings and moved the mouse, there it'd be – the pebbles and the oyster beds, the sun glinting off the sea like it does in *L'Avventura*. You know, the film by Antonioni...'

He looked at Linda, waiting for a nod that she understood the reference. But Linda just looked blankly at him. Giles scratched his chin.

'Sounds silly, doesn't it?'

Linda shook her head and put her hand on his arm.

'No. No, it doesn't.'

Giles smiled weakly and sighed.

'It took us a long time to get here – such a long time, but...'

Giles looked around the room – everything he had worked for. This was his kingdom. The only one that mattered to him.

'I can walk out the front door, down the road – pick up a perfectly ground flat white on the way – and I'm on the beach.'

Linda smiled. It wasn't a self-satisfied smile, or a smile of triumph, but one of relief – finally, the missing piece of the puzzle. This was what she had been waiting for, the clincher.

She knew now what needed to be done to get Giles to the coronation.

Nerves of sterling silver, they said at the Palace, and they weren't wrong. It was one of the reasons she'd beaten off strong competition to nail the job as Director of Royal Changeovers in the first place. She knew when to watch and listen and when to speak – and she had that knack of seeing things other people didn't.

'It occurs to me, Giles… I'm just busking here but, think about it for a moment: what if I said you could split your time between here and London? You commute up to London every day for work?'

'One day working from home.'

'Sure – but you're up in town for most of the working week. And you get home what – eight?'

'Sometimes closer to nine.'

'So it's the weekends that matter most.'

'I suppose.'

'Then I think being King could really work for you. You see, there's no reason you need to stay in London the whole week, just – let's say, three days a week. Four at the most. That's only two or three nights away from Whitstable. And then there are the holidays. You might not know this, but the royal family actually spend most of their time on holiday. When you add it all up, they only work about ten weeks of the year in total. So, when you're not working, you could come back…'

Giles pointed loosely to the floor – come back here?

Linda shook her head and made an apologetic face.

'Unfortunately, you couldn't carry on living at Number 242. I know you've done a fantastic job restoring this place but, you know, a three-bed terraced house, even if it is the best part of Whitstable, isn't really appropriate for a royal residence. The security, for a start, would be impossible. But I think – if you'll allow me – I've got a solution.'

～

Here was another reason Linda Blair got the top job – she did her research. Within half an hour she was standing on the porch of 242 Cremorne Road, Whitstable, flanked by the two bay trees, speaking to representatives of the world's press.

His Majesty King Giles the First, she told them, had graciously accepted the throne. Henceforth he, Queen Imogen, Princesses Lily and Daisy, would be travelling up to London for royal business weekdays. On weekends they would return to Whitstable where, for the next four years, Whitstable Castle would become their royal residence.

Peter and Jane Go to Town

by Guy Deakins

'Why do people start wars?' Jane blurted, obviously perplexed by the images on the television.

Peter looked towards the room where his younger sister Jane was lazing on the sofa. He wasn't used to this kind of interaction. His day was more often than not filled with the kind of sentence more suited to his two-dimensional life.

We like sweets.

Where is the ball?

Watch Pat run!

He placed the wooden building blocks down onto the playroom carpet and sat back on his haunches. He looked about the room he'd played in so much as a child and thought on the question.

'Why, indeed, do people start wars?'

After carefully making sure his statement of swastika'd defiance was clear for all to see, he stood, brushed his smart beige shorts down and walked through the archway to the living room. He stood behind the sofa, yet again absorbing the harrowing images of another country tearing itself apart.

'I think,' he began, 'People start wars because the military industrial complex demands it.'

Jane snapped her head around and glared at her brother.

'You and your fucking conspiracies, Peter! Nobody believes that shit!' The words escaped her mouth with an unexpected malevolence that took Peter aback.

'I mean, why do people allow wars to happen? Some idiot decides to declare war on another idiot, but it is never them that fights. It's the rest of us mugs.'

Peter studied his sister's gentle face, traced the line of her blond bob to her neck. She would be a good Frau in the New World Order, he had no doubt, but she'd have to watch her tongue.

'Look at it like this.' Peter decided to try another tack. 'Humans are not dissimilar to sheep. We follow strong leadership. Most of the time, we stand in the field consuming what amounts to nothing much at all – that is, until we are threatened. Then we panic. It is in our nature to look around for a strong decision. If that decision is made by a madman, it doesn't matter, we follow the decision precisely because it is a decision. Before that decision, there was panic. Before that panic there was calm. We all remember the calm before that panic and we want to return to the calm, so we hope that somehow, somewhere, calmness is possible.'

Jane looked back to the television and then to her brother. With a very deliberate action, she lifted her right arm, her index finger pointing to the TV. By happenstance the image of a dead child flashed onto the screen. See Jane point.

'Are you saying that those poor sods have asked for this? They followed a madman into hell to find peace?'

Peter looked at the screen impassively for a good minute, then his gaze returned to his sister.

'The media spreads social panic. Nothing more. The politicians offer us safety. It worked for Hitler.'

He shrugged, turning as he did so.

Peter smiled to himself, knowing full well his sister would explode into a fiery ball of unrepentant rage at his suggestion. Pat, the red-setter, who had up until this point been quietly sleeping on the sofa next to Jane, decided to investigate the bin in the kitchen. Jane watched him go, her ire rising. See Pat skulk.

'How dare you! Those poor people are stuck between a mad tyrant and bunch of insane religious fanatics! They did not ask to be in this war! They did not ask to be bombed into oblivion!'

Peter, who had continued to walk from the room, stopped at the door. He let his hand wander up the door frame, feeling the contours of the late Victorian woodwork.

'They were quite content to live under the tyrant when the oil was flowing and they were making money. Grazing sheep. Nothing more. Nothing less.' His hand found a notch in the wood. He remembered it had been made when he and Jane had fought and he had slammed her head against the trim. She had spent the day in hospital. See Jane's bandage.

He smirked. He had supposedly spent the day locked in his room with no privileges for punishment. In reality, he had spent the day reading Mein Kampf again. The smirk turned to a smile. See Peter's salute!

Peter remained at the doorway, enticing Jane to respond. See Jane run!

He could feel the force of Jane's anger approaching, imagined her curled fist ready to strike the back of his head. Experience had taught him to wait, allow the fist to begin its descent before side-stepping. Her hand duly crashed into the door frame and she recoiled, a wail of anguish escaping her lungs. Feel Jane's pain!

He turned and grabbed her hair.

'You do not understand war, because you do not understand what drives us Lieben. Humans are sociopaths. Do you know what I mean?' He pulled her hair tight as he pushed his grimacing face into hers.

She tried to shake her head, sobbing as she did so. See Jane cry.

'Humans cannot find peace because biologically we are never at peace. We are by our very nature violent and controlling and angry. Why do you think people make so much money helping other people try to find it?'

He pulled Jane's head back until she lost her balance. She

fell and he let go, allowing her hair to flow through his fingers, but, just at the last moment, at the very last opportunity to inflict more pain, he grasped. The action caused a mass of blond to remain in his palms. She wailed, and lay prone on the floor face down.

Peter bent over her, allowing the hair in his hand to drift gently onto her shoulders. She could hear the smile in his voice. Hear Peter's hate.

'You know the problem with you liberal types? You can't accept the truth. Humans love war. We breathe it. We exude it. If we didn't, it wouldn't be on the news. That's the truth. We actually enjoy watching suffering. If we didn't it wouldn't be in films, in books, in computer games, in our history. It releases dopamine. It de-stresses us. Makes us feel happy in the knowledge that our shitty life is not as bad as somebody else's shitty life. We can all breathe a sigh of relief and walk on.'

He watched as Jane tried to surreptitiously clench her fist, ready for another onslaught. He knew his sister too well. Feel Peter's contempt.

He stood back and aiming precisely for a spot just below the ribs, kicked her as if he were trying to kick a rugby ball the length of the pitch. She screamed, her body jumping two feet in the air and coming to rest as an agonised ball on the fireplace carpet. See Jane break.

He stepped forward again.

'Humans start wars because we can. Humans start wars because it is another way for the strong to control the weak. We have done it for hundreds of thousands of years. The truth is, nobody cares. Not one person on the planet cares. We all strut around speaking platitudes and shaking our heads, but the whole sad, piteous, bollocks honest truth is, beyond our nearest and dearest, we, don't, give, a, flying, fuck.'

Jane's voice had been reduced to a whimper. She lay on the rug wishing her mother would come back from the neighbour's house, but knew it would be a long time. Her mother had taken a bottle of wine. Then she would come home with 'one of her heads' and go to bed for the rest of the day. Jane's insides hurt, her vision was blurred and her knuckles stung. Peter remained, his malicious presence hovering somewhere above her. She closed her eyes against the pain. Her body throbbed every time she took a breath but she could sense, just the merest perhaps, victory was still in her grasp as Peter stepped back slightly. Somewhere close by, her brother, was waiting for the opportunity for the coup-de-grace. She would be ready.

She lay still. The floor board under her flexed. She knew instinctively he was about two steps away. She tensed as she sensed the pressure change. One step closer, just one step. Wait girl, wait for your moment.

She felt the floor yield again. Now! Feel Jane's wrath.

Eyes still closed, her left arm darted out from under her, grabbing for the poker that she knew lived beside the hearth. With an upward thrust she caught Peter square on the chin. He staggered back. Run Peter run!

Jane jumped to her feet and slashed the iron through the air. Again and again she made contact, her brother's flailing arms uselessly defending his head against the onslaught.

See Peter fall!

It was over.

Peter's lifeless eyes stared at the flecks of dust swimming in a shaft of sunlight.

Jane stood over him panting. Her ribs hurt, her head was swimming. She looked about. The room was a mess of blood spatter and broken furniture.

She stood back, wiping her brow with the back of her shaking hand. What next? Hear Jane think.

Lips pursed, she nodded once, decision made. Still holding the poker, she walked to the front window and looked out through the net curtains into Cromwell Road. Not a soul stirred.

Jane turned and calmly walked back through the rooms

to the French doors which led from the playroom into the garden. Pausing only to pull her sleeve over her hand, she turned the handles, pushed the panes of glass with the very tips of her fingers, walked outside and closed the doors behind her with her heels. The air was filled with the smell of ozone from the beach. Somewhere children were playing, a light aircraft was passing overhead. All was normal. An ancient climbing rose that had been trained long ago to arch over the doors caught her attention. A solitary flower, defiantly free of restraint, jigged lazily in the late summer breeze. She cupped its pink folds in her bloody hand and took a deep, deep lung-full of its heady talc-lemon scent. She'd always loved this rose. It reminded her of dad, of his warm earthy hands and sad tired eyes. Still gripping tightly, she allowed her arm to drop, pulling the petals away as it went. The feeling of the silken rose remained on her fingers and palm making her suddenly feel unclean. She dropped the poker in the grass and looking down at her hands, rubbed them furiously, trying to destroy the sensation. Having only succeeded in making the feeling more intense, she stood alone in her world, wringing her hands whilst looking out over the now unkempt garden, at the hidden toys, and missed opportunities. See dad hang.

The feeling of stained emptiness subsided as quickly as it had begun, the sound of the children and a school bell returning her to the immediate reality.

Searching out the poker, and with her back still to the doors, she took a deep breath and swung the heavy metal implement in her left hand. See the glass break!

Taking one last arrogant sniff of the air, she pirouetted, wiping the poker's handle clean with her sleeve as she did so. Treading carefully through the broken door, she tiptoed through the house to the front door. She opened it, dropped the poker and, leaving the door swinging ajar, reversed her journey. She coolly walked back into the room where her brother lay and stopped, hands on hips. Jane felt the urge to just stare at him, to study his broken face, but a random thought entered her mind. Had he moved? What if he was feigning?

She edged forward, nervous, unprotected by the abandoned poker, aware of her brother's furious temper. She grabbed a cushion from the sofa and held it to her chest as she edged sideways towards him. With care, she knelt next to him fist raised, ready to strike, craning her neck to hear if there was a chance that he was breathing, then deftly smothered his face with the pillow. She held it firmly over his face for a full count of two hundred and then released it. Feel Jane's relief.

Carelessly discarding the cushion, she sat back on her haunches, studying his features. He looked quite peaceful, his broken socket stare not quite focused on the ceiling, his mouth fixed in an odd, dislocated grimace. He looked like an indignant fish, surprised to be on the monger's slab. She rested the back of her sore hands on her thighs, exhausted, exhilarated. Looking to the heavens she stifled a laugh, both hands immediately clasping her open mouth. A frustrated tear ran from her left eye, pooling at her lobe. She snorted and wiped the itch away with a knuckle. Was it joy or pain?

She allowed her hands to drop, her concentration returning to her brother's corpse. Leaning in, her venomous mouth almost touching his now deaf ear. Sense Jane's hubris.

'No, Peter. People start wars because they think they can win.'

Hear Jane scream.

Nanny Crabbe

by Kerry Mayo

Interview by Bethany Blair for her blog,

Bubblicious (Media Studies homework project)

'HELLO, NANNY CRABBE. MY NAME IS BETHANY. I'VE
COME TO TALK TO YOU ABOUT HOW OLD YOU ARE.'

Nanny Crabbe looked away from the TV and saw a young
girl with a switch of dark hair so straight she must have laid
her head on the ironing board while her mother was doing the
sheets. She watched as the girl edged into the room, mobile
phone held out in front of her like a Geiger counter.

And, of course, right behind her was that silly childless
woman, Mary, with the nervous tics. However much she
wanted the world to think she was coping since her useless, but
rich, twit of a husband ran off with his Procurement Manager,
she was failing miserably.

Nanny Crabbe sat up a bit straighter. She'd nearly been off
for a nap; that nice man who looked old even though he was
young but now he was getting old and growing into his looks,
always sent her to sleep in the morning with his calm voice
and giggly sidekick.

'Turn the telly off, Nanny, so you can talk to Bethany,' Mary
said in a voice that sounded like she was talking to an idiot.
In fact, as long as she'd been living here, which had only been
a couple of months, Nanny Crabbe didn't think she'd heard

Mary speak to her any other way.

She pressed the red button and waited. Jittery as fillies, the pair came further into the room, not that there was that much further to be had.

Mary pushed Bethany towards a hard, wooden chair next to Nanny Crabbe's spongy armchair, one of an old three-piece suite from at least thirty years ago, while she stayed by the door.

Bethany sat, phone still outstretched towards the old lady, who swatted at it as if it were a fly.

'OH NO, NANNY. I'M RECORDING AN INTERVIEW. IT'S GOING ON MY BLOG. JUST SPEAK INTO THE PHONE.'

Nanny Crabbe leant forward and held her lightly whiskered chin over the phone. 'Bugger off.'

Mary tittered her embarrassment.

'OH, NANNY, YOU ARE FUNNY,' said Bethany, through lips dripping shiny goo Paul Hollywood would be pleased to judge on top of a fancy cake. Her blackened brows and over-emphasised features reminded Nanny Crabbe of the tarts that used to stand outside the old Long Reach Tavern on Borstal Hill when Nanny Crabbe was young, calling to any man or boy who passed, their guttural laughter following the young girl down the hill as her mother prodded her in the back to go faster.

'ANYWAY,' said Bethany, 'I'M DOING A PROJECT FOR SCHOOL AND MRS SANDERS TOLD MY MUM YOU WERE VERY OLD AND IT MIGHT MAKE A GOOD INTERVIEW FOR MY BLOG.'

'She did, did she?' said Nanny Crabbe, eyeing up the other woman. 'Did she also tell your mother that I'm deaf?'

'ER, I DON'T THINK SO.'

'Good. Then stop yelling.'

Bethany flushed as pink as her blusher and mumbled a 'sorry'. She lowered the phone and rested it on her knee, right over a rip in her jeans that needed seeing to.

Nanny Crabbe said nothing as Bethany unfolded a piece of paper with typed questions on it.

'So, Nanny Crabbe, how old are you?' said Bethany, without an ounce of deference.

Nanny Crabbe had taught Paddington Bear all about hard stares, and she gave Bethany one now.

'How old do you think I am?' she asked.

'Er,' said Bethany, glancing uncertainty at Mary. 'Sixty-five?'

Nanny Crabbe cracked a smile, an eight-toothed smile but a smile none the less. 'That's really old, is it?' she asked.

'Oh, yeah. My nan's like fifty-eight and you look a bit older than her although my mum says my nan was born with grey hair and a set of dentures.'

Bethany snorted but quickly quietened under Nanny Crabbe's gaze.

'See that picture?' Nanny Crabbe asked, nodding to the one on the plain wooden nightstand next to the single bed with its orange candlewick bedspread that dominated the tiny room. 'That was me and my third husband, George, on our wedding day.'

'Third husband?' said Mary, from the door. 'I didn't know you'd had three husbands.'

Mary received a stare this time; even though the eyes were more of a milky latte than the hard espresso of her youth, they still gave quite a jolt. 'There's a lot you've never bothered to ask, my girl.' Mary looked at the floor.

'My third husband,' Nanny Crabbe continued, 'died in 1981. We'd been married thirty years when he passed. Terribly sad. He fell off a ladder putting some lights on the roof at Christmas time. Fell onto a pair of antlers, Blitzen, I think it was, in this whole sleigh scene he'd created on the front lawn. Punctured a lung and that was the end of him.'

Bethany lifted her phone and took a photo of the picture without asking.

'Why aren't you wearing a white dress?' she asked.

'Didn't have much money in those days, just after the war.

My cousin had that two-piece made for her wedding and I borrowed it. Besides, it doesn't do to wear white third time around.'

Bethany looked at her piece of paper. 'So, my mum says Mrs Sanders is very kind for taking you in after her own mum died recently...'

Nanny Crabbe looked around the tiny basement room that still had an exposed waste pipe from where the washing machine had been moved upstairs when they built a more accessible utility room, just before Mary's Stephen had upped and left. 'Very kind,' she murmured.

'When she knew she hadn't long left, Mummy said I was to look after Nanny Crabbe,' said Mary, 'just like her mum had said to her.'

'So you've spent a long time living with other people?' asked Bethany.

'Longer than you'd believe,' said Nanny Crabbe.

When Bethany was gone, and Nanny Crabbe was sure that Mary wasn't going to reappear, she eased out of the chair and reached for a small wooden chest on the bottom shelf of the bedside table. She stroked each of the pictures there in turn and even kissed one or two. Only when the box was safely stowed did she finally close her eyes and have that nap.

Interview with Sky News following
Bethany Blair's blog going viral

Nanny Crabbe had been allowed upstairs. It was nice up there, all new soft grey leather sofas and glass coffee tables. Could have done with a bit of colour though, rather than the black and white prints with nonsensical patterns that were on the walls.

Mary had got herself all worked up and was twittering on to

the producer like they were old friends.

'Is it ok if we film over here, Mrs Sanders?' the young woman with a clipboard, a stopwatch, an iPad and two mobile phones asked.

'That's fine, of course, and please, call me Marie.'

'Why would she when your name is Mary?' said Nanny Crabbe, but the ambient noise of low-level chatter and cameras and equipment being pulled into place drowned her out. Come to think of it, Mary did look a bit different. Gone were the dowdy patterned blouses and elasticated-waist slacks. Today she was wearing a beige blouse with a fine leopard print and a pair of snug-fitting black trousers with a silver strip down the outside seam of each leg. She was thinner than when Stephen had been around, from pining or in an attempt to get him back Nanny Crabbe couldn't tell. She sat, forgotten, on one of the grey sofas as the equipment was pushed and pulled into position.

At last, they were ready. The interviewer was definitely past her prime but so well preserved Tiptree should ask for the recipe, Nanny thought. She was stick thin with a big round lollipop head, coiffed into a bob that didn't move, even when the sound technician tugged on the cord from her earpiece to the battery pack and nearly pulled her head off.

'NANNY CRABBE?' The producer was smiling down at her like they were old friends despite not even introducing herself in all the time she'd been there. 'I'M ELOISE. WOULD YOU COME OVER HERE?'

Nanny Crabbe stood. Another yeller, she thought. She followed her over to the sofa by the window, with the view of the sea and the Red Sands forts, declining the reluctantly proffered arm.

A young man fixed the microphone to the lapel of her cardi, taking great care not to touch her. Repulsed or respectful, Nanny knew not which, but the web of lines covering the skin on her chest gave a glimpse of the future not many youngsters were keen to see.

Then they took light readings, fiddled with cameras and, finally, the interviewer sat down on a chair next to her – one from the dining set with a plum-purple seat and clear plastic frame. Cheap-looking tat in Nanny Crabbe's view but she was sure they cost a fortune.

'Good afternoon. I'm Melanie Holmes and I'm here with Nanny Crabbe, subject of a recent online sensation after a schoolgirl's hilarious blog went viral. Nanny, how does it feel to be the subject of so much media attention?'

Nanny looked directly at the camera. She knew she wasn't supposed to but, like the woman had said, it was her moment. 'It's nice. Like my wedding day all over again.'

Melanie laughed; a head toss and a flash of carefully dentured white. 'Which wedding would that be? I understand you've had three husbands,' she said, tinkling what Nanny Crabbe presumed Melanie thought was a charming laugh.

'Funnily enough, I suppose my second wedding was the best. My first was all very quick, if you know what I mean, but second time round was a big affair. We had a big party at the Bear and Key. Seventy guests. Fancy sandwiches and everything.'

'What was your husband's name?'

'Samuel Borgenstein. Sam. He was Jewish but we never let it affect our marriage.'

Melanie looked confused but didn't pursue it. 'And how long were you married?'

'Nigh on sixty years,' said Nanny Crabbe, with a smile. 'Love of my life, that man. He died trying to rescue his family from those bastard Nazis. He travelled to France on a boat from Dover. He planned to reach Germany and trace his nephews and their families but I never heard from him again.'

Nanny Crabbe saw Melanie look over at Mary, who twirled her finger into the hair at the side of her head. Melanie smiled at Nanny Crabbe but it didn't reach her eyes, or even her cheeks.

'Do you need to take a break?' she asked.

'I'm fine,' said Nanny Crabbe. 'I might be old but my bladder can hold more water than the Gorrell Tank.'

Later, when everyone had gone, Mary shooed Nanny Crabbe back downstairs. She brought her a tray with some leftover sandwiches and a mean glass of port and lemonade. On her way back out, she stopped and said, 'I'm not fooled, you know. You might pretend to be a confused old lady but I know you're not.'

'I don't know what you mean, dear,' said Nanny Crabbe, wishing she could be left in peace to tuck into the sandwiches before they curled any more.

The Sky News interview aired the next day and a Twitter storm broke out about whether Nanny Crabbe was having everyone on, or should be left in peace in an EMI care home.

Calculations over the two interviews were quickly made and, although the maths had everyone calling 'fraud', at least one person made the discovery of the names of two families who had died at Treblinka which were the same as Nanny Crabbe's husband Sam's unusual surname.

Doorstep interview with Harry Gallagher, Investigative Reporter with the Daily View

Nanny Crabbe's second nap, 1.45 to 2.15 during Neighbours, what utter tosh, was interrupted by the sound of the doorbell. It rang three times, the additional bell in the basement level being right by her chair.

There was a pause before it rang again, and again.

Mary was obviously out, not that she'd told Nanny Crabbe she was going anywhere, nor God forbid, that she offered to take her along.

The doorbell rang again, and again.

Nanny Crabbe pulled herself to standing and shuffled to the base of the stairs.

The stairs were narrow enough that she could hold the rail on each side. She gripped as hard as the mild arthritis that had just started in her knuckles would allow, and pulled.

Step-by-step she progressed up the stairs, almost matching the chimes of the bell with each step. Finally, she was at the top. Whoever it was, they were still there, a shadowy shape showing through the opaque glass at the side of the door. Nanny Crabbe put the chain on the door before opening it.

'Nanny Crabbe?' the man said in a voice that defined him as a bit of a geezer.

'Yes?'

'Harry Gallagher from the Daily View.' He flashed her some photo ID he could have Photoshopped on his computer. Oh, Nanny Crabbe watched Crimewatch, she knew about these things.

'What do you want?'

'To talk to you. I've got an appointment.'

'No one told me.'

'Can I come in?'

'No. Bugger off or I'll call the police.'

Nanny Crabbe shut the door but didn't go back downstairs. She picked up Mary's sleek silver house phone that looked like a vibrator. Oh yes, Nanny Crabbe watched the Love Honey ads on Quest Red.

The man stayed where he was but left the doorbell alone. After a few moments, the letterbox flap opened and a pair of lips appeared, the bristles making a funny beard and moustache around them. 'I've done my research, Nanny. I know what happened to your husband, Sam.'

When Nanny Crabbe got home Mary had worked herself up into a right state. 'Where have been? I've been worried sick about you.'

Nanny Crabbe eyed her up and down. 'Worried your cash cow had walked out on you, were you?'

Mary had the good grace to blush. 'I don't know what you mean.'

'Don't forget, Mary, I'm not fooled by you either. I know you've been taking money for these interviews I've been doing. Only you forgot one today. Nice young man, bit pushy at first but very interesting once I got talking to him.'

'Oh! The Daily View,' said Mary. 'I completely forgot. Stephen rang and asked to meet so I went.'

'He calls and you go running? Have some pride, child.'

Mary prickled. 'I suppose you could tell me a thing or two about marriage,' she said, 'what with your years of experience.'

Nanny Crabbe's eyes flicked to the dining table. On it was her memory box, the papers spread across the table top. 'What are you doing with my things?'

'Just having a look through,' said Mary, gleaming. 'Very interesting reading. I found your marriage certificates – all three of them. Including one that says you married a man called Arthur in 1839 which...' Mary spluttered and waved her hands around, '... would make you over 200 years old.'

Nanny Crabbe crossed the shining marble floor to the table, careful not to slip, and picked up the papers Mary had been reading. Most of them were yellow with age, curling at the edges or falling apart along the creases.

'I'm not over 200 years old,' began Nanny Crabbe.

'Of course you're not,' interrupted Mary, 'because that would be ridiculous.'

'I'll be 200 next May 15th,' said Nanny Crabbe. Mary's mouth fell almost as low as the cleavage-revealing top she wore. A couple of squeaks came out but nothing else.

'Where's the money, Mary?' she asked, putting her paperwork back into the box.

Mary's jaw worked up and down before she managed to say, 'What money?'

'The money you were paid for the interviews. According to that brash young man who came this afternoon, it would have been quite a pretty penny.'

'I – I – I,' stammered Mary.

'How much was it? In total?' Nanny Crabbe asked, picking up her box. She walked towards Mary who took a step back. 'Ten thousand? Fifteen?'

'E-e-eighteen,' said Mary, recoiling from the wizened old lady in front of her.

'Good girl,' said Nanny Crabbe, admiringly. 'I'll expect my nine tomorrow morning in cash. Call the rest an agent's fee and something for my board and lodging.'

She started walking away, back to the front door.

'Where are you going?'

Nanny Crabbe paused at the door. 'After the journalist and I had a little chat, he persuaded me to go and see that nice doctor at the Vogler Institute, at the top of the high street, and he said he would pay me quite a lot of money if I went in for a study into my longevity. And the journalist will pay me for exclusive access to my story, very handsomely too.'

'What do you need money for at your age?' Mary spat.

Nanny Crabbe pulled herself up to her full 4 ft 10 in. 'The doctor thinks I might be aging three times as slowly as everyone else. Imagine that! So I could have quite a while longer to live, Mary, and I can't wait to inherit this house. The doctor has a penthouse I can stay in so you can keep your shabby basement that's not fit for a cat, useless creatures though they are, and burn all my old clothes for all I care. I've got what I came for.'

Nanny Crabbe spoke through a gap in the door and a man pushed it open for her. A taxi was waiting on the drive.

'Bye, Mary,' she called, as the taxi driver took her box and stowed it in the boot for her. 'Close your mouth, dear, it's most unladylike.'

About Writers of Whitstable

by Jo Bartley

Whitstable is a truly creative town. You'll find arty graffiti on our high street, poetry slams in the Umbrella Cafe, the annual WhitLit literary festival, and dozens of artisans and craftspeople demonstrating creative pricing with their organic smoothies.

You'll also find the Writers of Whitstable, which has been running since 2013.

It's a simple enough idea. Writers read each other's short stories or chapters, then get together to give feedback and improve each other's work. The group has earned its acronym 'WoW' due to its tremendous growth. Our creative town has filled the meetings with more than a hundred writers, and the group has published three books. And alongside the regular group there are now three spin-off groups helping writers focus on improving their novels. If you visit the Marine Hotel on a Monday night, you'll find a WoW group talking, writing, and working on their projects.

A feedback group is a simple concept, but every member needs a set of complex skills – skills they might not know they have. Like the mythic story structure "The Hero's Journey", WoW writers possess many heroic attributes.

Bravery

To accept criticism and listen to what others think of your work takes courage. It's easy to hide away and hope a story works. But brave writers seek constructive criticism and listen hard. They have the strength to trust their own instincts, and then make plans to improve their work.

Honesty

To give helpful feedback to another writer takes tact. It's not easy to tell someone a story wasn't perfect. But WoW writers always try to be honest with each other. We respect each other enough to confront things that might be hard to hear and offer encouragement along the way.

Generosity

The writers who come along on a Monday night will spend their Sundays reading other members' stories and making notes that are full of thought. This isn't all about them, it's about giving their time and attention to other writers trying to improve.

Perseverance

Some members of the WoW novels groups have shared a chapter a month for two years or more, improving their novels as they go. They know it's about making time to write. That way they can submit something for review at each meeting.

On top of this a feedback group's purpose is to give writers more work! Writers take notes and use them to rewrite stories.

So, you see WoW writers are a heroic bunch!

And as the Hero's Journey makes clear, heroes have flaws to overcome too. Our writing journeys are never easy. We often face the monster of self-doubt, we meet the beast of procrastination, we need to overcome challenges managing time and meeting goals. This is particularly hard when work and family responsibilities take priority. Then there are those writers who have no clear goal. Every hero needs to find a quest.

People think WoW is 'just' a Monday night writing group, but I see it differently. To my mind when we get together, we are a band of heroic adventurers, looking out for each other, and sharing a mission to learn and improve our writing craft. We are better together and stronger when we help each other. This group brings out the best in ourselves.

I'm lucky to be involved with WoW, because on top of all the rampant heroism I get to read entertaining stories and have a laugh with some lovely people.

People come and go, trying the WoW group when they feel a need, and this works fine. One or two writers have even outgrown the group to find agents and publishers. (Well done Sue and Vicky!) We are lucky to have Lin White as a member, Lin uses her time and skills to edit and project manage the group's anthologies. We owe Lin huge thanks; without her you wouldn't be reading this book you're holding.

If you enjoy writing and have an interest in joining WoW we always welcome new members. We can't promise it's an easy group to join, but put on your hero hat, and join us on a Monday night.

Joanne Bartley
Writersofwhitstable.co.uk

About the Authors

Jo Bartley

Jo founded the Writers of Whitstable group in 2013 and is thrilled that the group has gone from strength to strength, the monthly meetings have involved over a hundred local writers and led to three spin-off groups for novelists. Jo works for an education campaign group and is a school governor at Herne Bay High School. In her spare time Jo puzzles out the clues to a 27 year old French treasure hunt, writing about the mystery at goldenowlhunt.com. She runs storyplanner.com a site for planning novels, and is soon to launch writerlink.org, a website to set-up, manage and promote writing groups.

Nic Blackshaw

Nic fell in love with words as a small child and a love affair that began with the spoken word, soon progressed to the printed form as reading opened up new worlds and the chance to see life through others' eyes. As the relationship deepened the writing of words followed but life and career intruded and they grew apart. Fortunately the split was not final and Nic returned to writing fiction, after a long estrangement, with a wealth of life experience to draw on. The two short stories in this collection are the first fruit. Nic is also working on a novel.

Guy Deakins

Guy Deakins BA (Hons),BSc (1/2), ANC (Hort), is, to put it simply, an eccentric. An artist cognoscente, he creates therefore he is. From a writing point of view he has written fiction since the mid-1970's. Indeed, he won awards both for his poems and short-stories whilst at school. Eventually he progressed to long-form successfully publishing his first major book. 'The Atheist Messiah' (2005) was published online in serial form and gained a following just shy of 100,000 readers. He has since written for various publications as himself as a garden consultant or under his alter ego's Peter Panshadow and Patricia Rölande (who is still in the doghouse after getting sued). In spite of these experiences, he still writes to this day and is publishing another book online as we speak.

R.J. Dearden

R.J. Dearden is the published author of *The Realignment Case* and has appeared in the past two WoW anthologies. He lives in Whitstable and divides his time between family, work and procrastinating about writing.

Grantt Ennis

Grantt Ennis is a Kent native who really needs to leave it at some point and see other parts of the world – or at the very least, other parts of the United Kingdom. Unfortunately, Grantt suffers from a rare form of madness known as an overactive imagination that he was assured he'd grow out of. He never did. This affliction causes him to constantly craft meticulous worlds in his own head that he just has to write down. Many of these worlds fade into blessed obscurity, but some rare few are currently in the process of self-realisation in the form of numerous unfinished novels.

Grantt lives in the middle of nowhere in the countryside just outside Canterbury where his madness is managed by his wife and dogs. They make sure that he gets up to as little mischief as possible, while still encouraging him to build these fantasy realms. He is also the director of a tabletop gaming company, the result of a happy accident, which allows him to, you guessed it, make miniature worlds, but also play with lasers. Maybe he just never actually grew up.

Duarte Figueira

One of Duarte's earliest memories is listening to his grandmother and great-aunt sitting knitting in the kitchen of their farmhouse in Northern Portugal telling each other stories about real and imaginary people, stories of love and hate, kindness and revenge, brutal reality and magical escapes. After too many years of drafting and editing work reports and publications he is writing to recapture the pleasure he had then, sitting at their feet, soaking those tales in. Luckily, his family and cats tolerate this ridiculous self-indulgence.

P.J. Ferst

Phillipa Ferst joined wonderful W.O.W. in 2018, two years after self-publishing her futuristic children's book *DomeKidz*. She started writing aged six but her unfinished opus, *Pony Mad* got lost in a house move. Deciding to read instead, Phillipa narrowly escaped death by trying to fly like Peter Pan.

Fast forward fifteen years and Phillipa is in the Middle East, writing silly sketches to make learning English more fun. Zip on fifteen more and she's honing students' study skills at Canterbury Christ Church, publishing academic articles and co-writing a teacher resource book with her HOD. Now retired and WOW supercharged, Phillipa produces stories with happy endings, plus poems and sea shanties, performed locally. But a cunningly disguised memoir is brewing. Will it need to be censored for the grandchildren?

Aliy Fowler

Raised on a farm on the North Devon coast with no television as a distraction, Aliy spent a lot of time reading (when she wasn't making secret hay-bale camps or roller skating in the empty silage pits with her brothers). All the reading ultimately led to her studying foreign literature at the University of Keele; which in turn led to a Diploma in Technical Translation at the University of Kent. On realising that technical translation was not as much fun as hanging out with the university Ski Club, she opted for a further year as a student (this time doing Computer Science). Two decades later she finally escaped academia to pursue a freelance career. She now fluctuates between web design, photography and writing.

Prior to this anthology her only published pieces were about Prolog Programming and Computer Aided Language Learning. These lacked interesting characters and well-paced plots, but may have helped a few insomniacs.

Nick Hayes

Nick has been writing since an early age but has yet to break into the Big Time. If sales from the anthology go well he will buy a third speed boat and holiday again in his favourite cabin in the Maldives. He possesses a good imagination that served him well in his twenty two years in teaching.

Today he occupies his time as a youth worker in Herne Bay and Whitstable while also attending local spoken word events with a range of questionable poetry. His chosen topics are himself and mental illness. The two are not unrelated.

He urges anyone to buy this book. Or else jump up and get involved yourself!

Helen Howard

Helen began to think about becoming an author one day, at the tender age of 9 when she won a story competition at primary school. The story she wrote was about two girls who ran away from home but returned when the food ran out. The prize was half a dozen eggs. As an adult she tried her hand first, unsuccessfully, at short stories and plays aimed at a radio audience. Writing at work took her into non-fiction: writing textbooks, learning materials and training packs. Shifting away from non-fiction towards fiction proved to be a bit of struggle but the support of the Writers of Whitstable group has been invaluable. These days Helen sometimes writes poetry and enjoys dancing, singing and growing her own food.

Kate Keane

A Whitstable native, Kate watched the transformation of her childhood small seaside town from afar for many years, until gradually it drew her back. Never happier then when in library or a bookshop surrounded by words, she always dreamed of writing stories herself but life somehow got in the way. She is now working on a number of other pieces which are in various stages of completion, and is hopeful that she has finally overcome her phobia of committing words to a page, or screen.

Away from words, whilst juggling her portfolio career and family life, Kate is often to be found walking in the woods soaking up the tranquillity or on the beach herding an over-enthusiastic Labrador.

Kerry Mayo

Kerry Mayo started out writing about spunky princesses but would get bored and behead them before they met their prince. Five-year olds can be so ruthless...

As time went on, her ability to focus increased and she is now a Kent-based writer whose books include From This Day Forward (2017), Catch, Pull, Push (2018) and non-fiction book Whitstable Through Time (2014). Her Soul To Keep (fiction) and a companion walking guide to Whitstable Through Time (non-fiction) will be published in 2020.

She has also been published in the women's magazine market with numerous short stories and two serials and her short stories have also appeared in three anthologies. She also enjoys scriptwriting and has had two short films produced and a radio sketch broadcast.

Gillian Rolfe

Gillian has spent a lot of her life in libraries. Mainly working in them, hiding in them, being inspired in them and quite often having a little doze in them too. She has always written stories but only recently started to commit them to paper before that they just swished around in her head. Having swapped shelving stories for writing stories she is now realising how difficult it is to resist Netflix and chocolate biscuits to concentrate on writing something. Studying with the Open University has helped focus her efforts and hopefully any day soon she may even graduate.

She has lived in Whitstable for many years and shares her home with one lovely fella and two very over opinionated cats.

Ellen Simmons

Ellen became a true lover of literature when she read the Harry Potter series aged seven and has never looked back.

She went on to study English Literature and Creative Writing at university to see if she had any ability to write herself, and enjoyed being part of a group of writers so much that it made sense to find such a group when she returned home.

Her latest project focuses on two women who form an unlikely and life changing friendship with a common goal to change the views of social media and how those of a certain age and size should no longer be invisible.

Ellen writes mainly to break up the dull mundanity of everyday life, and will continue to do so until magic truly exists. Or her Hogwarts acceptance letter arrives in the post.

Lin White

Lin is an avid reader, and has been making up stories in her head for as long as she can remember. Writing started with fanfiction, but tackling original fiction was the logical next step. To date there are several novels in various levels of completion, plus a bunch of short stories.

In her real life, she has been involved in publishing and education for many years and currently works as an editor, typesetter and proofreader, helping other writers to polish up their work ready for publication.

She also runs regularly, and enjoys life with her husband, three sons, two cats and a dog.

Richard White

Richard wrote nothing but letters and film scripts until after several professional lives, mainly in the film industry. Returning from two years in the Caribbean he discovered writing, and started two novels, which remain a private endeavour.

In 2005, with his partner Rose MacLennan Craig, he wrote, produced and directed a play at the Edinburgh Fringe, resulting a series of others, until in 2015 the last of these, *The Mythmakers*, was produced in venues in Scotland, California, London's West End and New York. Other plays were collaborations with the Bonnington Playwrights, with whom he still writes.

Over these years Richard has also written short stories which now seem to be finding a home in Whitstable. Perhaps this is the start of a new professional life?

John Wilkins

John enjoys imagining the stories behind the news, considering what might have happened and what it might be like for the people involved. With the support from Writers of Whitstable he has contributed stories to the previous two collections and completed a novel in the month of November. For the rest of the time he continues to try and support others either as event director of Canterbury parkrun or as a volunteer trainee counsellor.

David Williamson

David is an original member of WoW group and designs our anthology book jackets. David is a self-published author with titles including The Lovers of Today and specialises in short observational stories, often with unexpected twists.

Beyond the Beach Huts
features stories set in
Whitstable

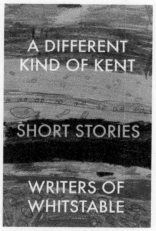

A Different Kind of Kent
travels wider, to cover the
whole of the county